LOST *in* HIM

HARLOE RAE

For smacking a lofty goal on the ass and saying,
"I've got this."

Also, to those looking for an escape in whatever shape
or form that might take.

PLAYLIST

"It Only Gets Better" | WILD
"Please Notice" | Christian Leave
"Falling" | Harry Styles
"What a Time" | Julia Michaels, Niall Horan
"Trying My Best" | Anson Seabra
"Birthday Cake" | Dylan Conrique
"A Little Bit Yours" | JP Saxe
"Is It Just Me?" | Emily Burns
"Lease On Life" | Andy Grammar
"I'm With You" | Vance Joy
"Chasing Stars" | Alesso, Marshmello, James Bay
"Girl" | SYML
"All the Pretty Girls" | KALEO
"Crystals" | Of Monsters and Men
"Flashed Junk Mind" | Milky Chance
"Fire and the Flood" | Vance Joy
"Need the Sun to Break" | James Bay
"Happiest Year" | Jaymes Young
"I Guess I'm in Love" | Clinton Kane

Listen on Spotify!

"It's an interesting tale about how the princess rejects
her riches and flies free from the castle."
My story isn't quite so glamorous.
Well, not the part worth telling.

After my parents tried marrying me off
to the wealthiest investor, I ditched their
sheltered nest and set off with my own
agenda.
This summer is my chance to begin again.
Fulfill the dreams that were previously ignored.
The adventure starts at a secluded cabin in
the middle of nowhere.

That's where I find him avoiding civilization.

Nash Hudson is a broody recluse holding a major grudge.
With stormy eyes and a perpetual scowl to match, his dark
mood tries to steal my sunshine.
I take his hostility personally, only to discover he doesn't
like anyone.

Little does he realize that my stubborn streak rivals his.

As it turns out, Nash is the tortured hero
my love story is missing.
Too bad he's very reluctant to fill that role.
Thanks to a little luck—or a strike of lightning—he's
forced to face me.

I'll break down his walls as if this soul
searching depends on it.
Or maybe I'll end up getting lost in him instead.

"What appears to be broken might've stumbled
on purpose."—Nash Hudson

"It wasn't my intention to get lost, but that's
where I found myself."—Penny Blaire

LOST *in* HIM

PROLOGUE

Penny

THE PRESSURE CRUSHING MY CHEST THREATENS TO LEVEL ME, but that doesn't stop the announcement from breaking free. "I'm leaving on Monday."

My father—the mighty Alastair Theodore Winchester—places his cutlery down with methodical grace. The deceptively calm motion has my posture immediately going ramrod straight on reflex. There's not a speck of food on his face, yet he takes an extended minute to wipe his mouth with a pristine cloth napkin. This move further instills his deliberate and calculating control over the room. My knees quake under the table while discomfort pinches at me.

Finally, after what feels like an hour, my father lifts his steely gaze to mine. "Pardon?"

Interrupting our meal with idle chatter is forbidden. Too bad for Daddy Dearest, I quit following his rigid rules months ago. That doesn't shrink the lump in my throat, though. "I'm moving out. Permanently."

His stony expression doesn't so much as flicker. "That's almost amusing."

"I'm serious." It's a feat to squash the petulant whine that demands escape.

My father stares at me as if I'm a mere blip on his radar. "We've already discussed this, Penelope. You're scheduled to study abroad this summer."

I blink with concrete coating my lashes. What he thinks I'll be studying while stranded overseas is an unknown I don't care to venture into. Besides, I just graduated with a joint degree in communications and marketing. It's a small miracle that my overbearing parents allowed me to attend college, not to mention actually finish.

With more courage than I've ever managed to scrounge up, I return his unwavering focus with a determined glare. "I'm taking a trip, yes. But somewhere I chose on my own."

At this point, my mother offers a low tsk. The fact she willingly cracked her dutiful silence screams volumes. "Listen to your father, Penelope. Venice is gorgeous this time of year, and you've never been. You'll be happy to get away for a few months."

"Yes, I certainly will." I'm nodding too fast and jerk the robotic motion to a sudden halt. "That's what I'm telling you. My flight takes off early Monday morning. I'll be gone until mid-August."

She sniffs and reaches for her wine glass. "I'm afraid to ask where you're planning to go."

"Then don't bother," I snip.

"Penelope." Reprimand is thick in my father's tone.

Fire singes my cheeks at the scold fit for a rotten toddler. "I found a cabin to rent. It's secluded and safe and small. Just right for me."

My mother waits, her lips pinching tighter with each passing second. "Must I drag each detail from you?"

The urge to roll my eyes twitches my left lid. "Must you know my whereabouts at all times?"

A resounding smack against the polished wood table makes me jolt upright. When my gaze swings to the man responsible, I find him seething. "Haven't you caused enough trouble by disrupting our dinner? You forget your place, daughter."

The reminder is wholly unnecessary since his demeaning beliefs are permanently etched on my skull. I'll never be an equal in this archaic environment. That's just one more reason why I'm leaving. My older brothers didn't suffer this unrelenting hold from our father. They were allowed to do whatever their reckless spirits desired.

Me? I've been trapped since conception. I'm little more than a bargaining chip, with no wiggle room to speak of. It's no wonder I'm chomping at the bit to shed this sheltered existence. I'm nearly twenty-two, but have less control than most toddlers. That's about to change in three short days. They no longer have the power to control me.

"Let's pretend I didn't mention anything. The food is getting cold." Not that it matters. The meager portion on my plate will remain untouched.

My mother makes another disapproving noise in the back of her throat. "So you can disappear into the night without a trace again? I think not."

"Whose fault was that?" Just swerving close to that memory makes my skin crawl. It's been months, yet the betrayal feels like a fresh wound leaving me raw. I was expected to accept my fate with a grateful smile.

"We've already taken the blame for that… oversight." The last word seems torn from my father's steel trap. It still pains him to admit defeat.

I don't hesitate to exploit that sore spot for my advantage. "Which is why you shouldn't have an issue letting me go."

Early signs of forfeit flicker in his stone mask. Just that slight pinch between his brows is enough to tell that I'm making an impact. "Are you sure that's wise in your current condition, Penelope?"

"And what condition might that be, Father?" Flinty ire sparks off my squared posture.

"Don't be coy. It's unbecoming."

A smile that most likely displays the very tactic he's accusing me of using curls my lips. I'm more than cued in that he's referring to my two stints in the emergency room about six months ago. First, I crashed the Aston Martin I'd been given for my birthday, and not long after that, I ingested a sizable handful of peanuts. While my allergy to them isn't deadly, the reaction was bad enough to land me back in the hospital.

If it wasn't an accident in both cases, that blame would also rest heavily on his shoulders. I can't be too upset over the fact I was admitted, albeit very temporarily.

Bayside Regional is where I met Dr. Larsen Belle and found my backbone. It's also where I received her expert advice to choose my own path. The chains my parents shackled to me were solid, but I know that I possess the strength to break free. No one has the power to trap me in a situation other than me. If I didn't make the choice to leave, that was my own damn fault. She gave me the courage to take a stand against their reign.

Not that my newfound resilience was instantaneous. I had faltered and floundered while initially wading into these uncharted depths. Before my botched engagement party, I'd been a dutiful sheep confined in the pen of my father's making. I didn't believe I could escape my gilded cage. Turns out I was wrong. The night I skipped town felt like the first moment I could actually breathe freely.

All it took was my disappearing act—and my so-called fiancé getting arrested for embezzlement—for my parents to call off the arrangement. I almost snort at the reminder, disturbing as it might be. That sorry excuse for a man never laid a finger on me, but he certainly would have, given the opportunity. I'm thankful the truth of his crimes came to light before he could lay a twisted claim to me.

I fork a limp lettuce leaf with zero intention of eating. My stomach is a churning jumble. "You still treat me like a fragile artifact best left behind a thick wall of glass."

With that recited line from my therapist, the great Alastair Theodore Winchester cracks. His expression turns thunderous, a brewing storm darkening his already foreboding features. "There's good reason for that."

My eyes narrow on their own. "Not anymore."

Meaty fingers curl into a fist on the table. It probably needles him beyond agony to surrender his prized pawn. Not that he hadn't planned to do just that all along if the deal hadn't flopped.

"You're my responsibility, daughter. That won't change."

"But I'm an adult, and fully capable of caring for myself."

Vibrant brownish-green eyes the same shade as mine appraise me with a disproving glint. "That has yet to be seen."

Heat stings my cheeks with that proverbial slap. "Only because you won't give me the opportunity."

"That's a faulty perception. You have all there is to want at your disposal, Penelope."

"What I want can't be bought."

"Typical nonsense," he spits. "As if I don't provide your every indulgence. Get your priorities straight."

"They are."

"I disagree."

A rather unladylike snort spews from me. "That's what's typical."

There's a protruding vein in my father's forehead that begins to throb. "I will not be disrespected, especially when you've already caused a fine disruption with this drivel."

As if I could ever cause him a deplorable offense that won't roll right off his ego. The very thought is laughable. "You told me I could do as I please after the Nathaniel Hollingsworth fiasco."

A quiet squeak reveals the methodical pause he takes while tracing the rim of his scotch glass. "And what do you call these last six months?"

The urge to wither under his judgment shudders through me. He's referring to the so-called free rein I've been granted since the news of my intended's crimes was splashed across the media. Nathaniel was the lucky suitor my parents plucked from the shallow selection pool. His connections and assets would further stretch my father's already monopolizing reach. Or so it appeared on the surface. Turns out, that sleaze was a con artist. I would've been his next payday. Imagine the scandal.

The thought alone smacked some much-needed sense into my parents. For a brief period, I even believed they would let me live free. My optimistic attitude even led me to brag about their drastic change. What a fool I was.

Their restrictive grip fell slack, but I didn't take advantage. The possibilities were endless and overwhelming—and more than I could manage. My college courses were online, but I used the rigorous demands as an excuse to stay put. That error in judgment has cost me dearly.

The relief my parents expressed once I returned home was short-lived. It only took a week for old habits to resurface and familiar patterns to take hold. I quickly found myself once again stuck behind glimmering gold bars in the gilded cage. That's precisely where I'm perched at this very moment.

I'm not convinced they would've let me fly the coop anyway. Not then. The shift in our dynamic was too fresh and uncertain. But now? I'm ready to test the limits.

"Well?" My father's impatient prompt is paired with an arrogant lift of his brow.

Those shackled musings go slack when I jolt to attention. "You only gave me enough wiggle room to pacify me. I accepted those scraps like a toddler with her first taste of sugar. The reality is far less tasty. A sorry excuse for the guilt you supposedly felt."

His complexion has taken on a ruddy hue. "Are you trying to tell me how I feel?"

Snarky confidence might be pulsing through my veins,

but that doesn't mean I'm stepping in a careless trap. "We're getting nowhere with this."

"As I mentioned when you carelessly ruined our meal to begin with."

I lower my gaze to conceal an exaggerated eye roll. Formalities are expected and guarded, which makes my impulsive reveal that much worse. What a tragedy it would be for this lavish farce to appear flawed.

Dinner at the Winchester household is an upscale affair regardless of the guest list. This table is too large for three, more suitable for two dozen feasting on overpriced cuisine. The display is comical, ostentatious, and proves just how far removed we are from each other. In this setting, we're mere strangers forced to stomach this uncomfortable burden.

After a solidifying breath, I lift my chin to restore the stand-off. "I just wanted to give you fair warning that I'm leaving."

"The answer is no." His stern expression prepares to reprimand me without another utterance.

"I wasn't asking for permission."

A muscle leaps in his cheek, most likely attempting to avoid the upcoming collision. "Do I have no say over my only daughter's future?"

"Your opinion has already been noted on several occasions."

"And yet you insist on defying me."

"This isn't your choice."

Alastair must recognize the absolution in my terse retort. There's no swaying me, not with my heels digging in deeper with each passing beat. "We can discuss this further tomorrow."

Heat stings my eyes at yet another dismissal. "I need to discover myself, Father. That isn't much to ask after the trauma I withstood."

"Trauma," he complains with a scoff. "Don't be dramatic. That situation has been properly dealt with. There should be no lingering effects. If there are, we can schedule an emergency session with Doctor Jenkins."

I'm fuming inside, the sizzle crackling in my veins. This is his reaction whenever I expose a slice of emotion that wavers beyond the plastic veneer he expects. If only we could all be detached robots like him. "I'm not being anything other than realistic, Father. You need to let me leave, like you promised."

"Quit with the theatrics. It doesn't bode well for your case." But his features soften into a semblance of negotiation. "Where is this cabin located, Penelope?"

"In Minnesota." The northern state beckons to me with its ten thousand lakes and countless shoreside rentals. It's the rustic retreat my heart longs for, and about as far removed from the tropical heat of Bayside as I can imagine. It will be a much-needed change of scenery.

"Must you go so far?" My mother manages to wrinkle her nose through the layers of Botox. She complains about the distance, yet they planned to send me across the Atlantic.

I send her a flat stare. "It's just over three hours by plane. Very accessible."

My father steeples his fingers. "How will you fund this excursion?"

"I've saved every cent from the bookstore." The job is a small allowance they afforded me after a heated debate on my eighteenth birthday.

My mother sips from her wine, deciding to rejoin the initiative. "How will you survive financially on that piddly sum, dear? They pay you only—what, twenty-five dollars an hour? The lifestyle you're accustomed to will burn through that in a week."

"Fifteen dollars an hour," I correct her. The look of shock

and surprise on both my parents' faces is almost worth the admission. "I'll find another job."

If necessary, I have the money my grandfather left me to stay afloat while I decide what direction to take. It doesn't hurt that the place I'm staying is extremely affordable. I could probably last there for a year without having to worry. But by no means do I plan to be an idle mooch for long. I want to gain a solid foundation for myself to stand on. Step away from my family's shadow. That's another trick I learned from Dr. Belle. I'm going to reinvent myself for the better.

It will be an adjustment, but I'm prepared to prove myself. Not to mention determined. My stubborn streak reaches far and wide, a trait I inherited from Father Dearest.

"You're not properly trained for any lucrative career options." My father's reminder is salt in a festering wound.

I can't conceal my wince. "Who says I need training to find a job?"

Allister grunts while smoothing a palm down his tie. "Any business worth working for. Whoever hires a pampered socialite hellbent on reckless behavior is a fool."

"And I look forward to meeting them." I jut my chin.

He crosses his arms, seeming to arrive at a decision. "That makes one of us. We'll send Henry with you. He'll protect you until your rational logic returns."

The cramp in my belly clenches tight before easing with a whoosh. My independence doesn't have a price tag. "A hired guard to spy on me? Not happening."

"You expect me to approve this charade without trusted eyes on you?"

"Yes," I rush to say. "I'll give you the address and rental site information."

His unyielding force wavers, a steep frown betraying him. "What good is that from where I sit?"

I take a risk, reaching to rest a palm over his fist. "Don't worry about me. I took care of myself just fine after deciding not to marry Nathaniel. And that location wasn't meticulously researched beforehand."

"Reckless," my father spits.

"But it did the trick in a pinch." I never revealed where I ran off to in November. That's a secret spot I intend to keep, just in case. They don't need to know.

All they ever aspired for me to become was polished arm candy. But I'll prove I'm worth far more than a lucrative merger.

My parents exchange a glance thick with indecision. It's my mother who pipes up. "I'll agree on one condition."

As if that will deter me one way or another. "What is it?"

"You'll answer when I call."

My lashes flutter fast enough to cause a gust. "I'll do my best."

It's my father's turn to set his terms. He leans forward, the chair groaning with effort. "If you come across any… gentlemen that spark an interest, I expect a complete background check to land on my desk prior to any entanglements."

Another ridiculous request I have every intention of ignoring. That doesn't stop me from pasting on a patronizing grin. "Sure, Father. You'll hear the moment a guy so much as crosses my path."

CHAPTER ONE

Penny

GRAVEL CRUNCHES BENEATH THE TIRES AS I APPROACH MY home for the next three months. At first glance, the log cabin is just as described—quaint, rustic, and cozy. I can't leave out what I'm most excited about, either—the secluded factor.

Trees swaddle the clearing that the wooden lodge is nestled in. A mirrored reflection from the lake glitters in the background. The sight has an instantaneous impact on me, dislodging the knot between my shoulder blades. In all my years, I've never seen anything quite so serene. Not that I've experienced much beyond the scope of my father's choosing. That lens is currently blowing wide open. This isolated treasure cove is all mine.

The engine's quiet hum almost seems invasive. With a quick stab to the ignition button, that mechanical purr putters before falling silent. The resulting hush crackles along my nerves. Only wilderness remains, beckoning me in with a welcome embrace.

I step from the car in a whimsical trance. The quiet is absolute and startling. I'm almost afraid to breathe for fear of disrupting the peace. My craziest, most inventive imagination couldn't conjure this level of natural beauty. Branches sway with a soft breeze while birds chirp to announce my arrival. It's the optimal location to begin again.

A smile quirks my lips at the reminder. I'm taking a page from Dr. Belle's book and reinventing myself. She's got the right idea, if my rapidly growing confidence is any indicator.

Penelope Blaire Charleston Winchester is no more. I tip my face to the sky while walking toward the porch. Pride radiates from me as the past melts away. The identity I have been forced to endure my whole life has shed from me—sliced and cropped into a sleek Penny Blaire.

The lockbox opens with a click, releasing the key into my waiting palm. That slight weight hitting my skin feels like salvation. I don't hesitate to stride inside my fresh start.

Feet twirling in a slow circle, I study the modest interior. Fresh linens and sunshine fill my nose as I breathe deep. It's small, but it's beautiful. The layout is similar to a studio apartment, with only the bathroom separated from the rest. A clever furniture arrangement creates division across the single room. Wood boards and warped metal are used as paneling. Thick logs have been repurposed into several cute decorative pieces. Some might consider it plain or cramped, but I see endless potential sitting on each surface.

My mood soars higher as I explore farther into the space. There's nothing boastful or showy about this place. It's practical in design and purpose. The space is neat, tidy, and well maintained. Random knickknacks and personal touches grace the walls and shelves, revealing the owner's modern style. Every item appears unique, chosen specifically to fit with the other pieces in this rare collection.

In short, it's simply everything I've been missing.

A shrill tune cracks into my peaceful bubble. I dig the pesky interruption from my pocket, but all traces of irritation vanish when I glance at the screen.

"Hey, Lou." Happiness dances from my voice.

My bestie huffs down the line. "Oh, you do remember I exist."

I laugh at her dramatics. "How could I forget the greatest friend to ever grace me with her awesomeness?"

"Yet you left me," she mutters.

"The invitation still stands. You already skipped out on my birthday." I walk my fingers along the blue sofa, similar in shade to the still waters tempting me to take a swim. The fabric is plush and alluring, so I collapse onto the cushions with a sigh.

Meanwhile, a strangled noise escapes Elouise. "Don't put that blame on me. You were very specific about this trip being your gift."

"To myself," I laugh. "Feel free to stop by and share a cupcake with me."

"I can't survive in that inhospitable climate. This girl needs heat and beaches."

I glance out the window. Warmth bathes the land while a sandy shore hugs the lake. "There are both right where I stand. This isn't Antarctica."

"Might as well be in the winter."

"Good thing it's summer, huh? I planned accordingly."

Another affronted noise squeaks from her. "It's happening already."

I pucker my lips in return, fully aware she can't see the expression. "And what, dare I ask, is that?"

"You're drinking the punch and it's spiked with Minnesota nice." A low hum as she arrives at some decision. "You'll never leave."

My eyes roll on their own. "Okay, Drastic Donna. The rental agreement is set for three months. I'll be outta here by mid-August."

"And back in Tampa?"

"Absolutely not." The very idea squeezes my throat in a tangled knot.

"Brat," she mutters. "I'll never see you again."

I stand from the pillowy comfort with a stretch. "That's not possible. We're life partners."

"Could've fooled me."

"Don't be salty. You're rarely in Florida," I counter with a huff of my own.

My bestie is a high fashion model constantly on the go. If I hadn't told her before leaving, it probably would've been several weeks before she noticed my absence. Not that she'd ever acknowledge our growing distance—purely physical, of course.

Elouise sighs, still carrying on in airy exasperation for several seconds. "Just admit it. You abandoned me."

"Not even a little bit," I retort.

"Whatever. Give me the tour." A rhythmic alert chimes in my ear as she requests to FaceTime.

I accept with a laugh. "Can't wait? I just walked in the door."

Her beautiful smile is prepared to charm me. "Then it's perfect timing. We'll wander together and get the vibe of this humble abode that stole you away."

"All right," I agree and tap the screen to flip the camera.

Elouise appears riveted at the view of my main living section. "That couch is super cute."

"And extra squishy. My butt approves." I pivot to showcase the kitchen and dining area.

"Good thing you aren't staying with anyone else. That table barely seats two."

I shrug while turning to the bed and dresser pressed against the south wall. "One spot is all I need."

"You're being awfully modest."

"This is the new me."

"Penny Blaire," she coos.

"Has a fancy ring to it, eh?"

"So posh." Elouise leans closer as I approach the last corner left to explore.

The bathroom is narrow and short, but the tub is clawfoot with a stainless spout that gleams in the sunlight. The urge to scrub the flight and drive from my clammy skin suddenly takes top priority. "And that's the end."

A slim brow cocks upward. "Where's the rest?"

"What do you mean? I showed you the entire thing."

"That's it?" Her tone reaches shrill levels, as if the very thought is offensive.

"You act like this is a dingy shack." Defensive barbs steel my voice.

"Well," she scoffs. "Not far off, if I've seen all of it."

I frown at her pinched expression. "How very snobbish of you."

"Oh, please. We were raised in filthy riches. What you're currently drowning in has me concerned for your sanity. Where's the television?"

"I have my iPad."

"Please tell me there's Wi-Fi." She very well might implode if I don't.

"It's super fast. And the cell reception is good too." Those details were listed in bold on the rental website. I may want to reinvent my life and take some time away, but that's far from wanting to go completely off-grid.

"Thank goodness for small miracles. There's no way I believe you're—"

"I'm happy. Very much so," I interrupt. Heat flares across my cheeks at her assumption otherwise.

Elouise must catch the conviction vibrating from me since the camera is still pointing at my surroundings. "Okay, sorry. It's just not what I was expecting."

"Then it's a good thing you're not living here." I offer a final span of the cabin to emphasize my point.

"What little there is looks nice. I especially like the wood furniture."

My gaze trails to a bookshelf that fits just right underneath the window. "It's almost as if the pieces are made for this place."

"Maybe they were."

I tap the screen to flip the view back on me. "It's probably a local vendor. Maybe I'll find a shop on my adventures in town."

She nods while studying me. "Do your parents know how you're living?"

I give her a flat stare for that comment. "They know enough."

Her lips quirk at the edges. "I still can't believe they released you from their clutches. Willingly, I might add."

"As if they had a choice."

"Oooooh," she exhales with added flair. "Someone found her backbone."

"And proud of it."

"You go, girl. I'm proud of you too." Elouise lifts a palm as if we can exchange a high-five.

I return the gesture. "Thanks, Lou."

"Still butt hurt that you left me."

"We'll see each other soon. Come visit me." My tone borders on a plea purely for her benefit.

"Where will I sleep?"

"We can share the bed, like old times."

"What are we going to eat?"

A scoff signifies my waning patience. "Didn't you hear about the local restaurants? Besides, I can cook."

"Yeah," she snorts. "Okay."

Now I give her a glare. "I'm not completely inept. Believe it or not, I already stopped at the market to get basic supplies."

Her hand flutters to her chest. "That's shocking. Like, actually."

"Thanks for the overflowing confidence." My eyes roll on their own agenda.

"You're welcome. And just for that, I'll consider a visit. Very short." She holds up a sliver of space between her thumb and index finger.

"Better than nothing," I accept with a shrug.

"Aren't you going to be lonely? Let's face the truth, Penny. You're a social butterfly who needs a flock."

"Do butterflies have flocks?"

She mutters something unintelligible under her breath. "That's beside the point. You'll be climbing up the walls soon enough out there in the sticks."

"The town isn't far from here. I spotted a few bars and restaurants while driving through. Maybe that's where I'll have dinner."

"Alone?" She sounds horrified by the prospect.

"The goal isn't to remain alone for long," I tease.

"Ah, right. Get some. It's about time." Elouise dances in place, shoulders shimmying.

"I'm in no hurry." But a thrill zips through my belly at the potential company I might find. More uncharted territory to conquer on this trip.

"Yeah, yeah. You're soul searching, not looking for a date. The last thing I need is for you to find Prince Charming and move there permanently."

"Might not be so bad. You can rent the neighboring cabin and find your own happily ever after." I saw a few while searching for mine.

She inspects her flawless manicure, brushing off invisible dust. "Maybe I'll take you up on that. I'm already bored."

"It's been three days since I saw you. Isn't Kyler keeping you occupied?" The jest in my voice is a jovial beat.

Her cringe is exaggerated. "Ugh, gross. That's so over."

I predicted that outcome after noticing his obsession with his own reflection. "You'll find someone better."

"Obviously," she mutters. "That bar isn't set high."

Which gets me thinking of a more suitable companion. "I might get a dog."

"What?" Her pitch raises several octaves.

"A dog," I repeat. "There's a shelter not far from the main road. Already did my research."

My parents never allowed pets at our house. That's probably one reason I'm eager to fill that bitter emptiness in my heart. But more than that, I've always been an animal lover. There's a gnawing ache inside of me that's desperate to be soothed. I'd probably fill this cabin with furry friends if I could.

As if hearing the direction of my internal desires, Elouise cuts through the silence. "How will you get the pound pooch home when this trip is done?"

I think on that, my eyes straying to the window and picturesque view beyond. "Where's home?"

A pained noise escapes her. "I've lost you to the simple life already."

"Don't be dramatic." But she's not wrong. There isn't a single ounce of me that wants to return to Florida. Not in a permanent sense at least. "I'm just exploring my options."

Elouise's eyes shimmer with honesty. "That's what I'm afraid of."

CHAPTER TWO

Wᴵᴛʜ ᴀ ꜰɪɴᴀʟ ꜱᴡɪᴘᴇ, ᴛʜᴇ ꜱᴛᴜʙʙᴏʀɴ ʀᴏᴜɢʜ ᴇᴅɢᴇ ɪꜱ properly sanded into a smooth curve. I drop my arm with a groan. The limb hangs heavy, muscles cramping from overexertion. My entire body has the consistency of minced meat. It might've been wise to quit hours ago, but I couldn't leave the project unfinished.

A cramp seizes my lower back as I rise to my full height from the concrete floor. Rune jolts to attention at the sound of my stilted movements. The loyal mutt trots over from his bed in the corner. He's an abandoned drifter, chased from his home like me. Our bond snapped into place the instant he wandered onto my property, and we've been inseparable ever since.

I automatically bend to scratch behind his silky ears, simultaneously tugging the AirPods from my own. A dull thrum remains while I recalibrate to the quiet in my shop. "I'm all right, boy. Just sore."

Rune whimpers and nudges me with his wet snout. His concern shoots a spark of warmth through my stony chest, threatening to crack the impenetrable surface.

The urge to press against that hollow ache twitches my fingers. Instead, I rub my abused palms together with a choppy exhale. Maybe sleep will find me easily for once.

"It's been a long day. What else is new," I mumble the last part to myself.

Not that there's any reason to make that distinction. Talking to my dog is the only interaction I get. That point gives the impression I'm having an actual conversation and allows me to feel more… normal. Whatever that means.

Rune cocks his head, waiting for my next move.

Low grumbles complain from my gut. Dinnertime came and went with the setting sun. A glance at my watch shows it's two o'clock in the morning. I often get lost in the task and go all night. This could've easily been one of those times.

"How 'bout a snack before bed, huh?"

He bumps my hand again, adding a lick for good measure.

"Lead the way," I command with a swat at the door. "Let's go."

Sawdust and ripe musk clog my lungs while I trudge to the exit. Dusty particles cling to my damp flesh like a scratchy coat, evidence from the table I just whipped up from scratch. It's a beautiful piece—soft pine with subtle details carved in that showcase my signature design. The customer should be pleased.

I step into the darkness, my eyes straining for several blinks to adjust. The chill greets me with a cool embrace that I pause to accept. Raw silence streams in and does the job of replacing the music I'd been blasting moments ago.

But not completely.

There's a noticeable disruption to the usual calm this slight reprieve should bring. Aside from the chirping crickets and lazy lapping of the lake greeting the shore, I hear a fast beat pulsing through the trees. The hypnotic type that had been pounding into my ears on repeat.

Irritation is a swift blade stabbing into my exhaustion. I'm suddenly alert with a very specific disturbance to attack. The woman I rented the Monroe lodge to is wreaking havoc on my predictable routine. She should be snoozing with the Sandman, not blasting a song similar to his name. A scoff berates me, the irony not lost in context. But I rarely find peace long enough to dream.

This stranger is pissing all over what I work tirelessly to achieve. That escape is earned, reaped, and vital. My gaze narrows into a fine point while I tread across the space separating our cabins. Motivation to uncover and neutralize this problem guides me through the pitch black. I don't so much as catch my boot on a stray rock.

Rune keeps pace beside me, nose to the ground. The whispered brush from our hurried strides syncs with the booming tempo. That pulsing rhythm rolls a fresh wave of irritation over me. She's already labeling herself as a nuisance on day one.

Her reckless behavior is almost a taunt, a blatant reminder that I failed to include a noise violation section in the recently updated contract. It's never been a problem with previous tenants. They appreciated the quiet surroundings and chose this location for that exact reason. I'll need to deliver a harsh warning to stop her from ruining my sanctuary further.

Reality smacks me in the face when her porch appears straight ahead. Tension snaps taut as I slam to a halt. What the fuck am I planning to do? Confront her? Just the thought churns bile in my empty stomach.

I could knock to gain her attention before blending back into the shadows. Cowardice is inky sludge that clogs my veins. That's not bound to terrify her or anything. She's staying by herself in the woods, for fuck's sake. Although, it might be best for her to leave. Maybe a strongly worded email is more appropriate.

With these possibilities plaguing me, I shuffle forward on autopilot. That is until the view through her bay window brings my feet to an abrupt standstill. The scene from within steals my breath and I choke on pure shock. A young woman is dancing in plain sight, wearing nothing but her bikini. She twists to the side while shaking her firm ass. That's when the light exposes her skimpy outfit for what it truly is—a lacy bra and matching thong. I gulp at the gravelly grit in my throat, mesmerized by her bold actions. The strange heat scorching over me is another issue entirely.

Who is this temptress and what is she doing alone in the middle of nowhere?

Without any chance for answers, I'm stranded in this trap she set. The vision she presents is too damn intoxicating. I can't recall the last time I was this close to a woman.

Hair the shade of golden wheat spills down her slender back. Flawless skin kissed with sunshine holds a tantalizing shimmer of sweat. Smooth, toned legs twirl her across the floor. My blood turns to fire at an alarming rate when she dips and puts her lush cleavage on display.

Any trace of cold is chased off by the show she's unknowingly providing me with. Her motions are fluid and free, as if no one is watching, which is probably what she assumes. I drop my gaze as shame crawls over me. A pest she might be, but that doesn't give me the right to creep on her.

Rune whines and scoots forward on his ass, more than ready to meet our noisy neighbor. Unlike me, the mutt is overly trusting and enjoys the company of others. His eager insistence to make friends might betray my hiding spot if I continue leering.

An unwavering conclusion sinks in as I fight to keep my eyes averted. I'll have to approach this complication while maintaining my distance. The twitch at my upper lip is unexpected. Just one more unwarranted reaction she's wrenching from me.

Before I'm caught in a compromising position, I turn on my heel, an alternative course of action already brewing to fermentation.

CHAPTER THREE

MY TORSO EXPANDS WITH A LONG INHALE. THE AIR OUT here is so fresh, so clean and crisp and rejuvenating, that I get a little dizzy. Energy swells to the surface and I bounce on my heels.

A morning run is the best way to rebound after a restless night. I had trouble sleeping, which is rather rare. It was almost four o'clock when I finally ended up hitting the mattress. A few miles around the lake will empty the jitters from my mind and get me back on track. Maybe an afternoon nap can be added to the schedule. Lounging in a hammock sounds divine, the potential delivering a lazy smile to my lips.

But that won't happen if I don't get my butt in gear.

I thrust my arms straight up to alleviate the lingering stiffness. The porch floor creaks beneath my soles as I step forward into a lunge. A central focal point looms ahead during the familiar warm-up routine. It's almost too easy to get lost in the motions, but this time I have a gorgeous backdrop to admire.

Vibrant colors bathe the landscape. From leafy green to wildflower purple, I'm surrounded by natural beauty. Countless birds serenade me with a cheerful tune. Another deep breath to complete the stretching phase.

This is exactly where I'm meant to be.

That's when a hear a slight flutter, like paper blowing in the breeze. A glance to my left reveals that's precisely what the sound is. My forehead pinches into a furrow when I snatch the note tacked to a railing post. My gaze is quick to devour the bold handwriting, sloppy as it might be.

To the Monroe lodge occupant,

This is your first and only warning regarding excessive noise disturbance after hours.

Be considerate of your neighbors, who don't appreciate being kept awake.

You're not the only one on this shore.

Signed,

Management

Fire singes my cheeks as I read over the words again. The hit is formal, direct, and effective. I've never been a rulebreaker, and the reprimand is shocking.

This feels unjust. Unwarranted. My music wasn't that loud. It's not like I was having a party. But even if I were, that shouldn't be an issue. The nearest cabin is out of sight.

Ingrained teachings from my past demand restraint. It's been hammered into me since birth to act calm and collected. If I never expose weakness, people can't take advantage. What a crock of shit.

I glare at the note as a gloomy shadow attempts to blot out the rising sun, seeming to reflect my plunging mood. It's difficult to not take this personally. Someone must have complained about me, which is a bitter pill to choke down.

But I have come too far, both physically and emotionally, to allow a stranger to dictate my newfound freedom. If this person has an issue with me, let them say it to my face. The backbone Elouise mentioned yesterday steels with that notion.

I widen my scope to the bigger picture and allow clarity to take root. This is a minor blip that I can smooth over. The *how* might be complicated. Even now, as I stand on this porch, I only have the owner's email address as a point of contact. He didn't provide a phone number.

Hurried movement diverts my attention from the proverbial slap on my wrist. I crumple the paper in a sure fist while waiting for what's approaching. Grass rustles and leaves crunch. My breathing accelerates and I picture the worst. But bears aren't common in this area. The half-hearted research I did months ago suddenly feels less adequate than tissue paper in the rain.

As if conjured from my heart's desire, a lone dog jogs into the yard. The fluffy wanderer moves with purpose to narrow the distance between us. Perhaps I should be afraid, but I've always been too trusting where animals are concerned.

I lower to my knees and extend a hand as a peace offering. He—an assumption on my part—doesn't hesitate to complete the required sniff test. Air seizes in my lungs as his wet nose proceeds to carefully judge me as friend or foe. He ends the thorough inspection with an enthusiastic lick. I giggle at the ticklish sensation and reach to scratch his shaggy ears. A quick peek under his belly confirms my earlier guess. He's very studly indeed. Another amused tune bubbles from me. My visitor tilts his head to one side in that adorably curious manner.

The medium-sized pooch is a mash of several breeds—Husky or Shepherd most dominant, if I had to guess. One eye is blue, and not many carry that trait. The other is a brown so dark it appears black against the speckled white fur.

"You're a beautiful boy, huh? What's your name?" I check for a tag on his collar.

The word 'Rune' gleams from a silver disk dangling from the ring. No other information is listed. My focus returns to his eager expression. His tongue is cheerfully lolling to one side of his open mouth, with slobber dribbling free. There's already a puddle forming on the ground.

"Where are you from, Rune?"

A cheerful yip answers me, paired with feverish tail wagging. There's room for interpretation. Not that I was expecting otherwise. There's just something about chatting with a pup that comes naturally. Or I'm already desperate for a companion. Either way, it's a nice reprieve from my inner dialogue.

He seems all too happy to hang around. With that wiggling butt planted on the ground, Rune nuzzles against me for more pats. I have to admit, I'm not familiar with this situation. Surely someone is close behind or searching for him. I continue lavishing him with attention while waiting for his owner to arrive. There's not much I can do other than keep him occupied.

That's when another visitor crashes through the trees along the wooded path. This one is far louder and… more masculine. I struggle to stand from where I kneel in the grass. My jaw goes slack when the man comes into full view.

His wild gaze scours the area. A noticeable calm loosens the tension when he catches sight of Rune, who's quick to welcome him by scampering around his towering height. Rather than stick near the newcomer, though, Rune reclaims his spot next to me. The guy flicks flat disinterest in my direction before refocusing on the dog. My initial glee dims somewhat, which is silly and romantic—and misplaced. I don't know him, but damn… do I ever want to make his acquaintance.

This stranger has to be the hottest man I've ever seen, and that's really saying something considering the company I've been forced to keep. The highest-paid IMG models would lose their jobs to this guy.

He's nothing short of striking. A tall, broad stature with power emanating from his wide shoulders. Hair the color of dark chocolate—my favorite indulgence. But it's his eyes that steal my ability to concentrate beyond him. Like a cloudless sky and just as endless. Those bright blue depths lull me into a false state of calm, pinned on me or not. He won't meet my imploring gaze, but I don't misinterpret that as fear. This guy could probably fight a wolf and win.

The space between us swells with warmth until moisture

pricks my brow. A furious, guttural rumble sizzles off him. He's probably sick and tired of women drooling over him. I've met him for all of two seconds and have already joined the horny harem.

In the next instant, he clenches his eyes shut. That seemingly insignificant action rips me from the floaty bliss. Then thunder enters his expression and I shiver. Still no words are exchanged.

I manage to untwist my tongue from its tied position. "Um, hi. I'm Penny."

He ignores my greeting and presence entirely. His gaze remains locked on Rune, who's still planted beside me.

Unease tickles my throat. "Is he yours?"

Nothing, not even a nod.

No problem. I can stumble through this awkward stage for both of us. "He's only been here for a few minutes. Do you live close?"

The man flares his nostrils, an indication that he hears me. Regardless of his refusal to exchange pleasantries, he doesn't flinch or cower. The silence stretches until jitters crawl under my skin. It's like having a conversation with a tree, albeit an extremely handsome one.

He still doesn't look at me. A stab of something mean lodges in my belly. I'm well aware that I'm not in my tip-top form, but acknowledging my existence isn't too much to ask for. It's not like I'm demanding a lingering glance that builds into a sultry smolder. The visual is enough to make my imagination melt.

His blatant disregard decimates my polished demeanor. I tangle my fingers until the knuckles turn white. A downward glance reminds me of the run I was about to take. That will smooth these jagged edges he's created.

"Uh, so… is there something I can do for you?" *Or to you,*

I add mentally. Suspicion hints that he wouldn't appreciate that comment.

Simmering fury rolls off him in waves as he stands too still. With a snap of his fingers, he beckons Rune to heel at his side. The dog glances between us, somber and hesitant. Conflict whimpers from him.

"Does Rune belong to you?" It deserves repeating based on his reluctance.

The man's blue eyes flash to mine for a mere beat before skittering away.

His behavior suggests submission, but I'm no fool. He bleeds pure dominance. His lack of eye contact is most likely a snub, or he isn't comfortable giving it.

A delayed and startling realization slams into me. Maybe he can't talk and I'm offending him with this insistent questioning. I'm struck with a fiery blow of alarm straight to my chest.

As if to soothe my guilt—or stoke my irritation—the man disproves that unspoken theory.

"Rune," he states with authority. "Come."

The command in his growly timbre makes my knees quake. I fumble to remain upright, fanning the embers erupting across my skin. The fluttering somersaults in my belly aren't appreciated. I shouldn't be having such a strong reaction to him. He's just a man, an extremely surly one at that.

"Come." He snaps those powerful fingers again, demanding that his command is promptly followed.

Rune lifts from his haunches and glances at me, an apology drooping his stance. His mismatched eyes are rimmed with indecision.

"Go on," I urge with a shooing motion. "We're in enough trouble already."

The silent brute emits a gruff noise, as if I'm turning his best friend against him. It shouldn't be that easy. The scolded pooch whimpers again, nearly cracking my heart in two.

I return to my crouched position and offer the pup a farewell pat. "Feel free to visit whenever, Runey-boy. The cabin gets lonely."

The comment is a last-ditch effort to get a rise from the broody stranger who refuses to speak. Sure enough, all I'm met with is chilled silence. Shocking.

I've been in therapy long enough to know this guy is dealing with some sort of… something. That's as far as I'll allow the assumptions to wander. His issues aren't my business. The rudeness might be a defense mechanism, but that's no excuse to be an asshole.

Rune dashes back to his owner, bathing his extended hand with overzealous licks. The man bends to accept sloppy kisses on his scruffy cheek. He reciprocates their joyful reunion by treating Rune to a belly rub. Their tight-knit connection and familiarity reflects in each anticipated move. The tender moment softens me to the brute.

As if just remembering my close proximity, the guy shifts to his feet with jerky motions. He turns to begin a hasty retreat with Rune trotting beside him.

"You still haven't told me your name," I call to his back.

He visibly stiffens, tossing me a quick glance. No words tumble from those full lips. Just a harsh, menacing stare not quite directed at me.

"Guess I'll call you Thorn." I mimic the act of plucking one from my side and tossing it at him.

His steely glare intensifies for several sweltering beats. I almost blot my forehead from the intense heat he's blasting at me. Those blue eyes swirl with the promise of retribution. I'm not much for revenge, but I also refuse to be a doormat.

Been there, done that, and never going back.

I wiggle my fingers at him, pasting on a wide grin for good measure. "Until we meet again, Thorn."

CHAPTER FOUR

A PITIFUL WHIMPER BREAKS ME FROM THE TOXIC CYCLE swirling in my brain. It's a needed relief. My thoughts have become putrid sludge after obsessing all morning. That doesn't mean I've forgotten the responsible party. I glance at my so-called friend, the only being I've relied on in years.

"This is all your fault."

Rune releases another sad sound, face dropping between his paws. The sight threatens to weaken my resolve. Dammit, I'm a mess. I rip my gaze away from him with a snarl.

"You're not getting off that hook that easily."

He blinks those different colored eyes at me. The picture of innocence. Unguarded and pleading. That leads me straight back to another pair I recently got lost in.

I was so transfixed on everything else last night that I didn't see them. Now she pummels me with the full force of those hazel depths. Gray swirls with brown, a storm brewing on the horizon. How fucking poetic.

Penny.

My boots pound on the cement while I resume pacing. That woman is nothing but trouble. She reminds me of dreams better left forgotten. Optimism, kindness, compassion. More than that, she's the embodiment of a bright future. But all that's left for me is darkness and shadows.

I'm not afforded the privilege to escape this prison. Seven years in solitary isolation will cripple a person mentally. I've lost the ability to have a fucking conversation. Not that I'd break my silence for her. The lie drives a hot stake through my temple.

Penny.

The name plays on repeat, haunting me on a continuous loop. It seems so innocent and prim, yet has the power to obliterate me. An image of the countless ways I'd break for her soon follow.

"Fuck." I grind my molars until an ache blooms. "Damn temptress."

Rune offers a noncommittal noise, most likely in agreement. He was all too quick to fall under her spell. If I hadn't arrived when I did, he'd probably have adopted her as part of his inner pack. The resulting attachment would be cruel to sever.

"Traitor." I glare at him again.

He snorts, tail thumping on the ground.

"If only we could all be so calm." My agitation forms dust clouds that I choke on. That doesn't mean I stop burning a path into the concrete. It's not like there's anything else I can do.

Penny.

I've been replaying her introduction for hours. It's seared to memory at this point. Her voice is softer than silk, and equally as devastating.

Her identity wasn't a secret. I have her basic information from the paperwork, but hearing the delectable syllables curl off her tongue has awoken something that's been buried deep beneath the surface. Five minutes in her presence has rattled the solid foundation I've spent years building. She makes me want things I've long since abandoned. To flirt and fight and fuck. Be the charming punk I used to be. That's what truly causes this riot in my blood. But I can't allow my walls to crumble. That's how the enemy invades.

There's a reason I stay secluded in these woods. People can't be trusted. I learned that lesson early on and it was fucking harsh. That's trapped in the past, the steel door reinforced with betrayal. It's done and dealt with, but not wiped from memory. She's a reminder of what I left behind. I can't invite those complications to my house, even if she's already right next door.

Penny.

The interest was mutual. Maybe that's what really dangles me by the balls. I might not get along with people well, but even I could feel her attraction to me. Rosy cheeks and parted lips. A lingering glance I could feel stroking my cock. She couldn't stop fidgeting. Desperation to watch her squirm under other circumstances surges to the surface. I chase those fantasies off with a scoff.

Any initial desire she may have felt has been snubbed out. My reception toward her made sure of that. Penny tried to engage with me, and I gave her a cold shoulder. It makes me look like a simpering coward, but I'm not afraid. I don't want to imagine what she thinks of me. A sour gurgle bubbles in my gut.

It's not that I can't talk. She heard my growled commands pointed at Rune. The choice is mine, and I avoid it by any means necessary. A hollow pang reverberates through my chest. It's a frigid souvenir of who I've become. All that remains is an empty shell. Anything of value or substance is gone. No one can bring those parts of me back.

Not even her.

Penny.

Her parting remark taunts me. She plans for our paths to cross again. I'd be lying if I didn't admit that the possibility intrigues me.

She had the audacity to give me a nickname. *Thorn.* The implication is a crock of shit. As if I'd ever get close enough to prick her.

But I almost smile. It actually sounds pretty badass. Leaving my mark on her doesn't sound like such a chore either.

"Dammit," I bellow to the ceiling.

Rune flops to his side with a gruff moan. He's done listening to my shit. Can't say I blame him.

I need a distraction before I lose what little sanity lingers. My furious gaze settles on the tools scattered across the bench. I haven't been able to concentrate on work. The gnarled oak trunk remains untouched in the corner. It's going to be a custom table base if I ever get myself straightened out. But I find myself too preoccupied to even pick up a sander.

The limited options lead me outside. Maybe a swim will help clear my head. Rune is fast to agree, loping ahead on the path as if he can read my mind. The water shimmers with a promise of peace from this internal battle. I'm already anticipating the bite from the cold as my boots hit the sand.

A not-so-distant gasp whips my focus to the left. What I find brings my progress to an alarming halt. Penny is wading waist-deep in the calm depths. Her creeping pace suggests she's still adjusting to the temperature. It seems she's infiltrated this domain as well.

"Fuck," I spit. Indecision pummels me from both sides.

The blonde bombshell isn't aware that she has company. Her hesitation reaches me on a breeze. "Brrr, brrr, freaking *brrr*."

That almost twitches my lips, but I recall the purpose. I was attempting to escape this woman's witchery. My spine steels when she eases forward a few inches. She's invading each corner of my sanctuary without an ounce of remorse.

The lake would be big enough for both of us if we weren't neighbors. It was a mistake putting her in the cabin next to mine. I should've assigned her to Pine or Birch farther away. It's not like anyone else booked them. But I couldn't keep her in my sights if that were the case.

The ulterior motive gives me pause. I can't be thinking like that. She's causing too much damage as it is. The last thing

I need to do is pay more attention to her. That doesn't mean I'm going to hide. This shore is mine, dammit.

As if to announce my territorial claim, Rune leaps into the shallows with a resounding splash. Penny twists in our direction, eyes hidden behind oversized sunglasses. Shock unhinges her jaw and she drops into the water. She immediately springs upright with a sputter. A loud shriek follows close behind. Her arms form a protective cocoon to ward off the chill. I grunt at her scrambled display. The lake is still damn hostile in late May and takes some getting used to. She just got a harsh lesson of her own.

Clarity attempts to take root in my muddled brain. Penny wasn't trying to warm herself up—she was trying to hide herself from me. Maybe the little vixen is modest. Didn't appear shy this morning, or in the middle of the night. I absently wonder what might happen if I strip down to my boxers and join her.

"Are you just going to stand there?" Her fists are now parked on those curvy hips, erasing any assumption of bashfulness. The seductive visual she willingly provides will tent my shorts in mere moments. She's too effective at getting under my skin.

I wrench my eyes from her with a muffled curse. Rune is already paddling her way. His sleek form will reach her in seconds.

"Seriously?" The word is a gritty punch.

He slows, but not completely. The conflict ripples and swells. I'm just as drawn to her, which means I need to double down on my resistance.

Summer hasn't officially started. She just arrived and will decimate my control for months to come. August is a faraway blip on the radar. I can't avoid altercations with her, but I can at least try to lessen their impact—otherwise, nothing good will come from them.

I'm still the one to retreat. For now.

CHAPTER FIVE

I SIP AT MY STIFF COCKTAIL—FAR MORE VODKA THAN SODA—AND scan the dim interior. There's not much to see beyond faded posters, dusty shelves, and wobbly tables. The dank smell reminds me of a long-forgotten basement. In short, this bar is… incredible.

A snort shoots from me, disrupting the alcohol swirling in my glass. If only my parents could see me now. They'd never step a pompous foot inside a dive like this. It would be so far beneath them that they'd practically shrivel up on contact. Maybe that's why I feel right at home at the humble establishment called Timbered Tavern.

"You're new." The distinctly feminine voice comes from directly over my shoulder.

My eyes are already narrowed into a skeptical squint as I turn to acknowledge her. The snarky guard is warranted—I've already been bitched at by three local women in the ten minutes since I arrived. This one's smile is a pleasant change, but that might be a fake front for her to land a painful strike.

I quirk a brow, willing to entertain her inquisition. "What gave me away?"

"Other than the wince you let off with each sip of Greg's legendary overpouring?" She juts her chin at my drink, brown hair managing to shine in the dark room.

"It's very strong." The sickly slosh in my stomach is proof enough.

"And tastes like cheap shit," she laughs.

My nose wrinkles as I dare to swallow another gulp.

"It's… no, it's not that bad," I insist, laboriously downing the stuff with a smile plastered on my face.

She levels me with a quirked brow of her own.

"You're a terrible liar. But I suppose you'll build up a tolerance eventually like the rest of us lifers." The woman thrusts an open palm at me. "I'm Lydia."

I clasp her proffered introduction in a quick shake. "Penny."

She slides her skinny ass onto the rickety stool beside mine. "What brings you to Bumfuck, Nowhere?"

"Is that where we are? I might be lost." I glance around in mock concern.

A bright smile highlights her pretty features. "Funny girl. I appreciate the humor. We don't get many visitors in Hacken, especially a single lady."

I can't say that's a surprise, but still. "Even with that concert venue at the edge of town? Excel Entertainment?"

She waves a dismissive hand. "The renovation was a total bust. They only host concerts once a month and the talent isn't that impressive."

"Really? That seems like a waste."

"Meh." She shrugs. "I stopped paying attention."

My mouth dips into a frown. "Bummer, I was hoping to catch a show."

"Oh, you can. Probably snag front row too." Lydia wiggles her brows.

I rub my palms together. "Ah, that sounds promising. What about backstage passes?"

"That's not a thing 'round here." She pauses to give me a once-over. "Where are you from?"

Rocks drop in my belly. "Tampa."

She reels backward, the ancient stool creaking in protest. "Florida?"

"Yeah?" Not sure why that comes out as a question.

"Long way from home," Lydia mumbles almost absently.

"I didn't belong there. Consider this my second chance. It's just getting started."

"And you chose this hole to begin again?" She stabs a finger into the wood counter.

"Yep, and I couldn't be happier."

"Wow, I'm gonna need something strong to wash that down with." She signals to the bartender, who I assume is Greg. "I'll have whatever you gave her."

He saunters over with far too much swagger. The wink he tacks on only adds to the cheesy display. "Comin' right up, hot stuff."

Lydia clucks her tongue. "Don't get smart with me. We're not getting naked tonight."

"We'll see how you feel after this." He slides the glass across the chipped bar. The clear liquid splashes over the sides.

"Sloppy," the sassy brunette mutters.

"If the drink fits the customer," he returns with a crude stroking gesture.

"Ass," Lydia jests.

"Hussy," he retorts.

Her light eyes flash with vengeance. "Oh, you better take that back."

He crosses his beefy arms, a cocky smirk tilting his lips. "Gonna make me?"

I'm fully invested in their entertaining banter until Greg struts off to help someone else. "Are you two…?"

"Absolutely not. He's just very well hung." She holds her hands at least a foot apart. "When the kitty demands a good and thorough dicking, he's the one to call. I'm done with him, so feel free to get your hump on."

I choke on my drink at her forward comment. "I see."

She plays with the straw between her teeth while assessing me. "Prude?"

"Virgin," I admit in a hushed whisper. My flushed cheeks give me away for miles.

Her jaw drops. "I thought those were a myth at our age."

"Not when you're raised under strict rule."

Air hisses from her. "That doesn't sound good."

A drawn-out huff signals my agreement. "But I'm here now."

Lydia leans in with a conspiratorial wink. "And looking to pop your cherry?"

Nerves create a jumble in my throat. I gulp against the clump. "Eventually."

"Greg would very eagerly help with that." She blindly swats in his general direction, but he's not really my type.

My mind flashes to Rune's broody owner. Now that's a mighty fine example of chiseled male glory in full definition. Oozing testosterone from his pores. My mouth waters just recalling the glimpse of his sculpted torso through the thin shirt he wore yesterday. How badly I wanted him to ditch the threads and jump in the lake. The chicken shit vanished before I could suggest it. Pretty sure I heard him cursing my name while stomping away.

I'll give him a reason to nibble at my bait. It's just a matter of casting the line in the right spot. He won't be able to resist a taste. I giggle at the mental image of reeling him in. My research on fishing is already coming in handy.

"You sure about that?" Lydia's voice knocks me from the lusty musings.

I blink the remaining smoky tendrils from my vision. "Huh?"

"Looked like you were picturing getting busy with our bartender," she drawls with saucy enthusiasm.

The mere mention is a wet, soggy blanket slapping against my feverish loins, effectively extinguishing any trace of heat. "No, not at all."

"Too sexy?" She smacks her lips at Greg.

"Too easy," I counter. Not to mention taken by my new friend. Something tells me she doesn't actually want me to sleep with him.

She props an elbow on her knee, sighing wistfully. "Ah, he's definitely eager to please. Won't put up a fight."

As if that's appealing. Bile threatens to choke me. "Hard pass."

"I totally get it. You didn't save yourself just to be plucked by the town bull." At my blank look, she clarifies. "Everyone's had a ride."

"Charming."

"Quite."

Maybe this will be considered overstepping, but she seems like the type to appreciate loose boundaries. "And you're okay having sex with him while he's with so many others?"

Lydia wags a finger. "Oh, we're totally over. I plugged the plug after catching him banging Bimbo Bettie."

"But before that?"

"Well, no. Not really." A cringe pinches her expression. "But it's slim pickings in these parts. That's just the way it is."

"How… unfortunate." It makes me wonder how many girls are getting busy with Mr. Surly Silence.

"It's whatever. Most girls get clingy and possessive, but don't worry about me. I'm not like them." She hikes a thumb at the vicious trio that offered me such warm welcomes with sharp claws.

I mirror their haughty glares aimed at us. "What's their deal?"

"They're just worried you're gonna swoop in and steal the only available men in Hacken. Jealous wenches. Stay far away and you'll be fine." Lydia waves at them with her middle finger.

"Noted."

"Also, if you're looking for decent tail, I'll take you to Walton or Thymouth. A bit of a drive, but high-quality stock in the meat department."

I don't recall those on the route, but Hacken was barely a speck. "Were you born here?"

"And raised. Anything you need, just ask. I'm a walking map and gossip column rolled into one." She blows on her pointed index fingertips.

Her intel on everyone within a fifty-mile radius sparks a thought. "Do you know a guy who lives off Timbered Lake or visits regularly? Seems to be the quiet type. He has a dog named Rune."

She scrunches her face. "I don't think so."

Disappointment deflates my posture. "Damn."

"Why do you ask?"

"I've had a few… minor mishaps with him." But that's being extremely generous. He seems to barely tolerate my presence.

Recognition suddenly sparks in Lydia's gaze. "Oh, wait! Is he ridiculously hot? Like, could instantly impregnate you from one smoldering glance?"

I'm nodding in supremely jerky fashion. "Very much so."

"Super broody and mysterious?"

"Yes."

"Didn't talk to you?"

"Not a word." I slurp at the remains of my drink.

"That's Nash Hudson. He owns the Timbered Forest lodges."

I spit out my mouthful of vodka. "What?"

Lydia's brows hike skyward. "Nash Hudson?"

My pulse beats to a staccato tempo. "Do you have a picture?"

"I wish." She bites her lip with a moan. "But it would keep me up all night."

Me too, I agree completely for my benefit.

He'd make gorgeous wallpaper. It wouldn't be too difficult to capture a candid. Creepy? Probably. An invasion of privacy? Most definitely. Is that going to stop me? Undecided.

"He's the owner of the Timbered Forest lodges," I recite dumbly.

"You're catching on." She pats my head in a pacifying manner.

"That's where I'm staying. In the Monroe lodge."

"And?" She rolls her wrist to motion me onward.

That asshat is the one responsible for the oh-so-sweet complaint that was tacked to my porch. I did a bit of digging into the other cabins on the property. All sit empty.

The only peace I'm disturbing is his.

"It's perfect," I whisper.

She squints at me. "How so?"

"I can smoke him out." The idea makes me positively giddy, a thrill zipping up my spine.

"You don't seem devious, but should I be concerned?"

"For me? Without a doubt." I shove away the scheming that tries to instantly take shape. "This is above my paygrade."

"And now you're losing me," she mumbles.

"Just… thank you." I grip her upper arm impulsively, then remember we're not on that level of friendship yet. *Note to self: must contain my excitement.* "It's brilliant and reckless and just what I need."

Her sharp gaze narrows on me. "I might've underestimated you, newbie. You're feisty."

I clutch a palm to my chest. "That's the nicest thing anyone has ever said to me."

"Um, wow. I retract my last statement. You're more of a magical unicorn who poops rainbows."

"Are you trying to make me melt?" I fan my face with a breathy exhale.

"Greg's potion is working wonders." She points at my empty glass. "Another?"

"Sure, we're celebrating."

"I'm always down for a good time." She snatches her fresh drink before Greg can set the glass down. "Cheers to finding whatever you're searching for."

A grin slips over my mouth easily. It's as if she's reading my mind. "I'll drink to that. You've just given me an advantage in this fight."

He'll crack eventually, and now I have the means to get a step or two ahead.

Lydia lets a whistle loose. "Damn, I didn't realize you're feuding. Is he your enemy?"

"Only if he insists on it." But I've always been more of an attack with kindness sort of girl.

"Oh, the sex will be explosive." She mimics her head blowing up. "I'll be demanding all the dirty details."

My toes curl in my flip-flops. I can't picture how that would go, so it's best not to include it as an option. "That's not going to happen."

The guy can't even look at me for thirty seconds without storming off in an angry rant.

Her laugh is ready to call my bluff. "How else will this end?"

"No clue." This situation is another unknown for me to cross. I tap my lips, attempting to untangle the snag. "But I'm going to find out."

CHAPTER SIX

Nash

I SET THE NEXT LOG AND PREPARE TO STRIKE. A SWIFT DOWNWARD arc splits the piece into two. Set, strike, split, repeat. Replenishing the firewood supply takes priority with a guest on site. Penny probably burned through half the stack in her cabin already.

The seamless repetition comes to a screeching halt. I'm supposed to be keeping her far from my mind. A foul curse reinforces my resolve.

By some miracle, we've managed to maintain our distance over the past few days. That doesn't mean my thoughts don't stray to her at every available moment. Rune's constant insistence to visit our neighbor only aggravates the situation.

The hellhound in mention is gnawing away at his bone, only pausing to implore me with those mismatched eyes, seeking the truth I'm trying to evade. Or maybe it's my imagination. Most likely the latter.

These meddling distractions are precisely why I startle from the vibration in my pocket. Email notifications are rare. Even more so after filtering customer order alerts through my website.

I grab the discarded rag and wipe my brow, the axe dropping to the dirt with a soft thump. The debris coating my hands is a lost cause. With a harsh tug, the phone rests in my calloused palm. A single swipe and the message appears—prim and proper.

From: Penny Blaire
To: Timbered Forest

Today at 11:39 AM
Subject: Please advise

Dear Mr. Hudson,

I wanted to bring an urgent matter to your attention.

I've spotted a strange man in the woods on several occasions. He won't acknowledge me or answer simple questions regarding his identity. I'm afraid he's lost or something.

If I'm being honest, I'm also worried for my safety. It's already a risk staying way out here in the middle of nowhere alone.

Can you please provide reassurance that this man isn't going to cause me harm?

Eagerly awaiting your response,
Penny Blaire (Monroe lodge tenant)

I like to consider myself a fairly level-headed guy. At least, under normal circumstances. Whatever that means. But it's definitely not this.

The words glowing on my screen are tinted with a red hue as my blood sets to a boil. She's claiming that I'm a potential danger. A threat that requires management to get involved. The sheer audacity shreds what remains of my pride. As if she weren't causing enough problems already.

My fingers are a furious blur as I type a response.

From: Timbered Forest
To: Penny Blaire
Today at 11:41 AM
Subject: Re: Please advise
Ms. Blaire,

Your concern is noted, but unnecessary.

I'm familiar with the man you saw. He's not a problem for you to think twice about.

Enjoy your stay in the Monroe lodge.
Nash Hudson
Owner of Timbered Forest Lodges

Her reply is almost instantaneous. As if she was ready and waiting for my response to come through.

From: Penny Blaire
To: Timbered Forest
Today at 11:42 AM
Subject: Re: Re: Please advise

Mr. Hudson,

How do you know it's the same guy? Also, how can you be certain he's not a threat?

No offense, but your word—by email—doesn't put me at ease.

On the edge of my seat,

Penny Blaire (Monroe lodge tenant)

A cramp seizes my lungs as I read her refusal to cooperate. I'm spitting fire while my fingers set to typing a response.

From: Timbered Forest
To: Penny Blaire
Today at 11:44 AM
Subject: Re: Re: Re: Please advise
Ms. Blaire,

If you're this upset about meeting a person out here in the middle of nowhere on your own, perhaps you should find a vacation resort more suitable to your liking.

I'll waive the early cancelation fee.

Best of luck at your next stop.

Nash Hudson

Owner of Timbered Forest Lodges

The whoosh that dares me to hit send is like a punch to my solar plexus. This could be a premature end to months of torture and agony. If she accepts the offer to leave, I'll return to my solitude as desired.

Numbness filters in, familiar and cold.

I don't want to admit that Penny's presence has been a welcome reprieve from the vast loneliness. She'll leave eventually. Might as well be sooner rather than later. It's for the best, dammit.

But the hollow pang spreads faster across my chest.

Relief is a stark and disturbing beast when the phone vibrates in my palm.

From: Penny Blaire
To: Timbered Forest
Today at 11:47 AM
Subject: Re: Re: Re: Re: Please advise

Are you trying to get rid of me, Mr. Hudson?

From: Timbered Forest
To: Penny Blaire
Today at 11:48 AM
Subject: Re: Re: Re: Re: Re: Please advise

Not at all, Ms. Blaire.

Feel free to do what you believe is best.

Your comfort should come first.

Let me know what you decide.

Nash Hudson

Owner of Timbered Forest Lodges

From: Penny Blaire
To: Timbered Forest
Today at 11:50 AM
Subject: Skip the formalities

If my comfort is important, you won't mind telling me about the stranger in the woods.

Who is he? Why won't he talk to me?

I don't want to be insensitive. Just hoping to understand.

The air whizzes from me in a deflating hiss. Revealing my true identity wasn't part of the plan. All I wanted was to stay out of sight and complete the property management duties as required. She's asking too much, yet barely anything at all.

Genuine compassion bleeds from her curiosity, demanding as she might be. Trust in her arrives too easily all the same.

A clenching knot attempts to suffocate me as I prepare my confession.

From: Timbered Forest
To: Penny Blaire
Today at 11:53 AM
Subject: Re: Skip the formalities

The man in the woods is me.

I choose to speak when there's a reason worthy of doing so.

From: Penny Blaire
To: Timbered Forest
Today at 11:55 AM
Subject: Re: Re: Skip the formalities

Should I be offended? Maybe. I'll let it slide for now.

Thanks for your honesty.

Also, can I have your phone number?

The request gives me pause. I stare at the words, my pulse thrumming a feverish beat. Gut instinct declares I should reject her outright, but this compelling interest in her still holds me hostage.

From: Timbered Forest
To: Penny Blaire
Today at 11:58 AM
Subject: Re: Re: Re: Skip the formalities

Why?

From: Penny Blaire
To: Timbered Forest
Today at 11:59 AM
Subject: This is obnoxious

Exchanging emails is old-fashioned and time-consuming.

Texting is much faster.

Or, if you prefer, we can try Snapchat.

I choke while reading that last option. As if I'd be connected on social media. That defeats the purpose of going off-grid. Not that I expect her to know that.

From: Timbered Forest
To: Penny Blaire
Today at 12:01 PM
Subject: Re: This is obnoxious

Texting isn't necessary.

Any requests you have can be sent here.

I'll respond at my earliest convenience.

From: Penny Blaire
To: Timbered Forest
Today at 12:02 PM
Subject: Seriously?
Why can't I have your phone number?

The relentless prodding against my well-established boundaries sets me into motion. I pace along the gravel path. Leaves and twigs crunch under my agitated stride. It's been years since I've sent a text. There's no point in forming the habit again.

With a refusal blazing in my veins, I stab at the screen with a curt reply.

From: Timbered Forest
To: Penny Blaire
Today at 12:04 PM
Subject: Re: Seriously?

It's personal.

From: Penny Blaire
To: Timbered Forest
Today at 12:05 PM

Subject: I repeat, seriously?

More personal than me renting your cabin?

From: Timbered Forest
To: Penny Blaire
Today at 12:06 PM
Subject: Re: I repeat, seriously?

Yes.

From: Penny Blaire
To: Timbered Forest
Today at 12:07 PM
Subject: Be creative.

I don't get why it's such a big deal.

From: Timbered Forest
To: Penny Blaire
Today at 12:08 PM
Subject: That's the problem.

You wouldn't, so don't bother trying.

I refresh after a frozen minute. No response appears in my inbox. My gaze is glued to the screen like a fiend in desperate need of a fix. I wait, bated breath locked in my lungs. Only silence finds me.

Maybe I've chased her off. I should be relieved, but bitter resentment finds me.

Not directed at her.

No. That's solely for me.

For a few minutes, I almost felt connected to someone again.

The stillness yawns and stretches, as it should. As it has since I arrived in this isolated location. I'm alone on purpose. This is my choice, how it's meant to be.

But the longing sneaks in while my guard is lowered.

The soulful yearning for compassion and comfort from another. The very desire I've tried to ignore. I was doing just fine until Penny Blaire barged in without warning. She's left me exposed. Vulnerable to the crater gouged into my chest.

I'm slowly dragged back into the dark caverns where I belong.

Where nobody else dares to enter.

Fuck that.

CHAPTER SEVEN

MUSHY SENTIMENTS AND ENDLESS DEVOTION BLEND INTO nonsensical jargon as my mind drifts once again. Not even my favorite romance novel can hold my attention. With a huff steeped in frustration, I toss the book aside and search for a different distraction.

I glare at my phone, as if the device is personally responsible for this ache. Nash hurt my feelings. The assumption that I can't empathize with or comprehend his preference for extreme privacy has left me sore and raw. Following close behind is guilt thick enough to chew on. I rub at the heavy force rooted in my chest.

Maybe I was too pushy. Selfish and stubborn. But dammit, he kept responding. Flinging barbs just as sharp and quick. It felt like an even match. The conversation flowed with our digital sparring. Until he tacked on that nasty retort as a final blow.

The more I think about our exchange, I realize my actions might've been inappropriate. Brash and forward while I was aiming for playful and witty. I don't know this man. He's a stranger. There's an explanation for why he's out here alone, perfectly fine not talking to anyone. One I'm not allowed to pry at. That's his secret to keep.

My knee bounces to a distressed tempo. I need a change of scenery. The dog shelter isn't far from here. It could be a quick visit, just to see if I bond with any available pooches up for adoption. I don't have to bring one home. Yet. That option has appeal enough to lift my butt off the couch.

As I'm searching for my keys, a telltale chime attempts

to send me off track. I try to resist. I really do. But the temptation is too strong. Besides, delayed gratification isn't nearly as satisfying. A haughty laugh trips from me as I scoop my phone off the coffee table. That opinion is coming from the girl with zero sexual experience. Real valuable.

The notification glows on the screen and gets my heart thumping.

From: Timbered Forest
To: Penny Blaire
Today at 1:17 PM
Subject: In case of emergency

612-555-0164

And cue the giddy flutters. I press a hand to my warm cheek. It's silly to be this excited about a phone number, but I've never done this before. Just text a man for the thrill of it.

And that makes me sound like a sheltered loser.

Guilty as charged.

I create a new contact, storing him under Thorn. More zippy glee shoots through me and I grin. Then my fingers are flying with a sugary sweet reply.

Me: You're forgiven.

My thumbnail is lodged between my teeth while waiting for the three little dots to appear. Nash doesn't leave me hanging for more than twenty seconds.

Thorn: I wasn't aware I needed forgiving.

Me: No? Then why did you cave?

Thorn: I didn't cave.

Me: I'm texting you, aren't I?

There's a pause, long enough to get my foot tapping. I'm probably overstepping again. Just as I'm about to pocket my phone, he adds to the thread.

Thorn: So it seems.

Me: And you're responding. Willingly, I might add.

Thorn: You're staying in a cabin on my property. That implies your well-being is somewhat my responsibility.

A visual of him caring for me—in multiple forms—springs forward. More belly swoops soon follow. I nibble at the smile curving my lips. His response gives me an idea. Goading him is just too much fun. More so, I want to keep him talking.

Me: Do you employ a tour guide?

Thorn: No.

Me: Can you recommend someone in town?

Thorn: No.

The prickles are extra pointy this afternoon. Too bad for him and his bristly armor. I'm not afraid to get poked.

Me: How about someone not from town?

Thorn: No.

Me: That's unfortunate. I often find myself lost while hiking and exploring. It would be helpful to walk the paths with someone familiar with the area.

Thorn: Get a map.

A snort spews from me. Chivalry is lost on this one. He might be, quite simply, the greatest challenge I've met. Good thing I set off on this adventure to conquer the unknown.

Me: I don't think a detailed layout of the area exists, unless you made one. This is your land, right?

Thorn: Just stay on the trails. They're properly marked.

Me: Will I find my way in the dark?

Thorn: If you bring a flashlight.

Me: Why are you being so difficult?

Thorn: Not sure what you mean by that. I've answered all your questions.

Me: Without providing a decent solution. Do you want me to get lost? Ambushed? Meander off in the wrong direction until I reach the Canadian border? Attacked by a bear? Any harm that comes my way will rest on your conscience. Are you prepared for that?

A lull hangs in the balance after I send that babbled rant. He's most likely chewing on a proper response to put me in my place. I'm being a diva on purpose, of course. Traversing in the woods—especially during the day—doesn't scare me. Not after staring down the barrel of my future shackled to a monster like Nathaniel.

But Nash doesn't know that. It serves him right for not coming with a warning label. In truth, I'm doing him a favor. Troublesome renters won't appear like such a hardship once I've moved on.

Besides, if Nash didn't want to deal with me, he wouldn't have sent his number.

Thorn: What do you expect me to do?

Me: Point me in the right direction.

Thorn: I already did.

Me: Not very well since I'm standing still.

Thorn: Don't let me stop you.

Me: That's exactly what you're doing.

I pace in front of the couch when the three dots appear and dance. Then he stops writing. Several beats pass before he starts again. The pattern goes on for a full minute. My gaze is burning a hole into the screen when his reply finally appears.

Thorn: You can borrow Rune.

The grin that cracks my face is cheesy as hell. I'm sure there's a scowl that rivals a thunderstorm on his.

Me: Great! When can I pick him up?

Thorn: I'll drop him off.

Me: I'll be waiting.

There isn't much else for me to do. I'm already dressed for action. My gym shorts, tank top, and tennis shoes are ideal for a warm afternoon exploring the woodsy scenery. With a bounce in my stride, I lock the door and skip down the porch stairs.

It only takes a few minutes for the sounds of approaching steps to reach me. Nash's place must be right next to mine, which is what I assumed after seeing him so close on the beach. His broad frame breaks through the trees. My mouth goes dry when I catch sight of his bright blue eyes. For a man who avoids others with ferocity, he has the magnetism to at-tract a horde. The impact is instant and intense. I'm drawn into those cloudless skies until it feels like I'm floating. It's devastating.

Rune gallops into the clearing with his canine grace and glory on display. His energetic incoming knocks me from my stupor and I lower to my knees with arms spread wide. He doesn't waste a second, dousing my face in slobbery kisses. I manage to tunnel my fingers into his silky hair as an anchor. Medium-sized he may be, but his enthusiasm can still topple me without much effort.

"I missed you, Runey-boy." A gruff noise comes from the broody Thorn rather far from my side. I ignore him, wisely choosing to shower the eager pooch with my attention. "Did you miss me too?"

Rune's tail could chop down a full-grown tree at the speed it's wagging. Happy yips further prove his joy at our reunion.

I rub at the scruff area under his collar, which results in him collapsing against me. My nails hit the jackpot and his hind leg begins to pinwheel. Strain bleeds from my muscles as I spoil him with extra love. There's just something about the unconditional affection from a dog that can't be beat.

A whimsical sigh hints at my relaxed mood. We could probably stay in this spot for hours, but there's hiking to be done.

"Should we go for a walk?"

His answer is a chipper bark, announced loud and proud.

"You can lead the way. Would you like that?"

He hops in place, bumping me with his wet nose. Several licks are added in for good measure.

"Okay, I'm ready." I stand with a stretch, catching sight of a dark presence nearby.

It's only then do I remember his owner looming mere feet from us.

I offer him a wave, fast and lame. "Thanks for this. I appreciate Rune's company."

Nash's blistering blue gaze burns directly into me. It seems he's no longer avoiding eye contact. Tingles erupt along the back of my neck. I'm frozen in this moment as he pins me in place with that smoldering stare. My tongue swells and I nearly choke on nothing but the crackling air between us.

"Should I text you when we're done?"

His blink is slow, lids hooded over those seductive depths. I'm certain he's trying to incinerate my common sense that begs me to tuck tail and get a move on. That's the only explanation for what spews from me next.

"Do you want to join us?"

CHAPTER EIGHT

Nash

PENNY DOESN'T WITHER UNDER MY STARE LIKE MANY OTHERS do. Quite the opposite as she lifts her chin and reflects my unwavering focus. The woman is vibrant and bold—and a major pain in my ass.

"No pressure or anything," she blurts. "I don't want to come off as pushy. Rude either."

I assume she's trying to make a joke, but her expression remains hopeful and extra sunny. She obviously hasn't felt how far she's already pushed the limits of my normal. The mere fact that I'm even standing here is hard evidence. It's been months since I've spent time with someone on purpose. That didn't seem like an issue until a certain blonde landed in my territory.

Hazel eyes study me with too much awareness. I subject her to the same scrutiny. Her tan complexion is flushed, chest rising and falling faster than typical for a relaxed state. Mine matches the erratic rhythm as I glance at her golden hair that's streaked with sunshine. The long length is swept in a messy knot on the top of her head. My fingers curl with a primal desire to yank on those glossy strands.

Lust billows feverish heat in my veins. I treat myself to another lazy perusal. Penny is too beautiful for this place. A precious and rare gem buried in dirt. That prods at a discovery I recently made. After our initial clash, I dug into her history. Or lack thereof.

The list of inconsistencies I've found about this woman is longer than the Mississippi River. She has secrets. Ones I find myself intrigued by. The fact she chose to live in this obscure location for the entire summer raises suspicion. A lone woman staying by herself was strange from the start. Her lack of wilderness experience and fear of traveling the woods only adds to the oddity. There's no question that this rural fortress tends to repel the female population. The rental history reveals as much. It tends to attract guys looking for a decent spot to fish.

As I continue leering like a creep, I find myself wondering about her story. Again. I've lost track of how many times my mind has strayed to this topic as of late. There's no explanation for why this curiosity hounds me, or why I give a single shit at all.

It's the demand for answers that keeps me close. Nothing else.

Soon the lies will stack higher than the walls I hide behind. But that doesn't change the truth.

Penny Blaire is a farce. The permanent address she listed on her application is a public library in Iowa. There isn't a chance that this posh darling is from a tiny town near Cedar Rapids. Not born and raised, at least. The hint of a southern accent betrays her, slight and infrequent as it might be. I'm not in the market for bullshit. The deceitful variety she's trying to sell shouldn't make a difference. Yet it does just that.

I've considered the very likely possibility that she's on the run for whatever reason. My resolve wavers whenever that thought enters the ring of my wayward obsessing. I'm the last person who can condemn her for attempting to start a new life elsewhere. On the contrary, I feel the steely lump in my chest softening at the prospect of us having that in common. What's more concerning is that I can't pry without fear of her returning the favor.

Penny is jabbing at my protective layers with each breath, and appears well aware of it. "Am I making you uncomfortable? Just figured you were sticking around, maybe waiting for an invite."

I grunt, tipping my face to the sky to search for a higher power to grant me tolerance. There's none to be found. Only the typical nature soundtrack, but Penny's chipper humming cuts into the white noise.

"Does that mean yes?" The innocent prompt is one more lash against my better judgment.

My gaze seeks hers without permission. Brown and green swirl in her bottomless depths, begging for my surrender. How easy it would be to fall. My breathing remains elevated, as if I just completed a five-mile run. I need space.

She's entirely too tempting and untouchable. I compel my body to retreat, but I might as well be trapped in stone. Control is a rapidly fraying thread.

Penny releases a drawn-out sigh. Wisps of stray hair shoot off her forehead from the effort. "Should I repeat the question?"

The urge to answer her is a vicious force ripping me in two. I waver as the opposing sides prepare for battle. In the end, this darling is difficult to deny. That's precisely why I don't. Not directly.

My focus dips low to the traitor guarding her side. "See you in a few hours, Rune. Be a good boy."

Without further detriment to my wits, I turn and stride off. A disgruntled huff smacks my cowardice in the back. I'm being a bastard on purpose. Serves her right for steering me in this warped direction. Even so, blatantly ignoring her is a dick move—not that I plan to change course anytime soon.

I keep my pace at a fast clip to avoid the tide trying to shove me in reverse.

"Seriously?" Stunned disbelief is evident in her tone.

My steps falter, which pushes me onward. Branches whip at my feverish skin as I aim straight for the trail. I vanish from the clearing but don't go far. As if I'm going to let her take my dog and disappear. The truth mocks me. I want to keep her close for the sake of my sanity. She's driving me directly to madness. It's only fitting that I compartmentalize this stint under the illusion of protecting her.

The excuse is flimsy, even to my own deranged brain.

I cut off the path and wait behind a tree. It's so damn quiet that my racing pulse feels like an angry stampede in my throat. She might notice me. My white shirt is a beacon. I remain still, the threat not enough to slap sense into me. The ability to leave is no longer mine to possess.

The shadows are my friends as I duck to dodge low-hanging obstacles. Darkness plagues my mood and it's her fault. But not really. Once again, I'm madder at myself for willingly strutting into this shitstorm. No one forced me to offer Rune as her guide. That's her damn intoxicating influence speaking. She might drive me to distraction, but I'll gain the upper hand before nightfall.

Penny stews in silence for a minute. Delayed acceptance expels from her with a harsh breath. Slow footfalls shuffle across the grass soon after. She chooses to go north with Rune jogging beside her.

Some deep, problematic compulsion sets me in motion. My tread is soft to avoid instant detection. It isn't lost on me that I'm walking the line with stalker-like tendencies. But I can't let her out of my sight. Not entirely.

If she gets lost, I'll be the one who has to find her anyway. This saves me trouble and eliminates the risk before it can occur. I nearly crash into a bush when Penny's lyrical voice serenades our surroundings.

"Who broke him, Runey-boy? Was it a girl? I bet she regrets that decision."

Now I do stumble, my fingers barely snagging the smooth

bark of a nearby maple. My calluses provide extra grip or I'd be flat on my ass.

How very wrong she is.

She hums, her sloppy bun bouncing to and fro with indecision. "No response?"

Rune's smooth stride doesn't hitch. The mutt is clueless on the topic. My social status was already demolished before he came along.

"Too personal?" She ruffles the white and black fluff on his head.

He bumps into her, but still doesn't pause. Instead, his nose does a quick inspection of the passing ground. My muscles lock as I wait for the alarm to be triggered. By some small miracle, he doesn't sniff out my concealed presence. That call was too close.

As if summoned by a cautionary tale, my house and shop come into view on the left. Now would be a great time to veer off and abandon this outrageous impulse. The twinge in my gut kindly suggests I take the escape route home. Mud squishes beneath my soles as I hesitate. I track the sway of Penny's flared hips in front of me. There's zero inclination to follow my moral compass.

Nope, the blonde bombshell is in charge of this screwed-up alternative. I don't stray from the course she sets.

A humorless sound rasps from me. I'm a crazed fool. That's the only logical explanation for why I'm still trudging behind them. Although, there's nothing logical about this.

In my defense, Penny invited me to join them. She probably didn't predict that I'd do so without her knowledge. This situation is fucked. Nothing about how I'm acting is normal. Although, to be fair, Penny is currently having a one-sided conversation with a dog. That elevates a brick of ugly unease from my chest. Maybe we have a few strange habits in common too.

I almost punch my temple. Thinking that way will open

old wounds, delivering nothing but pain. Penny isn't a woman I can fuck and forget. That means she's not a woman I can fuck at all.

"I've always wanted a dog. Might go to the shelter and adopt one soon." Her fast-acting attachment to Rune could be cured.

He snorts, the sound resembling a resolute refusal.

Even from this terrible angle, I see her lips twist into a pout. "Wouldn't you like a friend to play with? Humans are awesome, of course. But another pup to wrestle with? No exception."

The sun casts swaths of bright light along the dirt path. These glimmers split apart the chaos inside me. My thoughts drift with the leisurely pace. Once again, I find myself contemplating where the hell she came from. She's a puzzle I'd be thrilled to solve. Soft curves and supple flesh. Pliable under my coarse hands. Heat floods my system in an erotic gush. I shudder and wrench my mind from the gutter.

Penny squeaks when a slight breeze rustles through the trees. "You're so brave, Runey-boy. Are you going to protect me if a big, bad wolf leaps out from the bushes?"

He jumps in front of her while investigating the so-called threat. After Rune determines there's nothing to fear, he glues himself to her leg.

"Such a good boy. My hero," she coos. "I'll give you some chicken for dinner."

I swear he licks his chops.

My eyes roll to the leafy branches swaying above. She's trying to be clever, but I see right through her defenseless act.

Penny lifts an arm to touch a wide oak leaf. Acorns tumble from the disrupted twig. "Did you know your daddy wrote me a note? He told me I was being too loud. Who's out here to hear me?"

Me, that's who. Closer than she realizes.

"Maybe he's just jealous I didn't invite him to my party."

This incessant chatter is grinding my patience into mulch. Maybe she's aiming for naïve damsel or sassy defiance, but nobody is this perky without an artificial boost. That's my jaded experience talking.

I'm not paying attention and slip on a rock. Damn this woman and her infuriating nonsense. The snap under my boot is too loud to ignore, but Penny doesn't react. In fact, she just continues walking with that hypnotic gait. I'm helpless to keep tailing her like a lost puppy.

It doesn't take more than ten seconds to realize the change in her solo performance. "Not sure how you put up with him, Runey-boy. He's a happiness thief."

My dog sneezes but doesn't react otherwise. Good to know he isn't tossing me under the bus just yet.

"But he sure is sexy. Those blue eyes and bulging biceps. Not to mention the dangerous vibe he gives off. He's got that broody and broken combo going. Most women are suckers for a tortured soul. We want to be the one who can change him. Mend the wounds. It's a romantic notion I'm guilty of fantasizing about." She kisses the air. A breathy sigh accompanies her antics.

That proves my assumption. She's aware that I'm within earshot. Blood rushes hotter than molten lava under my skin. I'm quick to let loose a string of muffled curses.

Not sure why it's necessary to make me look stupid. Other than the obvious, I'm doing just fine on my own. Only one of us is currently camouflaged in the foliage. Didn't do a stealthy job either.

I don't move, passing the ball to her court. Might as well see how this plays out. Odds aren't in my favor, but I've never been a betting man.

More swing and allure accentuate her already fluid

motion. Her chin dips as she peeks over to the exact spot where I stand hidden.

Damn, I'm officially busted. Yet I remain firm in my stance.

Penny slows to a standstill, toying with a patch of over-grown grass. "We could stop by your place and check on him. I bet he misses you."

Rune cocks his head, tongue lolling out in comedic fash-ion. What a chump. Falling in line for the pretty girl. I thump my forehead on the closest tree. As if I'm in a position to be-rate him.

"Do you know the way?" Her focus is latched on me again.

My so-called companion dashes around her stalled form in tight circles. He'll lead her directly to me as if she hasn't already pinpointed me.

But he jogs off to resume their trek. Penny goes with the flow, letting him blaze a trail to who knows where. Definitely not to my cabin. This direction will take us around the lake. It's a decent hike, but we'll be at it for hours at this rate.

"It's really pretty in these woods. Have you lived in this area for long?"

At this stage, I'm willing to admit she's talking to me. Hope she's not expecting a reply.

"I never spent time in the country or true wilderness. Tropical beaches and ritzy mountain resorts pretending to be rural? Absolutely."

My snort is exaggerated. No one is surprised by that confession.

Pretty sure she tosses a glare behind her purely for my benefit. "This is exactly what I needed. That's what I told my friend. She thinks I'm crazy."

Again, no argument from me. I'm riding the insane train alongside her, though.

Penny kicks at the damp ground. Chunks of muck go

flying into the brush. She frowns and attempts to fling the gunk off her shoe. It's still our rainy season and these covered parts take months to dry out.

Another resigned sound wheezes from her. "Maybe I'm losing it, Runey-boy. I've spent the last thirty minutes having a conversation with a dog."

He's too busy pissing on weeds to notice her feigned distress. At some random bend, I've absently wandered onto the trail in plain sight. Guilt coils in a suffocating vise. This is wrong on too many levels.

Penny stomps to an abrupt halt. In the next beat, she whirls to face me with thunder in her features. "How long are we going to pretend you're not spying on me?"

I hold her gaze while carnal hunger gnaws in my stomach. There's a different question to ask. One I'm almost willing to voice.

How long will it take for us to ruin each other, Darlin'?

CHAPTER NINE

A HARSH TUG ON MY ARM MAKES ME STUMBLE, AND I narrowly avoid smashing head-on into a fellow pedestrian. Lydia clucks her tongue. "Watch where you're going, newbie. Minnesotans have a reputation for being overly nice, but they'll still cuss your ass out."

"Sorry, and thanks. Sideswiping an unsuspecting someone isn't on my weekend to-do list." I shake off the daze. "It's safe to say that I'm… distracted."

She tosses her dark hair with a scoff. "Yeah, I got the hint when you started blindly agreeing to everything. So, in case you missed it, we're going to a male strip club to watch the guys shake their schlongs."

"Um, what? I've never done that. Can't we see a movie instead?" I'm sure my complexion is on fire.

"Just fucking with you, Virginia." Her hip bumps into mine. "What has you miles away while we're supposed to be bonding over gossip and shopping?"

The three bags dangling from my arm show relative success with the latter. "Nothing much. I'm just taking in the sights."

"Uh-huh." She waves a hand in front of her nose. "I smell bullshit. Walton is great and all, but it's not worthy of starry-eyed, space-cadet mode."

When she called earlier, I jumped at the chance to visit the neighboring town. I'm in desperate need of a change in scenery, if that hasn't been made clear. Turns out that I'm still floating in Thorn-infested waters.

"Mr. Surly Silence," I mumble under my breath. That's the nickname I openly admit to giving him. Thorn feels too personal.

Lydia nods in understanding. "I don't blame you. I've heard amazing things."

I frown. "But you've never met him."

Or so she said. The intel she provided last week was based on common knowledge or rumors. That seems to be the case for most people in Hacken. There's a greedy cavern in my chest that likes the idea of him being this anonymous entity to everyone else.

She shrugs. "I'm just assuming. Don't make an ass out of me for trying to be empathetic."

"I can't when it's true, right?"

"Hell yes, girl!" Her whoop gains the attention of those nearby. She swats at their passing interest. "It's about time you get some action. Even if it's imaginary."

My cheeks burst into flames again. "It's not like that."

"It's absolutely like that. He followed you into the woods."

Acid churns in my belly at the way that sounds. The implication alone could be harmful. I suddenly regret sharing my most recent Nash incident with her. "Only because I had his dog."

She snorts. "Wow, you're clueless."

"Hey!" I lightly punch her arm. "That's not nice."

Her eyes roll skyward. "For real, newbie. He's mad about you."

"More like just mad." The man can barely tolerate my presence. There's no convincing me otherwise.

"Whatever." Lydia begins sniffing at a questionable rate. Her stomach growls soon after. My newfound companion doesn't bother hiding a wince. "What are the chances you're hungry?"

"Pretty decent." Queasiness aside, I could choke something down.

She steers me to a shallow alcove that hides a restaurant entrance. Benny Boy is plastered across the glass. "This place has the best pizza ever."

Little does she know that I've been to Italy, where they serve a cheesy pie unlike any other. I've also eaten at the most gourmet and renowned restaurants in existence. My refined palate wants to argue, but there's no sense in disputing her claim. "Can't wait to try it."

Lydia yanks on the door and ushers me forward. "You're in for a treat."

The delectable scents of fresh garlic, baking crust, and vivid spices smack me in my smug face. The smell alone has me scarfing down my previous spouting. Rich history and stories hang from the walls. Wide windows expose the kitchen, where several employees bustle about in organized chaos. It's humble but proud. I'm instantly in love.

A checkered floor leads us to the host stand. The teenager smacks her gum while studying a graphic with the seating layout. "Two of you?"

"On the patio, please." Lydia glances at me. "Unless you'd prefer inside."

"Nope, I'm good. Let's enjoy the weather." I'd hesitate if we were in Florida's humidity. Early June in this northern state is top-notch excellence that I plan to take full advantage of at every available opportunity.

She rubs her palms together. "Perfect. There's a bartender I want you to meet. Maybe he's assigned to that section."

The young girl makes a check on her chart, grabs two menus, and exchanges a knowing grin with my friend. "Chance is on the clock. I'll be sure he takes care of you."

Lydia blows her a kiss. "You're a babe."

We weave a direct path across the dining room. Most of

the tables and booths are empty. My wonderment must be obvious on my face.

"They just opened at eleven. By noon, there will be an hour wait."

My slack jaw swivels to Lydia. "Really?"

She wiggles her brows. "It's just that delicious."

The hostess pauses after we step into the warm sunshine. She gestures between a wooden picnic bench option and cushioned stools parked by the shaded bar. "Take your pick."

Lydia's stare is feasting on the man mixing a drink behind the counter. She lifts her chin in his direction. "Front and center, girlfriend."

"Enjoy your lunch and entertainment." She sets a place for us exactly where the eager beaver requested. Then she gives a conspiring wave before returning to her hostess post.

I give the guy a diligent once-over, but don't find anything to replace the one who owns permanent real estate in my brain. My focus slides to Lydia with a sigh. "So, what are we going to order?"

"Very funny." She knocks her elbow into my side. "But let's focus on a juicy snack to stimulate our appetites."

As if reading between the lines, Chance—his name is stamped on a tag for us to identify—struts over to serve us. "Good morning, ladies."

Lydia exhales while leaning forward. "It's a fine one, isn't it?"

"Definitely looking up," he responds in a gravelly timbre.

That's when my phone buzzes, giving me a start. I whip the device from my back pocket to see three text notifications demanding my attention. The sender is none other than the prickly landowner responsible for my consistent fever.

Thorn: How's your firewood supply?

Thorn: Do you need more or not?

Thorn: A reply this century would be appreciated.

This is the most Nash has communicated in days. Apparently, someone doesn't like being ignored. Not that I ghosted him on purpose. I didn't feel the vibrations while in motion along Main Street.

Me: I'm good, thanks for asking.

A second barely passes before he's typing.

Thorn: How's that possible?

He must be worried about my wood supply. I wondered why bundles of logs were left on the porch. Figured I missed the bonfire pit on my tour.

Me: I haven't used the stuff you already dropped off.

Thorn: Why not?

Me: No marshmallows.

The typing dots appear, only to vanish. A smile curves my lips at the familiar pattern. I hope he's chewing on my clever wit.

Thorn: I don't get it.

Me: You wouldn't.

Thorn: Where are you?

Me: Why?

Thorn: You're not at the cabin.

Me: What was your first clue?

Thorn: Your car is gone.

Frustration leaps from the screen. The fact he's noticed

my absence gets a twisted rise from me. I recognize the traitorous flutters and bat them down with a hush.

Thorn: Where are you?

Me: With a friend.

Thorn: Who?

Me: None of your business.

Thorn: Tell me where you are, Penny.

Ah, we're done with the requests. The instinct to act like
a stubborn brat slides into the driver's seat. My logical, mature
side can't be held responsible for what happens next. Besides,
we've been locked in this tension tango before.

Me: Make me.

"Why are you squirming like that?"

I drop my phone like a hot potato. The plastic case clat-
ters on the metal bar top. "Huh?"

Lydia is assessing me with far too much scrutiny. "And
you're blushing. Were you sexting?"

I force my gaze to hers, ignoring the incoming texts flashing at me. "No, not at all. Just answered some missed messages while you were occupied."

"Not anymore." She jerks a thumb to the patio corner
where her flirting partner is with another customer.

"He'll return momentarily."

"I thought you'd be more interested in him." She picks at
the cardboard coaster under her sweaty water glass. Not sure
when that arrived, or the matching one for me.

My hand tips left to right. "Not really my type."

Now her mouth slants into a crooked grin. "Too easy?"

"Something like that." I allow my gaze to stray sideways,
stealing a peek at the inconsistent flashing that has yet to cease.

Lydia's focus follows mine. Her brows spring upward. "Who's blowing you up?"

"Mr. Surly Silence," I admit with a sigh.

"Not so silent now."

"Nope." Not until I give him what he wants. I bite my bottom lip to trap the elation trying to escape.

I tossed down that haughty taunt and disappeared. Another sly look at the screen shows his extreme displeasure. A salacious thrill skates along my skin, eliciting a shiver despite the summer warmth.

Thorn: Better watch that smart mouth.

Thorn: Or better yet, don't and see what happens.

Thorn: Were you just teasing me?

Thorn: Dammit, Penny. Stop fucking with my head.

Thorn: Where are you?

Thorn: The silent treatment isn't cute coming from you.

That last one deserves a laugh—rich and throaty. Moisture blurs my vision with the sudden onset of humor. He's hilarious, this one.

"Oh, you're s-m-i-t-t-e-n." It's entirely unnecessary for her to spell the word.

"I'm not."

"Quit lying. I have functioning eyeballs." She motions from hers to mine and back again.

"Good for you?" I try to relax my features into a neutral mask.

Lydia snorts at my failed attempt. "What's lover boy saying?"

"He isn't happy that I got quiet." And that's being beyond vague.

"Answer," she urges with a shooing motion.

But before I can consider telling him to calm the fuck down, a large pizza appears in the space between Lydia and me. I guess the thorn in my side will have to wait. That's what he deserves for leaving me hanging. Last time, in the woods mid-hike, he stormed off after I confronted him. I had plenty more to say too. We'll see how he likes the reprieve.

With those temporary terms dished out, my lashes flutter at the sinfully high-calorie lunch. Nothing has made me gulp in preparation quite like this. Other than Nash. Dammit.

A snarky brow gets arched at my friend. "I don't remember ordering."

Lydia doesn't appear sheepish in the slightest. "Because you spent the last several minutes glued to your phone. Trust me, you'll love it. Don't be polite and deny yourself. Grab it while it's hot."

My mouth waters at the blissful aroma. Oregano, mozzarella, and pepperoni bless my nostrils while tempting me to devour the entire pie. I scoop a square slice onto my plate and reach for utensils.

"Absolutely not." Lydia denies my attempt with a light smack. "We're not prim and proper up here in these parts. You eat this pizza like it's your last meal."

Father and Mother would have a shit fit. That's all the motivation I need to pick up the steamy piece with my fingers. The savory rebellion hovers inches from my lips, just waiting for that final nudge. "If you insist."

"I really do." She chomps down on her slice without hesitation.

Envy gnashes my teeth. I'm quick to follow her lead. Gooey goodness explodes on my tastebuds. I go a little cross-eyed at the punch a single bite delivers. Just the right amount of crisp and grease and meat. The flavors combine into a blissful melody that I'll crave for days to come.

"Oh. My. Gahhh." I moan in decadent fashion around my next gobble. "This is incredible."

Lydia is already going for a third piece. "Didn't I tell you?"

"I had my doubts, but damn. This is a spontaneous mouthgasm."

"You're wel-come," she sings.

My hand swoops down on my next tasty victim. "At this pace, I'll need to be rolled out of here."

She swats my worry away. "Don't worry, I'll call for a lift. Or maybe Chance will help us out. Literally."

"That's true friendship."

"Damn straight." She winks at me. "Now, text your man before he loses his shit."

"Not my man," I mutter with added petulance.

Lydia sucks on her messy fingers, going overboard on the cleaning process once Chance takes notice. "Just remember I told you so."

Just then, another message pops up. Nash's ears must be burning. I give a giddy smile free rein over my expression.

Thorn: Will you answer if I say Rune is concerned?

The exploitation is too sappy to resist.

Me: Tell him I'll have pizza leftovers from Benny Boy. You can come get them later.

Thorn: I'll send him over.

And since I'm a glutton for Nash's broody darkness, it hurts my heart that he doesn't include himself in that scenario.

CHAPTER TEN

THE AGGRAVATED BURN IN MY MUSCLES IS SATISFYING, BUT not enough. Another *thwack* ricochets off the forest's perpetual silence. It's taken hours for me to reach this point. Sweat stings my eyes and a raw blister forms over hardened callouses. Little relief arrives to comfort me. Aside from the breeze off the lake, I've been baking in the heat. But sunset is fast approaching.

Soft purple bleeds into the cloudless bright blue above. That means my window of opportunity is shrinking. I'm already spent. A glance at the ground mocks me. Four more cuts. That's more than my arms can handle, but I won't quit.

Set. Swing. Strike. Split.

This scene is too damn familiar. It's not like I spend my days doing much else. Not until Penny broke apart the dull monotony.

The handle slips with my next upward arch. Once she enters my thoughts, it's almost impossible to get her out.

"Dammit," I grunt.

It's a fucking feat that I manage to finish.

The ax falls from my limp grasp. There's nothing left in the tank except the minimal effort required to fill the wheelbarrow. Each solid *thunk* as wood hits metal keeps me focused on the task. I don't pause until the last piece is tossed on top.

Whether Penny needs more or not, I'm determined to deliver. It's no secret why. But this is a means to an end. The less she has to complain about, the smoother my summer will pass. Getting rid of her isn't an option. The sharp sting in my chest is unwarranted. I can't allow myself to get attached.

This is just part of my usual responsibilities. I'd do the same for any tenant. The lie doesn't taste better, no matter how often I spew it.

But the firewood isn't all I have to offer.

I pocketed a brownish-green rock on the beach that reminded me of her. Not just the color. The shape resembles a heart, which is asinine, but that didn't stop me from collecting the damn thing.

The small object is cool against the furious flesh of my palm. It appears fragile, but the stone can withstand the pressure. I scrub over my damp forehead as more poetic shit spills from me. This isn't who I am. But that harsh denial doesn't sit steady in my gut. The man I've allowed myself to become is no prize either.

I've become little more than an empty shell, refusing to move beyond the surface. I didn't even realize how hollow I was until she reminded me of what I'm missing. It's a curse more than anything. Once she's gone, I'll go back to a cold and lonely existence without sunshine along the horizon.

She's just a beautiful distraction. A pretty face with the bad habit of getting on my last nerve. Someone to defy the strict and rigid boundaries I abide by.

But a snarl curls my upper lip at the superficial depiction.

No, Penny Blaire is far more than that.

She's given me a purpose again. A different type of peace that solitude cannot provide. Her breathy voice taunts me, teasing my own. Curiosity refuses to release me. Those torturous shackles demand to be fed answers. Yet she defeats my defenses with a mere swipe of her tiny hand. Decimates any attempts I'm foolish enough to try.

I'd probably welcome her into my home—my last standing, untainted sanctuary—if she asked. The thought of her invading my space sends a cold chill down my spine, but it's not entirely unpleasant. A tour of my workshop might make her smile. It's an idea I've entertained on more than one occasion. I still don't sleep, but I catch myself drifting off hoping to dream about her. Just further proof that's she's already gotten to me in these two short weeks.

It's significant progress barbed in chilled fear. I don't want this to end.

Penny's delayed responses reminded me of the years I've spent in nothing but silence. The hollow memories kicked off this downward whirlwind. I found myself desperate to reach her. It's fucked beyond reason, and I don't know how to resolve this ditch I've dumped myself in.

What she must think of me.

Bitter numbness spreads from my chest. I haven't heard from her since last night. Even then, she wasn't trying to reach me. She had pizza for Rune from her trip to Walton. I let him go, following a safe distance behind to remain unseen. They shared the leftovers. Penny spoiled him with affection. My dog ate up every scrap as if starved—of both pizza and affection, the traitor—while I stayed in the shadows where I belong.

Now an entire day has crawled by.

Rune's pitiful whine intrudes into my deprecating spiral. The sorrow in his eyes might drown me. It provides some incentive that I'm not the only one obsessed with the blonde darling.

I hang my head with a groan. "Yeah, yeah. We're going."

Spasms threaten to seize my exhausted muscles, putting me in motion. My fingers curl around the worn handles and I haul the wheelbarrow off its supportive legs. A muffled bellow rips through me and the weight trembles my knees. With a shove, I get the load moving forward to our destination. Rune leaps upright from his sprawled position to join me in the venture.

Uneven footing makes the three-minute trek take twice as long. The stockpile teeters when I hit a hole in the trail, drawing a curse from between my clenched teeth. She won't even care about this gesture to mend our divide. Not sure why I bother. There I go again with the babbling nonsense.

I'm a shameless asshole, but I still have morals. Either way, I refuse to let Penny assume the worst. Maybe that makes me weak or foolish or overly fixated. I've already proven to be all of the above where she's concerned. I'm done giving a shit.

That's what motivated my peace offering.

But I find myself making these impulsive decisions more often as of late. That's the only explanation I can provide for my erratic, reckless behavior. Sticky sludge dilutes my stoic character as I recall the possessive messages I sent. My mind is officially scrambled thanks to her.

"We need to cut the cord, Rune." I glance at him in my peripheral.

He just trots along as if I hadn't said anything.

"She wants to get her own dog. You know that, right?"

The noise he emits is noncommittal at best.

"It won't be long before she finds a decent man to warm her bed too."

The reality shouldn't make my blood boil. The handles creak in my grip as I allow that visual to sink in. She's not mine. Not even close. That doesn't mean I want her to be with someone else, though.

Uninterrupted isolation was what I sought after running from the past. I built my cabin and shop on this three-hundred-acre oasis with that escape in mind. The other three lodges were erected for extra income as needed. I rarely open them for rent since the cost of living isn't too high. Some strange inkling prodded me to list the Monroe lodge for the season.

And I continue to fume about that poor choice while

bringing her wood that she doesn't want. The irony isn't lost on me.

Remorse creeps in when Penny's cabin comes into view. Her car isn't parked in the driveway. In all honesty, I hate that she's frequently in town without me. It festers into black rot I can't escape. Soon it will spread until I'm nothing but a deranged beast. My stomach sinks, which only serves to further darken my mood. I can't depend on her to strike a match when the shadows turn on me. That will leave me in total disrepair. I've relied solely on myself long enough to get over this funk.

My glare swings to the wood stacked on her porch. Then I study the untouched supply in the covered shed. The bundles appear exactly as I placed them before she arrived. Not a single one appears disturbed, but that can't be right.

"How the hell does she make a fire without burning logs?" The question is purely rhetorical for my stubborn will to hear.

Rune takes it upon himself to sniff out the previous delivery. His conclusion matches mine. Go figure.

Penny wasn't lying yesterday. There's plenty left from last week. Maybe even all of it. She really doesn't need more. But that's her problem now, I suppose.

Perplexity aside, I gather the fresh cuts and carry them up the stairs. I repeat the process to unload. Stretch. Secure. Stack. Over and again until the pile is transferred to her porch.

Perspiration trickles down my temple. I swat at the drops and wrench the rag from my pocket. The dirty fabric does little to mop the sweat, but fuck it. My weary body sags against the nearest post. That's a wrap.

Gravel under tires whips my focus to the road. Penny's red coupe is approaching at a snail's pace. Shock probably has her foot easing off the accelerator. Either that or Rune's direct dash toward her. The lovesick hound makes my infatuation look like a tame kindergarten crush.

I'm transfixed as she throws the car in park and kills the

ignition. She pops open the door, but stalls for several seconds before getting out. The brief hesitation does nothing to calm the rushing wind in my ears. Anticipation becomes my nemesis.

Penny leaves the safety of her vehicle. I watch the distance that separates us shrink with her timid stride. That reluctance is a direct hit to my pride, but it's my fault. It's also mine to fix. I can't let her believe I'm this unstable man hiding in the woods. Although, in all honesty, there's probably more truth than not in that description.

Our gazes clash and hold, pent-up energy throbbing between us. That unsteady pulse hammers against my skull. Her breath wobbles with uneven bursts. I can't look away and it appears she suffers from a similar plight.

Suddenly, everything slows. The fading sunlight freezes into crystallized streaks. Branches and leaves cease swaying in the breeze. Rune finds a grass patch to nap on. The ground tilts until I sway, struggling to adjust. Static crackles in the air. Taut tension is almost visible between us, drawing tighter with each strained exhale. My rapid pulse stutters to a near halt. Penny must feel it too. The furious rise and fall of her chest turns sluggish. Her blink is weighted. I take a breath that seems to take an entire minute to heave.

One.

Two.

Three.

Before the fourth beat drops, the trance thaws as if it never arrived. Our lush surroundings spin on fast-forward to compensate for the temporary lag. We're yanked from the clutches of this unforeseeable hold. Penny gasps and rips her gaze from mine. That loss is an immediate shock to my system. I blindly grasp at the post to remain upright. There's something else I need to get a grip on.

The smile that curls Penny's lips is staggering. "We really

should stop meeting like this." I feel my nostrils flare with agitation. The next inhale streams fire to my lungs. I'm still stuck in turmoil while she makes jokes.

Surrender is for those ready to lose or quit. I won't go down that easily. It's just taking me longer than expected to gather my bearings. Good thing we're just getting started.

With sound logic propelling me forward, I stomp down the steps with my aim trained on the path home. Rune will follow if he chooses. I'm mere feet from a successful getaway when the hurt in her tone blocks my attempt.

"Are you ever going to talk to me?"

Little does she realize how increasingly difficult it is to avoid doing just that. A force I can't explain has me peering over my shoulder. Her hazel depths shimmer with unshed emotions. The sight would obliterate a lesser man. Even as a hardened husk, I feel a fissure crack into the steely layer concealing my jaded soul. Maybe that's her intention.

That sparks an awareness I hadn't previously considered. This might be a challenge for her. A novelty to behold. I'm almost stunned by the realization. The shine might wear off once I give into her.

The open vulnerability in my expression is snuffed out. A seamless pivot gives her a full-frontal view of my denial. I'm in control, dammit. She won't sway me more than she has already. Not today.

All she gets from me is a soundless refusal as I begin backing away into the woods.

Until we meet again, Darlin'.

CHAPTER ELEVEN

Penny

THE EPIC SOUNDTRACK FROM MY FAVORITE NETFLIX BINGE fades into a muted hum. Icy panic crawls up my throat and tries to suffocate me. Those frozen tendrils dig in until I gasp. A furious boom shakes the walls. The thunder is attacking with ruthless intent. That's not what has my nerves in an anxious tangle, though.

I clench my eyes shut as the wind pounds angry fists on the windows. The panes rattle, splashed with torrential showers. This is all too familiar, yet not what I'm used to.

There's no sensible explanation for my unhinged behavior. I'm not a stranger to storms. We're frequent rivals. That doesn't mean I'm not gripping the blanket with white knuckles. Besides, it's different bunking down alone.

The catastrophic tropical variety of storms sweeps through Florida more often than not during hurricane season. Those of us in an incoming path seek shelter as needed, prepare for the destruction, and wait for the tail to breeze past. It's terrifying and doesn't get easier, no matter how often you evacuate.

But this feels scary in an entirely different way. The small cabin leaves me little space to hide. That seems much more dangerous in these conditions.

Terror strikes deep in my belly when another clap of thunder wreaks havoc on the night. The pulsing fear wants my submission. *Screw that noise.* I flip a middle finger at the roaring rage currently whipping through the woods. But even despite my efforts, the false bravado does nothing to soothe these jagged edges.

Rumbles quake the ground hard enough to send my heart into severe palpitations. Frames rattle on the walls, preparing for their ultimate crash. The table in front of me quivers. Rain splatters on glass, the wet slap almost seeming to douse my feverish skin.

Even though it's barely five o'clock in the evening, the sky is dark and ominous. A warning swirls fast within the dense shadows. The howl from beastly gusts makes me jump.

I curl into a tighter ball, as if my ability to be compact will change the weather. Sweat clings to my forehead as a chill tickles me. The contrasting energies heighten my awareness. I blink from the stupor. I need a distraction. That's why I turned on a show in the first place. With that driving force, I train my sharp gaze on the glowing screen.

Almost immediately, my mind drifts again. Anthony and Kate blur into obscure blobs on my iPad screen. Not even *Bridgerton* can hold my attention.

I bang my forehead on the armrest, which doesn't satisfy the brewing frustration in the slightest. This sitting duck situation isn't doing it for me. But limited options plaster my butt to the cushions. Driving isn't happening. I can always phone a friend. Elouise will understand my fretting. We'll pass approximately five minutes before boredom sets in. Aggravation streams from my flared nostrils.

And that's when the power zaps off.

"No, no, no," I groan. I dart off the sofa for the nearest switch. The lights stay off no matter how fast I flick it up and down. It's a blessing this happened during daylight, but I can't see beyond the frantic pressure in my chest.

What happens once it's dark? That's a question to cause true panic. My teeth chatter for no reason at all. Perhaps I'm anticipating the incoming chill that's bound to draft in at any second. The threat of frostbite and hypothermia only belongs in winter. Maybe. This isn't stuff I researched.

One thing is certain—or more like two.

The dark won't hurt me. It's spooky, but harmless. But without electricity, I don't have heat.

I'm not bred for cold temperatures. The fireplace sits un-used. Built from sturdy stone and brick, the hearth is massively intimidating. There are matchboxes stacked on top. The long kind, for hard-to-reach candles, or a fire within the safety of a pit. All I have to do is strike one, toss it on the logs, and the fire burns. Right? That doesn't seem right. An insistent throb-bing kicks at my temples. I could Google how to get flames roiling, but there's not much time for experimenting. My city girl roots are showing, and they're fiercely inadequate.

I can drive to town, but then what? There's no motel. Lydia might have a spare bed or pillow. That possibility doesn't settle my worry. We've been friends for two-point-five seconds. Talk about an imposition.

It's totally fine. I've got this.

My shoulders slump when my mood shows no signs of improvement. No amount of positivity will scare off this fright. That allows more worry to assault me. My bare feet smack against the cool floor. I pace the length of the cabin while scrounging up courage.

Nash is my only practical option. I'll arrive on his doorstep and beg for shelter. That's not desperate or anything. Maybe I should text first—what, so he can deny me easier? Scratch that.

How we left things the other day leaves much to be de-sired. He doesn't want to see me. I shouldn't want to see him either. This stupid outage is a choice thief.

But I'll be honest.

The thought of being holed up with Nash Hudson doesn't sound too shabby. There's just something about him I can't es-cape, and it's not from our close proximity. No, our neighbor-ing cabins aren't responsible for this yearning in my heart. The ache is for *him*, but that pang doesn't emit pity. Compassion, maybe. I feel like we could be kindred spirits if given the chance.

After what feels like hours, the fury just beyond the walls has calmed. Meanwhile, I've managed to wrap myself into a hissy fit. There's still no power. A peek outside reveals that the torrential downpour has slowed to a steady drizzle. I can walk in this, accompanied by my umbrella. That gives me pause. Lightning hasn't struck yet, but it would be my luck if it did while I'm hoofing it next door. Maybe I shouldn't risk it.

My jacket with a hood will suffice. Knee-high boots too. I pocket my phone and other necessities. A glance in the mirror is comical. I look like a pissed-off kitty forced to endure a bath. He won't turn me away. My middle and index fingers cross over themselves as I vacate the non-comfort of my temporary home.

Crisp freshness dangles in the air, but that's the only pleasantness I'm afforded. A damp chill burrows into my flesh, invading the lingering heat from what the sun left me with earlier. This terrain is a freaking slop fest. I nearly fall on my ass seven times in the first few feet. Thankfully, the trees provide coverage, so the trail isn't complete sludge.

Stray droplets drip from overhead, adding to the persistent sprinkle. I blink the moisture from my lashes with a muttered curse. Any hope of staying dry has been officially dashed. Soaked denim clings to my legs. Goosebumps cover me from head to toe. My soles squish in the mud when puddles are unavoidable. Slow and steady is my best bet. It's not ideal, but I'm making my way.

At a bend in the trail, the burden on my lungs whooshes from me in a choppy exhale. I've never been so relieved to see a smoking chimney. That billowing plume is a beacon that I'm desperate to reach. I can only hope who I stumble upon is welcoming.

Nerves skitter down my spine and I shiver. I spotted what's

sure to be Nash's house last week on our botched hike. Those suspicions are confirmed when I spot a familiar wheelbarrow out front. He abandoned the rust bucket in my yard after his last great escape. That reminds me of the conflict I'm walking into. My pace resembles a snail while I inch forward. Then the wind picks up steam and shoves me onward. Hint received.

I lift my fist to knock, but the door swings open before I can. A very naked chest greets me. Masculine pride ripples off the smooth flesh filling my vision. The angular contours and sculpted definition put chiseled marble to shame. I knew Nash was fit, but the evidence is damning—mostly to my decorum and proper brain functioning. The air is sucked from my lungs. Any trace of saliva in my mouth is sucked dry.

He crosses stocky arms over the hard planes of his pecs. His ropey veins are on full display, and I might just faint. I've always been a sucker for arm porn. But that's not all. The deep grooves cutting into his abdomen flex under my salacious perusal. I very well might've been struck by lightning, and this is a very pleasant dream. Maybe he suddenly developed an allergy to cotton and shirts. What a shame.

His growly displeasure snaps me out of my leering. Yep, this is actually happening. I realize far too late that I'm just lurking on his stoop like a dumbfounded loiterer. My closed hand is still hovering in mid-air. With extreme caution—so he doesn't spook—I lower my frozen limb. His glare is ready and waiting when I peek up at him.

I'm skirting dangerously close to perverted territory. He's never going to let me inside at this rate. Can't say I blame him. I smack my lips and force my eyes to the ground.

The sand in my throat is laced with hot embarrassment. "Um, hi."

Nash doesn't respond or acknowledge me. Go figure.

"The power is out in my cabin. On one minute, and poof the next. Not sure what to do about that. Figured you could help me. I'm not in the market for freezing my butt off." The nervous babbling is a terrible habit I have yet to kick.

He just stares, his expression blank without an ounce of concern for my discomfort. That's probably because I was unabashedly gawking at his naked torso moments ago. Drool is most likely stuck to my chin.

"Did yours blow too?"

Nothing for several beats, then he nods. Progress.

"I didn't know where else to go."

His jaw ticks forward.

"Do you, uh, mind if I stay here until the storm passes?"

Conflict tightens his features into a scowl. I almost retract the request. Almost. But my scant options keep me rooted on his porch. He can accept that or not.

The pause that pairs with his deliberation is painful at best. I almost wither under his shrewd scrutiny, but my newfound backbone makes an appearance and keeps me standing straight. Another second might wreck me.

Thankfully, it doesn't come to that. Nash grants me entry with a forward sweep from his muscular arm.

My stiff posture deflates with a heavy sigh. "Thank you."

The warm interior quickly envelops me. I shudder from the unexpected onslaught. Seems the cold penetrated deeper than I thought. My jacket is soggy, water sluicing off onto the spotless floor. The rapidly forming puddle might as well be a permanent stain. Ingrained politeness has me shuffling sideways to the large mat meant for dirty shoes.

Turns out Nash is watching me through thinly veiled disgust. It's been ten seconds and I'm already making a mess. I wince while slowly unzipping the drenched garment. It lands on the rubber surface with a splat.

"Sorry," I whisper. "Do you have a towel? I'll mop that up."

He just shakes his head.

"Okay," I drag the word out with my discomfort.

Rune pops up out of thin air, his sleek and agile run barreling straight for me. I barely have time to brace before he's making a lunge for it. My knees hit the floor at the same moment his body collides with mine. He wiggles with glee on my lap, lavishing me with his signature sloppy kisses. I'm grateful for the save from further ridicule.

The giggle that peals from me is ridiculous. "Well, at least someone is happy to see me."

A hollow grunt comes from Mr. Thorny Pants.

When I peek over at him, he's tugging a shirt over his head. Bummer for my eyeballs and girly bits. It's for the best. I didn't come here for… that.

With the reminder cemented in my mushy brain, I refocus my attentions on the zealous pup. "I missed you, Runeyboy. Have you been good? I should've brought you a treat."

Excited yips are my answer. Then he licks every inch of my face twice.

"Are we gonna have a slumber party tonight? Can I share your bed?"

Nash's strangled cough interrupts me.

My reprimanded focus swings to his. "I mean, if that's all right. How long will the power be out?"

Why I continue asking him questions is beyond me. He seems to have the same thought and is ready for a reprieve. Without another glance, he strides to the far corner. There's a makeshift wall blocking that area from the rest. I hate how often he stalks off.

But that's when I truly take notice of his home.

The interior is illuminated by dozens of flameless candles. Three portable lanterns are lit and ready for use. A roaring fire is blazing in the hearth. Jugs of water sit on the dining table. There's a lingering aroma in the air that reminds me of grilled meat with extra char—just the way I like it. Tarps are stacked in a neat pile. Two comfortable-looking chairs frame an equally appealing couch. What appears to be a generator sits turned off in the center of it all. This man knows how to survive in the backwoods. Not that I'm surprised.

"Wow," I breathe while straightening from my crouched position. My feet twirl in a slow circle, much like the first time I entered my cabin. But this sight brings forth much more awe. "I've come to the right place."

Nash has space and supplies to spare.

Rune lets me off the hook, dashing off to his cozy bed beside the log pile.

I grant myself the opportunity to explore. It only takes a handful of moments before my host joins me. He drops a bundle on the sofa before aimlessly pacing in a square around where I stand. That all too familiar tension settles in my belly.

"Thanks again for taking me in."

Nash comes to an abrupt halt, blue fire burning in his eyes. His gaze makes a purposeful dip down my soppy form. I'm reluctant to follow suit, knowing what I'll find. Drowned rat trying to pass as a cleanly houseguest isn't a cute look. Ignorance is bliss and all that nonsense. Instead of facing reality, though, my focus remains pleasantly locked on him. He doesn't return the favor, forcing the issue.

"Yeah, I'm wet." I cringe while plucking soggy fabric between two fingers. My coat was little more than useless. So much for the vinyl material protecting me from the elements. It didn't cross my mind to take along a spare set of clothes.

He pinches the bridge of his nose in that exasperated way I've noticed. But it's more than that. His muscles twitch and bunch. He almost seems… uncomfortable.

My toes curl with the simmering magnetism in this small room. There's no release valve from the pressure cooker. His gaze is blistering, even hotter than the flames dancing away in the fireplace. I absently realize he's fixated on my chest. A peek down at the ladies reveals why.

Oh, sweet sacrifice. I'm whoring myself out. My lacy bra is visible through the sodden cotton. It definitely wasn't my intention to give him a peepshow. I wrap a protective arm across my breasts. Even through the chilled exterior, I feel my cheeks scorch.

He grinds his teeth, eyes still blazing at me. Then he's shutting down, ripping his fiery focus away, and heading for the door.

"Where are you going?" My voice gongs like an alarm.

Nash halts in his latest hasty retreat, forehead thumping against the wall. "Need some air."

CHAPTER TWELVE

Nash

ENNY'S SHOCK IS A SPUTTERED GASP. "YOU JUST TALKED TO me."

My heavy sigh is steeped in resigned acknowledgment. The upper hand had yet to be mine. This might clinch a win for me. "I did."

She lets out a squeaky noise. "You did it again."

A sneer gets aimed at the door that's still sealed shut. Freedom is waiting just on the other side.

"It's not a miracle," I finally retort.

"Might as well be," she mumbles.

Only if she's that easy to impress. In that case, her standards will implode if she gets a look at my dick. Better make sure that doesn't happen. Call me cocky, but I know my value in the sex department. Being well-endowed is just the tip of my talents. Too bad for Penny Blaire. I won't be responsible for her spontaneously combusting.

Maybe it would be fair retaliation after she's displayed such an appetizing sight for me to feast on. Her damn shirt is transparent. Only an innocent darling wears white while it's raining and doesn't consider the repercussions. The dark bra is no match for her pert nipples begging to be sucked. She probably doesn't know how tightly my control is being stretched.

Just beneath my skin, carnal depravity surges potent and hot. My dormant libido roused from hibernation weeks ago. I've been fighting these cravings ever since. But now, with her in my domain? Game changer. The instant she crossed my threshold, those neglected parts demanded relief.

The urge to maul her won't be silenced for long.

She might even welcome my advances. The reminder of her keen interest in devouring me is a fierce brand into my flesh. Hell, after the way she was ogling me on the stoop, I'd be willing to bet on her making the first move. That doesn't mean I should sully her with my filthy debauchery—yet.

I need distance from her. *Now.* I can't let the immediate onslaught overwhelm my rational thoughts.

Penny must detect my impending—and not at all surprising—escape attempt. "Are you leaving?"

"About to," I rasp.

"Why won't you look at me?" Her disappointment lashes my back.

I remain firmly planted in my cowardice. "It's best that I don't."

"Why?" Honest curiosity begs me to answer.

The question is unnecessary. Penny is aware that her shirt is in a nonexistent state. But I can't seem to deny her for long.

My booted feet revolve on a semi-circle axis as if compelled. "Better?"

Her smile is dipped in simple pleasures. "Much."

That makes one of us. I'm a starving man with a seven-course meal dangling within reach. My tongue damn near lolls out like Rune with a juicy bone. I need to get myself under control.

I blindly gesture at the couch. "There's a dry shirt for you. Boxers too, if your pants are wet."

"Oh, thank you." She rushes to the folded offerings. "Can I change in the bathroom?"

I'm already pointing in that direction. "By all means."

Penny squints at me before moving. "Don't take off, okay?"

I hang my head, a captive to her every request. "Fine."

Her hands clasp into a pleading gesture. "I'll be super quick. You won't notice I'm gone."

The soft tread signals her departure, but I can't watch her go. A grunt dislodges from me. How impossible that feat truly is when my legs sway to follow after her. This woman is turning me into an unrecognizable sap. Only because I'm allowing it.

I should've turned her away the moment she showed up on my doorstep. But that puts a glaring spotlight on this already whipped situation. She didn't even have to knock. I just so happened to see her coming, more than ready to receive her.

Those murky thoughts dissipate as Penny's hypnotic curves come into view. She must've hurried through the motions in order to get back in front of me within a minute flat. The new sight she presents might be worse.

I'd assumed getting her tits concealed behind a reliable barrier would solve the inconvenient arousal preparing to ridicule me. But the sight of her in my clothes flips a territorial switch. My resolve is suddenly taking a brutal nosedive into testosterone-infested waters. I want to stake a claim on her, one that she can't just take off when her shirt and jeans are dry.

She tugs at the baggy hem kissing her mid-thigh. From this angle, I can't tell if she's wearing the shorts underneath. The difference in our sizes only strokes my crazed desire.

"They're a bit big, but better than being wet." Penny fidgets under my blatant approval.

I gulp and wrench my gaze from her mounting temptation. In the next breath, I'm turning for a necessary reprieve from this erotic visual. The door is right there for me to use. My palm grips the knob like it's my salvation.

"Please stay. I don't want to be alone." The plea in her tone makes me weak.

Every primal instinct pumping in my blood demands that

I go to her. I find myself turning to face her before my mind comes to terms with the decision. It leaves me reeling, especially from the joy radiating from her smile.

"Thank you."

I keep my distance, my back damn near plastered to the wall. "Didn't do anything that deserves thanks."

"Yeah," she scoffs. "Okay, Mr. Humble."

"You and your nicknames," I grumble.

"Does Thorn bother you?"

I give a noncommittal shrug. It doesn't, but I'm not going to admit that. There are far more atrocious things she could call me.

Penny's concentration doesn't waver from me. "How long have you lived here?"

"About seven years."

"Whoa." She sounds genuinely surprised. "Always alone?"

"Until Rune came along."

Her eyes narrow. "How old are you?"

I snort at her straightforwardness. Twenty-seven is young by most standards, but I often feel ancient. "How old do you think I am?"

Her laugh is too pitchy. "That's just asking for trouble."

"Figured that's what you're after."

She tugs at her borrowed shirt. "Is this crossing the line?"

Another strangled noise trips from me. Too late for that. Every moment since she arrived has tested me. Besides, there are countless interpretations. I settle on simple. "Nah, we're good."

Silence creeps in like an offensive fart. Ill-timed, but unavoidable. I rock on my soles while Penny fiddles with her damp hair. No one wants to take credit, and moving forward requires stealth that the two of us sorely lack. The itch to evade this tension returns.

I fight it down with a distraction from earlier. As she

stands in my home, I find myself wanting to offer her solace and security. I quite literally gave her shelter from the storm. And what's more, she sought me out. That fact encourages me to fulfill her demands. I want to be the one who provides for her. Makes sure she's fed and clothed. Guarantee she's tucked in a warm bed at night. Offer the comforts that will keep her content no matter where she is.

The list spirals into a hazy blur.

Lift her burdens and share those she refuses to release.

Support her dreams.

Listen to her desires.

Care for her unconditionally.

I cut off those wayward thoughts with a cough.

The last one is alarming, and crosses every single line. That doesn't mean I can't see to her basic needs for now.

"Are you warm enough?"

"Uh-huh." Penny scoots closer to the fire, hands out-stretched. "I really like your cabin."

I nod in gratitude.

She gnaws on her bottom lip. "Don't get me wrong, your place is nice and tidy and maintained, but there are no personal touches."

"All my decorations and stuff are in yours."

"What?"

"I don't usually decorate the rentals. Most don't mind the bare bone-slash-skeletal state. But a woman? Staying for a whole summer? Figured you might appreciate some extras to make it a bit more livable."

The wonder in her stare clenches my chest. Maybe that was better left unsaid. "That's considerate."

I drop my gaze to the floor. "Sure."

Penny clears her throat. "I, uh, didn't get a chance to thank you."

My stomach twists at receiving more unnecessary appreciation. "Pretty sure you did five minutes ago."

Her eyes roll to the ceiling. "Not for the heart rock. I found it after you left the other day."

Damn, I'd almost forgotten about that little token. "Oh."

"That was also really thoughtful, you know, since we were on the subject." She kicks at the frayed rug near her feet.

"It's nothing."

"Not to me," she blurts.

I feel my face grow hot. "Okay."

Penny lights up the room with her grin. "I'll cherish it forever."

Fuck, this bountiful appreciation is making me uncomfortable. My skin is damn near crawling. I squeeze the back of my neck to find relief. "Great."

She pinches her lips together, most likely snuffing out a cackle at my expense. "So, what do you wanna do now that the required idle chit-chat is done?"

What she should be thinking about is what there even is for us *to* do. The slim pickings clog my brain. We can't even go outside without getting dumped on. That leaves us with more talking, awkward silence, or avoiding each other. A lingering glance at her rack squeezes another option from me. We could fuck. Furious demands to take her—hard and fast— rush to my cock. The resulting ache is one only she can satisfy.

I almost recite the choices aloud just to see how she reacts. That last one might get a good rise from her. But I won't act on the impulse. That would leave her hot and bothered. There's no way in hell I'm turning her on just to ease the ache with some other asshole.

Then I remember the food.

That's safe enough. Maybe. Further deliberation suggests it's a trap set with open jaws.

I scrub the indecision from my weary eyes. "Have you eaten?"

"Not since lunch."

"There's chicken on the stove if you're hungry. I just took it off the burner before you got here." Didn't even plate a serving for myself yet.

Her mouth pops open. "Ah, I was right."

I furrow my brow. "About?"

"It totally smells like delicious, charred meat." She moans and rubs her stomach.

I get harder than concrete from the way her saucy tongue already deems my food worthy of consumption. "Help yourself."

There's no way I'm joining her in that cramped kitchen. My dick is just begging for an excuse to slip inside her pussy. Even an accidental nudge would set me off. I don't need further embarrassment, thanks anyway.

Penny seems to recall something. "Wait, are your appliances running? I thought your power was out."

"I have a generator." My gaze follows hers to the one on the floor that's currently off. "Several, actually. Do you need one at your place?"

Her expression is blank. "For what?"

That almost gets a laugh from me, which is a huge accomplishment. This pampered darling needs a lesson or two in wilderness survival. Easily accessible quick fixes don't exist out in the sticks.

"You need a generator in emergencies. Especially when the power blows," I deadpan.

"But that's what you're for." A blush stains her cheeks as she winks.

"Right," I grunt. It's probably sad to admit how fast I'd run to her rescue each time she called.

Penny must catch the dip in my tone, wisely steering off the topic. "Will you have dinner with me?"

I'm about to agree, lips parting with the words. Then reality crashes in. I can't do this. Letting her spend the night is one thing. Sitting at the table while savoring a meal together doesn't fall under the same guidelines. She's already decimated my carefully laid boundaries. No one has ever stepped foot in my home aside from Rune. Yet here she stands, surrounded by my shit. It's too normal.

Too domestic.

Too off-limits.

I hold up my palms. "Nah, I'll give you space."

Her features take on a stricken pinch. "But I don't want to be alone."

"Darlin'," I let the endearment slip by mistake. Her eyes widen and I curse the slip. "If I stay, I can't be held responsible for what's sure to happen."

She lowers her chin, peeking at me from lowered lashes. "That's okay."

The fuck it is. She's too pure and sweet. I'd ruin her without trying. That could be fun for us both. Maybe her idea of a good time is bagging a bad boy.

I almost cave. In the end, I use the last scraps of my control to slam a barrier between us.

My stance turns defensive as I cross my arms and withdraw. "Stay inside and fill your stomach. Toss logs on the fire if it gets low. Rune will keep you company."

She wants to argue. It's plain to see in her rapid blinks and clacking teeth. "But where are you going? It's still raining."

"I've got work to do." My projects are done, but I can pretend to sleep.

Penny steps forward. "Now? It's late."

The last thing I need to do is invite her to tag along. "Take the bed or couch. Your choice."

"Wait," she blurts. "You're not coming back?"

Not if she's staying until morning. I'll seek refuge in the shop. At the last second, I decide to toss her a smirk.

"Don't worry, Darlin'. You're safe. Just stay put." Then I'm slamming the door and getting the fuck away from her.

Penny Blaire is proving to be many things. My inevitable downfall just moved to the top of her long list.

CHAPTER THIRTEEN

I GAPE AT THE DOOR IN UTTER SHOCK. THE BASTARD JUST ditched me. My muddled mind struggles to replay our exchange for what must have triggered his exit. Insulted pride ripples through every coiled synapse.

Nash expects me to blindly follow his commands and stay put like a good little girl. Unfortunately for him, I put that pitiful doormat to rest when I left Tampa. My calf muscles twitch to chase after him. But that's hasty. Inconsiderate too. The furious wind deflates from my flapping sails.

Maybe he really does need time to cool off.

After all, I just stormed in and stomped all over his privacy. The least I can do is heed his wishes. Just for a few minutes.

It only takes a second for my thoughts to wander elsewhere. My chest warms as I think about the rock he gave me. The firewood too. Not to mention his belongings are scattered in my cabin to create a more comfortable, cozy environment.

But the greatest gift of all? He gave me a nickname.

Darlin'.

A shiver attacks my toasty skin. When the endearment slipped from him, he had a southern drawl. It somehow makes the title that much more appealing. As if I need more reason to drool all over him. The change in his tone could've been my imagination.

I tug on my hair with a frustrated groan. There are so many things I want to ask him. The questions are piling up faster than I can count. I don't want to bombard him with unnecessary curiosity. Our talking status seems fragile at best.

The last thing I want is for him to reclaim his former vow of silence or whatever. For now, I'll have to be satisfied with the crumbs he's dropping directly in my path.

Without realizing it or not, he's revealing small pieces of himself. He isn't such a heartless prick. Secretive and grumpy? Absolutely. But there's a lot to discover under the broody surface.

Nash Hudson might be a closet romantic.

And I'm here for it.

My feet carry me aimlessly around while I try to pretend all is well. There are several comforts readily available and waiting to distract me. Dinner waits in the kitchen. Warm flames crackle from the stone hearth. There's a pillowy couch calling for me to relax. Heck, I could even take a bath in the impressive tub I spotted earlier. It puts mine to shame. But no. None of those options will calm the nerves bubbling in my stomach.

All I truly want just stalked off. Again.

One of these days he will flee toward me.

I surrender to impulse with a sigh. My gaze settles on the dozing pup curled near the fire. "Will you help me find your daddy, Runey-boy?"

He's on his feet without further prompting. His nails click on the wood floor as he trots to the door. When I don't move fast enough, he scratches at the chipped wood.

"All right, I'm coming. Don't get your fur in a twist." I'm a foot away from him when I remember it's still raining. A peek out the nearest window proves the drizzle has grown into a full-fledged downpour. No way I can stay dry now. "Well, that's fudging fantastic."

But the weather won't deter me, dammit. I rub my bare arms in preparation for the chill. There's little else I can do. My jacket is still soaked and useless. That's when I spot a hoodie hanging on a hook. The thick fabric is practically begging to be used.

I tug the sweatshirt over my head, the worn cotton offering a gentle hug. The large size generously covers me to my knees. "Perfect fit."

Rune yips in agreement while I tug on my boots. Thankfully, their insides stayed dry, or else I'd have to waddle in Nash's monstrous shoes.

And with that, I exit the cabin's heated embrace. Rune is quick to run across the yard. His form blurs into an unreliable guide. I squint while my eyes adjust to the dusky conditions. Overgrown grass swishes against my sluggish stride. Damp earth and new beginnings perfume the air. It's natural to suck in a deep breath, but I can't take my sweet time. Even with the hood over my head, moisture is already sinking in. Soon the massive garment will be dead weight.

As it turns out, I don't have to wander far to find Nash. There's a small building tucked behind his home. Process of elimination and good sense suggests that's where he's hiding.

Hinges squeal in protest as I shove inside. I abruptly stop in my tracks. The space is lit by electric lanterns, allowing me to see the agitated figure who appears larger than the walls can contain.

Nash is pacing in the center, fingers buried in his hair. At the rate he's going, there will be tracks worn into the concrete. He slams to a stop and whips his eyes to mine. There's so much icy hostility brimming in those blue depths. But I catch the vulnerability above it. I once again find myself contemplating what bothers this man. That weight on his shoulders looks too heavy to bear.

Rune enters the tense atmosphere with a chipper bark. His interruption severs the spell we'd been lost in. Nash wrenches his glare off me with a muffled curse. I nearly gasp as I'm released from those perplexing clutches. Aftershocks tingle along my nape.

Then I notice what lines the room. Jaw slack and eyes wide, I digest the treasures I just stumbled upon. My feet stumble forward on their own merit. I rotate in a full circle to appraise each expertly crafted piece. The hoodie's protective layer lowers from the choppy twirl, leaving me exposed to the slight chill. It barely penetrates beyond my surprise.

"What is all this?"

Nash moves to the side, done with his frustrated stomping. "My work."

He mentioned something along those lines earlier, just before his latest escape ploy. This isn't what I had in mind. Honestly, his reasoning sounded like a lame excuse. I figured he was just grasping at straws to evade me.

"You made all this?" I study a knotty log that's sleek, glossy, and wide enough to function as a stool. Maybe that's what it is.

His gaze tracks my interest. "Yeah."

"Wow." I'm compelled by some unseen force to explore the entire collection. Each object is different, and not just in the type of wood. Some chairs have more curves. The tables are a variety of heights and sizes. Shelves that are connected or stand-alone. A bench with ornate carving. Bookcases. Wall panels. Frames. Crates. Stands. Then there are more artistic designs that I assume are used for decoration.

There's one similarity across the board. The finished products are flawless. Unique, handcrafted items people would pay a small fortune for. That gets me thinking.

"Are these for sale?"

"Most are already sold."

That's an interesting twist, considering his strict aversion to people. He must have a system. Just one more mystery about this complex man.

Another thought occurs to me. "You made all the furniture in our cabins."

"I did."

"Wait." I whirl to face him. "What about the cabins themselves?"

"Did those too." His bland expression doesn't reflect pride or accomplishment.

I part and seal my lips five times before an articulate response forms. "That seems highly unlikely."

"Believe what you want." His nonchalant attitude is maddening.

"You built four cabins *and* this shop?" That last one gets tacked on for good measure.

Nash just nods.

"Alone?"

He shrugs as if my shock is unwarranted. "Had to hire a professional to ensure they're structurally sound and up to code."

"But otherwise?"

"Did it myself."

I smack a palm to my forehead to keep my brain from exploding. "How's that possible?"

Nash glances around the room. "Nothing else to do."

Questions fill my mouth until my cheeks are puffed out. I blow out the trapped air with a hiss. This must've cost a hefty sum. That means he has money, and a lot of it. Or did. Maybe he spent every cent building his lodges. The urge to ask how he pulled it off makes my temples hurt. Shaky ground warns me to tread lightly. It's not my business. Besides, the details won't change the obvious.

I whistle through my teeth. "You're really impressive, Thorn."

He scoffs. "Never heard that before."

"Only because you avoid people like their mere existence offends you."

A muscle leaps in his jaw. Touchy subject. "I didn't confine myself out here for the fuck of it."

"Gotcha." I sidestep that minefield and continue snooping. Nash doesn't complain as I peruse his creations. Rune suddenly flanks my leg, herding me toward a coffee table with subtle pressure. I kneel while smoothing a palm along the polished leg.

A groan fondles my eardrums from the other end of the room. The erotic sound snags my attention. When I peek over at him, a heavy pulse throbs in my lower half. He appears to be barely restraining himself. White knuckles clench around a hammer. His entire body flexes and goes slack on a restrictive cycle. Raw, carnal hunger billows from his stare.

I gulp when the temperature rises, the suffocating heat engulfing me within seconds. Inexperienced or not, it's plain to see Nash likes what he sees. This scene isn't entirely new to me. I've just never reciprocated the blatant lust dumped down my throat.

Men have made their disgusting intentions known on countless occasions. They leered at my cleavage. Grabbed my hips hard enough to bruise. Slung degrading comments to shrink my esteem. Took liberties that weren't offered. An ugly sneer taunts me as the memories flicker on a warped reel. The extra ballsy ones groped my ass while we danced at ridiculously overpriced fundraisers. Their crude affections left me feeling shamed and hollow.

They didn't want me, not in the sense that mattered. Those crooks sought what my connections could grant them. Well, that's not entirely true. It's my father's wealth and influence they were after. Nathaniel was the worst, and he almost won the grand prize. Nausea bubbles in my stomach just thinking about him. I hope he's suffering in prison. Good riddance.

But Nash? He might use me, but with our mutual pleasure as the sole priority. His unapologetic gaze promises to deliver satisfaction. That desire is rooted to the most basic, genuine level. I get a natural high off him that can't be bought. This brutal, savage honesty is what I came to find. I'm instantly hooked, and I crave more of what he's so freely giving me. It's simple and addictive and glorious.

I don't truly know what it means to be taken and worshipped by a man, but I have a feeling Nash would destroy me for all others. That reality is far too appealing.

Which is precisely why I have to pull the plug.

I turn away from the seductive sight before I suggest something highly inappropriate. Wobbly knees carry me to a set of rocking chairs. With my focus anchored forward, I don't see his approach. But that doesn't mean I can't feel him. His presence is stronger than the storm. My breath hitches with each prowling step. I'm attuned to him as if we're connected by an electrical wire thrumming with high voltage.

Nash's presence becomes a hot brand against my back. That near proximity causes a fever to ravage me. I'm suddenly sweltering, on the verge of going up in flames.

We aren't touching. Not quite. An inch or less is all that separates us beyond our clothes. Even through the thick cotton, his heat threatens to incinerate me.

He crowds my space, his body a towering cage I'm all too willing to perch in. "Couldn't listen, huh?"

I wheeze around the ball blocking my airway. A verbal response isn't possible. I settle for a quick head shake.

He dips lower. A steamy exhale ghosts along my neck, eliciting a shiver I feel deep inside. "What's in this shop is deeply personal to me."

I tilt my neck until my head bumps his jaw. "Am I invading?"

"Yes." His mouth is dangerously close to brushing my ear.

My lashes flutter until darkness swarms me. "Do you want me to leave?"

Nash's silence is deafening. Only our labored breathing sizzles across the stillness. He makes me wait for a full minute. Maybe longer. An erratic beat drums in my ears, doing little to soothe me. I'm ready to jump out of my clammy skin.

Eventually, he must deem me worthy to stay.

His next inhale is long and loud. "You smell like me."

My tongue swells from the heat in his voice. "Oh?"

He groans while drawing more of the scent into his lungs. "Yes."

I wet my lips as flames lick at me. "Is that good?"

"Very."

The urge to face him pummels me. But that would most likely shatter this intimate moment. It's that fear blending with rich lust keeping me grounded.

Nash makes me wish for things I've only read about in romance novels. More so, this man gives me hope that those whimsical fantasies can come true. The dream feels too real. I could almost reach out for that happily ever after.

Instead, I blindly grasp for the chair my front is plastered against. The solid surface provides me with a much-needed tether. I begin absently drifting my fingers along the smooth finish.

"Do you know what that does to me?" His hand hovers over mine as I trace the grooves.

We're so close to touching, but distance still lingers like chaperones on prom night. I want to feel the rough skin on his palms rasping against me. I want to feel the coarse stubble on his jaw leave marks on my sensitive flesh. My cheeks flare with smoky desire.

It's difficult to take a decent breath, leaving me delirious and flighty. I finally manage to bathe my lungs with fresh oxygen and recall that he asked me a question.

"What does it do to you?"

Nash emits another erotic groan that curls my toes. "These pieces are an extension of me. My visions and livelihood. I survive off this wood with passion and dedication. When you caress hours of labor with such care, it feels like you're stroking my bare flesh."

I'm dizzy with blood loss in my brain. There's a distinguishable sensitivity between my thighs. That slick heat that has nothing to do with rain, but rather this addictive man behind me. I'm consumed by him.

Then it happens. Warm flesh overlaps mine. My hand isn't visible beneath his. I stare at the astonishing sight while trying to remain calm. Desire wafts through the room in thick spurts. My pulse races until I'm breathless again. Spots dance in my vision as I try to stay standing.

I'm not sure what's happening, but I enjoy the rush beneath my skin. My entire life has been riches and spoils. It didn't take long to determine I wasn't motivated by material belongings. My internal compass leads me straight ahead, on a path framed in love and devotion. The type that can't be forced or manipulated. Maybe this is a sign, a memorable point from which to start the journey.

That's why I sag against him with my next breath.

Almost as fast, Nash rips his palm off me. "Dammit."

Cool air suddenly replaces the fire he'd been stoking. His absence is an instant loss, and not just to my balance. I right myself with a forward sway.

"What just happened?"

He scrubs a palm down his face. "Too much."

I've pushed him again. A scolded wince cramps my expression. "Sorry."

"It wasn't you." His gaze slides to me for a brief second before darting away again. "Well, not entirely."

The anger in his tone stings, but one glance at him proves that fury isn't directed at me. He's mad at himself. For what, I can't be certain.

I inch forward, only to have him retreat a step. "What's wrong?"

"You should go. It's late." He's denying me. Again.

I'm tired of rejection. Exhausted, really. "What if I stay?"

"That wasn't meant to be phrased as a request, Darlin'."

"You and your nicknames." I bite my lip as a fresh rush of heat attacks my face.

"Fucking hell." The growly noise he emits is primal and animalistic. If he's trying to dissuade me, that's not a proper strategy.

"That could be arranged," I whisper.

"No," he grunts. "Get some sleep."

"How about you?" I find it hard to believe he'll find comfort out here. There's not a soft surface in sight.

"That's not your problem. I'll see you in the morning." Nash shoves more distance between us without moving. His resolute resistance bounces off the walls. There's no sense in arguing.

I can only suggest so much before it looks desperate. Tonight has already proven to be… intense. We have months together. That reminder is enough for now. I'll choose to retreat. For his sake, and mine. I'm not happy about it, but I'll have to raise the white flag.

My backward motion is hesitant, reluctance a sticky tar weighing me down. But I leave him to his cherished solitude all the same.

CHAPTER FOURTEEN

RUNE CRASHES THROUGH THE BRUSH WITH ZERO consideration for my latest attempt at relaxing. I crack an eye open to watch him dash off at breakneck speed. Whatever enticing scent he's caught must be a good one.

Not better than the seductive temptation seared into my nostrils.

Penny in my clothes, smelling like me, is more arousing than any provocative fantasy. Then she went ahead and stroked my wood.

I'm about to pop some in my jeans right now at the illicit scene burned into my memory.

Each gentle caress from her fingers across those polished edges felt like she was appraising me. My dick twitches, already semi-hard just imagining a hesitant graze from those supple hands. Penny dug beyond the shiny exterior to find the scars lurking beneath. Her immediate acceptance was a balm I felt in my bones. A permanent claim I'll never be free from.

And I'm not certain I want to be.

It's been years since I've initiated contact with someone. In my shop, with Penny surrounded by me, I was compelled to touch her. That connection sizzles in my palm days later. I fist my left hand to ward off the unwanted reminder. The beer in my right gets crushed by association.

"So damn weak!" I shout to the dancing branches above.

Rune appears at my side, bumping his head against me.

His intuition rarely fails. Same with his loyalty, except when a certain blonde enters the field. But he knows me in some ways better than I know myself—there's no hiding from him. The pity in his mismatched eyes slashes at the wound festering in my chest.

"Yeah, boy. I'm screwed."

His whimper acknowledges unavoidable facts.

I'm already too invested in her. She's leaving in less than two months. We won't see each other again once she's gone. That's why I've kept my distance this past week.

It doesn't change the harsh reality I'm living. I want Penny Blaire to be mine. Even temporarily.

If that's all I'm afforded, I should accept the scraps with open arms.

Yet I don't move to make good on that concession.

I'll savor what little remains of my sanity while I can. Besides, it's a fan-fucking-tastic afternoon to appreciate the great outdoors. June in Minnesota is a luxury to indulge in. The warm climate before summer humidity strikes is tough to beat. I let my muscles go slack for another attempt at relaxation.

The can in my palm is still cool. There's a slight breeze off the lake. Rune has forfeited the chase against whatever poor creature teased his instincts. His resigned huff is muffled as he sprawls on the ground. I tug on the brim of my hat and settle in. Nothing can get in my way—physically, at least.

Rickety pine creaks under my ass as I recline against the worn seat. This chair is a classic, one of the first I made. The construction is shoddy, and that's being generous. That's why I'm quick to choose this relic. The frequent repairs remind me of how far I've come. Humble beginnings and all that. Better yet, those squeaky joints give me something to do.

Right after I finish this beer.

The can is about to kiss my lips when a distinctive chime

sounds. A smirk begins to tickle my mouth. I scowl to offset the expression.

Penny: Hi, Thorn.

I slowly blink at the message. As a man of few words, I don't prefer to mince them. This woman is the complete opposite. She slices and dices like a professional chef.

Me: What's up?

Penny: Just saying hey.

Me: Okay…

Penny: You busy?

Coors Light spews from my mouth. What a joke. Seems only fitting I respond with my own.

Me: Always.

Penny: Thinking of me?

Now I pause, gaze locked on the screen. Penny is many things. Being outright suggestive without a bit of situational foreplay isn't one of them. At three o'clock on a Saturday, there's a conclusion I immediately jump to.

Me: You drinking?

Penny: Maybe.

Me: It's yes or no.

Penny: Yes. Happy?

I can almost hear those hazel eyes rolling skyward. Her frustration steals the sharpest point from my own. Even so, I'm the furthest thing from happy.

Me: Where are you?

Penny: Are we playing this game again?

Fire flares under my skin despite the mild weather. She gets me hot faster than a desert heatwave. But fuck climate change. This is a personal attack.

Me: Are you going to follow the rules?

Penny: Probably not.

I bite my fist while staving off the feverish crash. Her bratty attitude is an enthusiastic stroke to my cock. She's probably unaware of just how starved I've been.

That's why I let her wait.

The wild thrash in my pulse makes me feel too unhinged. It's unpredictable and obsessive and demanding. If I'm not careful, I might not be able to pump the brakes when I see her again. Just one more reason I've reinforced the barriers.

I return my focus to the dense forest that seems to have no end. Leafy green blends with earth tones. If I look to the right, azure waters will greet me. This view is safe and familiar. Unlike the vivid splash of neon Penny drops into the mix.

The silence stretches for several minutes. Almost long enough to believe she lost interest. That's not the stubborn woman I've begun to know, though.

Then an automated chime breaks into the natural hush.

Penny: Hello?

Me: What's up?

Penny: You went quiet.

Me: Did you expect otherwise?

Penny: Ignoring me isn't your style.

A gruff snort streams from me. She would know. My abrupt disappearances are reserved as her special brand of torture. At least where these message threads are concerned.

I've learned to rein in my shit. Coming across as a crazed maniac wasn't doing me any favors.

The furious rush in my veins betrays me. As if I need another reminder of how this woman is warping me. Soon I'll be snug around her pinky.

Me: You started this, not me.

Penny: I wasn't trying to poke the bear.

Me: Sure about that?

Penny: Nope.

Me: Where are you?

Penny: Maybe I'm in my cabin.

I know she's not. Call me a stalker and I won't deny it. Her car wasn't there when I checked earlier. It's not that invasive to do a property sweep on my rentals.

Me: Don't lie to me.

The extended inhale is a necessary practice. Penny won't tell me her location until I command it. I'm beginning to think my girl has a kinky side. The claim is a cold shower in the middle of a blizzard.

She isn't my girl.

Not yet anyway. Dammit.

Penny: I wish you were here, Thorn.

Penny: You could prick my side.

Penny: Or somewhere else.

Penny: Maybe I'd let you choose.

The rapid-fire messages are a juicy steak fresh off the grill. My mouth waters for a taste. She's probably the perfect balance between sweet and tart.

We haven't seen each other since the storm, but that hasn't stopped our newfound texting habits. Our messages rarely veer out of bland territory into something spicier.

This is something else entirely. I don't hate it.

A different approach occurs to me.

Me: Who are you with?

Penny: You think I'm sexting with others around?

Me: You think this is sexting?

Penny: Yes?

The question mark proves my point. Such an innocent darling. She'll find out just how dirty things can get if I have anything to do with it.

Me: We shouldn't be sexting.

Penny: Why not?

Me: It's inappropriate.

Penny: I find that hard to believe.

Me: Like always.

Penny: It's not my problem that you mystify me.

Me: Fancy words.

Penny: They come easy when you're involved.

Me: Are you drunk?

There's no other explanation for her loose tongue. I guess it's her fingers in this instance. Those digits have proven to be daring and dangerous.

The smirk crooks my lips without warning, but fuck it.

Then I'm compelled to—once again—recall the startling comfort of her delicate skin underneath my roughed palm.

Penny's hand was tiny in comparison. The sight left me with a savage need to protect her, more so than before.

If she's overindulging, or overserved, someone should be looking after her.

Penny: I'm tipsy, but barely. Just enough to feel free.

Me: Tell me where you are.

Penny: On the patio at Timbered Tavern.

Me: Alone?

Penny: I'm with Lydia.

The name is familiar from our previous conversations. They seem to be spending a lot of time together. Whether she's a good influence or not has yet to be determined. I like to assume Penny has high standards for the company she chooses to keep.

Which reminds me.

Me: Is Greg there?

Penny: He's bartending. Why?

Me: Stay away from him.

Penny: Jealous?

Me: Protective.

Penny: Same thing.

Me: Whatever convinces you faster.

Penny: How do you know him?

Me: Even I hear about the town scum.

That man and I have had a few misunderstandings. Try as I might to avoid civilization, I'm forced to endure visits to the general store. Delivery services have yet to arrive in Hacken.

Besides, I'm not afraid to be in public. I just prefer to avoid people whenever possible.

Greg is a shining example of why.

Last time he crossed my path, his flavor of the week couldn't keep her eyes off me. His fragile ego didn't care for that too much. He compensated for his small penis by joking about my loner lifestyle. Real winner.

Penny: Don't worry. He's more interested in Lydia.

Me: He better not be bothering you.

Penny: Maybe you should come tell him that.

Me: Trying to get me arrested?

Penny: For defending my honor?

Me: It'd be worth it.

Greg is a douche who doesn't deserve the same air as Penny. It makes my blood boil knowing she's near him. Now I sound like a possessive asshole.

This is why I tried to resurrect my boundaries. It's proven to be a wasted effort. She appears hellbent on decimating any progress I've attempted. We've already come this far. I slump lower in the chair. Weariness from the constant battle drains my resolve.

Maybe I should let her lead.

Penny: Guess Rune isn't my only hero.

Sometimes I wonder if she reads my thoughts.

Me: I'm no hero.

Penny: I'll buy you a mighty steed.

Me: A pitchfork would be more fitting.

Penny: You'd snap that in half.

Me: Even better.

A telltale lull settles in. My phone goes quiet, the pause dragging until it becomes a period. There's nothing left to say.

The can in my grip is warm, much like the beer in it. That's my cue to get moving. I stand with a stretch, my rested muscles pinching and twinging. My chair creaks with a reminder of the promised repairs.

I'm about to haul the seat over my shoulder when that distracting chime bleeps. My pathetic resistance lasts three seconds at most. My fingers tremble with the effort. Even Rune grunts at my futile attempt. The glowing screen mocks my surrender, but I can't find a shit to give a crap.

Penny: I've decided something.

A smile cracks my lips. The reaction is beyond my control at this stage. If I'm going down, it might as well be in flames.

Me: What's that?

Penny: I can't call you Thorn anymore.

The drastic dip in my stomach is concerning. Must be acid reflux.

Me: Okay.

Penny: It doesn't fit anymore.

Me: Does that mean I'm no longer a pain in your side?

Penny: I'll admit no such thing. You just need a new one for purposes I have yet to reveal.

Me: Nash is fine.

Penny: Boring.

Me: Should I be offended?

Penny: No. Everyone needs a nickname.

According to her. I scrub over my mouth to chase off another grin. Not sure where that logic comes from, but she's rolling with it.

Penny: Don't pretend you haven't been calling me Darlin'.

She's right, of course. Somewhere along these threads, her nickname habit grew on me. I even allow my drawl to escape with the endearing term.

Me: What're you suggesting?

Penny: Hot stuff, baby cakes, sexy bear, bubba, cutie pie, stud muffin.

Penny: Just some ideas.

Penny: Feel free to give me your input.

My upper lip curls. These make me sound like an actual pet. Ugly offense curdles in my gut. Fuck that. She can use that list on some sorry loser looking to be humiliated. I'm tempted to quit texting Penny altogether after this stunt. That would save me a lot of trouble.

She must get the hint after I don't humor her with an equally ridiculous response.

Penny: None of the above?

Me: I'm good going without.

Penny: That wasn't an option.

Me: Thorn is fine.

Penny: You like it?

Me: I'll agree to no such thing.

Penny: Hey! You stole my line.

Me: Didn't see your name on it.

Penny: Speaking of, Thorn is a keeper?

Me: Just figured it makes sense since you're stuck with me.

Until she leaves. That serves to cool the warmth spreading through my chest. It's fucking pathetic that the reminder is necessary at all. At this rate, I'll give myself whiplash.

Penny: That's not a bad twist, Thorn.

Me: Glad you agree, Darlin'.

Penny: Does this mean we're friends?

Me: Is that a question adults ask each other?

Penny: I don't care.

And she doesn't. That's what I like about her, along with every other refreshing trait. I wonder more than ever what she's hiding. Secrets are my closest confidants, but those ugly shadows aren't fitting for her sunny personality.

Maybe she'll trust me more than whatever darkens her past.

But that's a slippery slope, much like this exchange as a whole.

Me: Gonna be home soon?

Penny: Maybe. Why?

Me: Wanna be sure you make it back safe.

Penny: You miss me?

Me: No.

But the real answer is plain to see. I've burned a solid hour messaging her.

Penny: Lies.

Me: Rune misses you.

That's the closest I'll get to admitting the truth.

Penny: Are you going to give me some wood?

I grunt at the erotic visual that immediately pays me a visit. Innocent darling or not, this tipsy vixen knows what she's doing. Her supply isn't at risk of running out. Not by a long shot.

Me: Do you need another batch?

Penny: If you're delivering.

Me: Don't I always?

Penny: Just admit you miss me.

Me: What's gotten into you?

Penny: A big Thorn.

Penny: Well, not yet. But maybe soon.

I choke on my spit. She's back to waving that juicy steak too close to my face. If she's not careful, I'll take a bite.

Me: Jesus, Darlin'. Think about what you're saying to me.

Penny: That's all I've been doing in my head. You.

And there goes my dick.

I snarl a curse as molten lust throbs through me. That fierce heat collects front and center. There's a nine-inch salute standing proud, ready to seek her out. If only she was able to soothe the ache.

Me: You're not talking very friendly.

Penny: Just easing you in.

Me: Afraid to ask.

But the suspense won't let me rest. The blood loss to my top half will assist with that.

Penny: Just let it happen, Thorn.

Penny: Bye for now.

My jaw goes slack as her delayed gratification appears on the screen. She's got me by the balls, which was probably her intent all along. I'm too stunned to reply, but the shock will wear off eventually.

Come morning, I'll get what's mine.

CHAPTER FIFTEEN

Penny

I ADJUST ON THE TOWEL AS MID-MORNING WARMTH SEEPS straight to my bones. The groan I set free into the wild is pure delight. Soft sand cradles me in a toasty embrace while gentle waves meet the shore in a soothing tempo. Calm bliss soaks my skin until I'm ready to drift off.

This is the stuff my childhood dreams were made of. Aside from the unexpected chill that likes to bite me in the ass every so often. But those sneaky surprises keep me vigilant.

After a run at dawn through the woods, I pulled on my big girl panties and jumped in the lake. It was so freaking cold that my nipples are still stiff hours later. A shiver attacks my limbs at the reminder. Next time, I'll dip a toe in first.

The thawing process is almost complete when a large shadow blocks the sunshine from hitting me. I lift a palm to shield my eyes and catch the culprit.

Steamy desire singes my lungs, but I manage to speak. "Excuse you."

Nash doesn't appear affronted. The bulky brute also doesn't move from his stooped sun-stealing position. I recognize anger in the ruddy hue that tinges his tan complexion.

Before I can contemplate his interruption further, though, Rune crashes onto the scene and begins a thorough cleansing cycle on my face. The fit of giggles I release can't be stopped.

"Awww, did you miss me?"

His licks gain momentum, and he adds a full-body wiggle to showcase genuine enthusiasm. If only we could all be so free and giddy.

My fingers delve into his thick fur for a well-earned scratch. "Well, I'm glad someone is happy to see me."

Rune yips, gives me a final sloppy smooch, then splashes into the lake.

"Such a good pup," I sigh.

The big man on campus has yet to speak. Blue flames simmer in his eyes and might be cause for concern, but I'm not scared of a little burn. Besides, my sunscreen is extra strength.

Nice try, Thorn.

"You'd like that, huh?"

Between doggy kisses and a front-row seat to a surprise eight-pack show, it takes a moment for me to process his restrained fury. The fog clouding my logic isn't doing me any favors either. "What?"

"If I step aside whenever you ask. Let you run me over."

"I'm lost," I mumble absently.

He sucks air between his teeth. The resulting hiss resembles a coiled snake preparing to strike. "I'm not a doormat, Darlin'. You can't walk on me without getting the filth flung right back."

"But you're blocking my sun." The explanation is too breathy to be taken seriously.

"I plan to do a lot worse than that."

"Now?" Pretty sure I just exhaled two-hundred-proof desire.

His head jerks with a sharp refusal. "Nah, I'll let you sit and wonder until it drives you to the brink of insanity."

It seems someone woke on the grumpy side and had surly sauce for breakfast. Not that I don't deserve his frustration.

The wince I offer is sincere. "Sorry about that."

"Are you really?"

The fine line I'm straddling wobbles with indecision. "That depends, I guess."

"On?"

"How mad you are." I slide on a hesitant smile to test the waters.

He scowls in return. "I don't like being toyed with."

"Then it's a good thing I'm not joking. Besides, there wasn't any mention of toys." Oh, my gosh. I need a muzzle before my face bursts into flames.

Nash crosses his arms into an imposing fold. "Stud muffin? Cutie pie? Bubba?"

Okay, the cheesy nicknames didn't go over well. Noted. "I was just trying to be funny."

"Am I laughing?" Damn, his swim trunks are in a tight twist.

"Tough crowd," I mutter.

"That's what you get messing with me." His tone is the harsh crack of a whip, yet he doesn't retreat. Maybe he secretly enjoys our banter.

Or I'm more delusional than my therapists ever gave me credit for.

That's when I take stock of my sprawled position. I slowly prop myself into an upright position that puts us on more even ground. Nash must notice my slight unease and plops into the sand beside me. Our next breaths are simultaneous sighs.

I laugh when he rolls his eyes. "How 'bout a truce, Thorn?"

"What will that get me?" His hypnotic energy draws me in.

Without conscious effort, I'm turning toward him. "What do you want?"

After our saucy exchange yesterday, I'd been half expecting him to pound down my door and demand satisfaction. Oh, hell. I'll admit that's what I was hoping he'd do. But no.

Nash is a slow burn, the extra broody sort. Now that he's here, blasting me with the full intensity of his stare, I don't know why I thought otherwise. The guy stranded himself on purpose. He told me as much quite clearly. I've done little more than piss him off with my silly texts.

In all honesty, Lydia is to blame. She gave me a crash course in dirty talk. I wanted to be bold for him. That's why I sought her advice. Not that I told her who I was planning to seduce. She could've guessed, and probably did. My friend is too kind to point out the faults littered all over this scheme. It's bound to be botched. Starting now, or even then, apparently.

Maybe I should've thought twice before testing my new skills on Nash. It didn't turn out too bad, though. By the tension throbbing in his veins, I'd say it was a roaring success.

Speaking of veins…

I give myself permission to feast on his bare torso. Again. This scene is all too familiar. Drool puddles in my mouth faster than I can swallow. The sun doesn't stand a chance against his potent presence. Blistering intensity.

In my defense, it's criminal for Nash to show up without a shirt on. He's playing dirty. Too bad for him, I'm not unarmed. I tug at the triangle barely containing my boob. This string bikini is as skimpy as they come.

"You drive me mad." His timbre holds a growly note to punctuate the severity.

"I could say the same." My tone is silky and civil.

He seems to collect the fraying ends of his control. "Where did you come from, Penny Blaire?"

"A land from far, far away." A place I prefer to ignore. I bat at the air for emphasis.

His brows leap skyward. "Did you just quote *Star Wars?*"

I wrinkle my nose. "No, pretty sure that's a galaxy. Not land."

"The fact that you even know is incredibly sexy."

A zing races up my spine. "I'll take that as a compliment."

The strangled noise he spews almost sounds like a chuckle. Almost. "Not sure what to make of you, Darlin'."

"Keep sweet talking to me and see what happens." I tack on an exaggerated wink because… why not? My filter is already blown to smithereens.

His gaze is riveted on me. "You give an identity to my ultimate fantasy."

Oh, that's a good one. I drag my tongue along my lower lip. "Likewise."

Nash furrows his forehead. "That doesn't make sense."

Yep, definitely delusional. A huff steeped in disgruntled defense parts my mouth. "Can you blame me? You're too hot. My brain is melting."

Masculine pride straightens his shoulders. "Quit trying to defuse me."

"You're the one striking a match." Meanwhile, I squint against the blinding physique stabbing my eyeballs. "Warn a girl before strutting onto her beach."

"This is my property."

"Does that mean you can come and go as you please?" *And why does that policy appeal to me?*

Something about him sneaking in the window gets my motor purring. He'd probably just walk right in like he owns the place. A snort escapes me. Yeah, the irony isn't lost on me with that one.

"Yes, I'm allowed to complete random inspections to make sure my cabins aren't being destroyed. Check your contract."

So literal, this one. "Your customer service leaves much to the imagination."

"Normally people don't demand more than the cabin. They know how to handle the woods."

"Ouch," I wheeze. "My deepest apologies for putting a kink in your busy schedule."

He grunts. "The sweet darling has claws. Maybe you'll learn to use them more often."

That's the first time the endearment slaps me as an insult. "Okay, wow. I didn't mean to be a burden."

Ghosts of Penelope Winchester's past rise from the ache in my chest. The blurry sting in my vision is completely uncalled for. I hate feeling like a problem. My parents are really good at announcing whenever I'm unwanted. Spoiler alert: it was almost daily.

I fought against their reign, but they broke me eventually. By thirteen, I was dutiful and obedient. Then they pushed too far, and I remembered who I could be. Who I'm striving to become.

Who I refuse to be ever again.

The man beside me is a tough nut to crack, and so am I. Maybe he's teaching me a thing or two. Either that or I'm overreacting.

This entire situation is far too close to home. I find myself connecting our stories again. Differences aside, I'm willing to bet we share similar wounds. There's a familiar darkness that covers his expression. Almost like we're kindred spirits. While I've refused to acknowledge mine, perhaps he's embraced it.

It doesn't matter right now. I won't stand—or sit—for his hurtful ridicule.

"You should go," I mutter into the calm surrounding us. It doesn't match the chaos in my veins.

Startled blue eyes search mine. "The fuck?"

"I won't bother you again." The vow hardens my heart, even if I want to cry. We might've had something real. The urge to retract my statement lashes at me until I almost sob.

But this is a fight for me. That's what I'm truly here for.

Nash rips his eyes off me with a string of muffled expletives. "What just happened?"

"I won't let history repeat itself."

Understanding thrashes in his gaze. "All right, Darlin'. I'll go."

The lump in my throat tries to steal any semblance of a response. I manage a curt, "Thanks."

Nash pushes to his feet and stalks to the dirt path. His gait reflects the thunder just beneath the surface. Before he enters the woods, his parting blow hits me. "Just for the record, you're never a bother to me."

CHAPTER SIXTEEN

I DO AS PENNY ASKS, BUT I DON'T GO FAR. THE TREES PROVIDE the illusion of a signature retreat within moments. Once she's hidden from view, my stride slams to a stop. Feverish pacing begins almost immediately after.

"What the fuck just happened," I mutter.

Forest debris crunches under my soles. The twigs underfoot snap, mirroring a crack at my ribs from a blindside punch. It's tough to breathe. This fresh distance between us rips at what little stability I have left to stand on. Our conversation turned so fast that my head started spinning. I'm still dizzy from the onslaught.

When I found Penny on the beach, I decided to confront her. Maybe tease her with similar methods that got to me so easily yesterday. The plan was idiotic to begin with. As if I could actually even the score. All I did was upset her. Go fucking figure. This is exactly why I don't people.

I can't let history repeat itself.

That sentiment from her hit me hard. I can relate, more than she knows. Reckless impulses were my main meals growing up. My father built his legacy on nothing but taking risks and good fortune. Too bad that luck didn't last. I tug at my hair while harsh reality forces me to accept the facts once again. The chance he bargained for, the one that could change it all, cost my parents the ultimate price with their lives.

Their perceived agony delivers an ache to my chest that makes it tough to breathe. They didn't deserve that fate, yet chose it all the same. It didn't just take them either, as I'm surrounded by bitter memories and solitude.

But my loss isn't what matters right now.

One thing is certain.

Penny isn't that innocent when it comes to the gnashing jaws of pain. To what degree, I'm not sure. The shadows in her expression are genuine. I saw those dark tendrils wisp across her features in stark clarity. The signs are too familiar, as if they're my own. She's running from the past—a previous existence better left buried—and somehow ended up here.

With me.

That's some shitty luck.

A startling realization has my erratic motions skidding to a halt. I've become the villain in her story. My mind whirls with the sentence slammed on me. That's unacceptable. There's plenty of bad shit with my name smeared all over it, but causing Penny more pain doesn't belong on the list. She's the only person who's made an effort for me in all these years. It might seem insignificant to her, but those attentions—no matter how small—mean everything to me.

Maybe I should leave her be. That's what she wants. But I can't even bring myself to think that. Just the thought of her never speaking to me again is gut-wrenching.

Muffled sobs pierce the toxins flooding me. The broken sound shreds my heart. I'm stumbling back to the beach before my legs are sturdy.

Rune is parked next to her, licking the sorrow from her cheeks. Loyal mutt. I can't fault him for picking sides. Penny is the obvious choice in any contest. Pure and good and hurt by my spiteful words. Shame buckles my knees and I nearly crash to the ground.

It's staggering how much this woman already means to me.

Penny must hear the commotion behind her and visibly

stiffens. Not surprising, since I have the grace of a drunk elephant. I drag in some much-needed balance as I slow my approach. She peeks over her shoulder. Wet lashes blink at me. Splotched skin and red-rimmed eyes are my undoing.

"Fucking hell." I devour the distance separating us before she can tell me to stop.

There's no space for hesitation. With more care than I've ever shown, I scoop her off the sand and cinch us in a bonding embrace meant to last. The move is clumsy and strange, but gets the job done. She's flush against me in the next second. Unfiltered sunshine flows off her exposed skin. My bare upper half is quick to return the favor, blanketing her in the fever that rushes just beneath the surface. A foreign remedy settles me. The calm that follows is a shock to my system and I almost jolt. That's the only explanation for why heat assaults my vision. I slide my eyes shut to ward off the burn.

Just like talking, I've developed the habit of avoiding physical contact. It wasn't necessarily on purpose. The idea of blending individual warmth into shared heat is actually arousing. It just never happened for me. Quite the opposite—I was left with a numb sensation whenever I tried holding someone close. The dull reaction left me feeling more empty than usual.

But the electric sparks shooting off my skin right now? That's what I've been missing. This thrum under my skin is sudden and slightly alarming, but a welcome relief all the same. It turns out I'm not detached. I just needed the right person to reach me.

Before this, we haven't touched for longer than seconds. Our conversations are stilted and mostly via text. None of that registers or makes an impact. This is just… finding comfort in each other. The fact we happen to be mostly naked doesn't hurt.

That's when I realize Penny is stiff and unresponsive. Her reaction fills me with doubt. I loosen my grip until her feet almost touch the ground. The slack I grant seems to knock her from a stupor. Her resistance melts, and she collapses into me with a sigh.

Penny loops her arms around my waist in a smooth motion. Her reciprocation is encouraging, to say the least. I tug her impossibly closer, my hands caressing her bare curves. Her body feels fragile compared to my much larger build. If I squeeze too hard, she might shatter. That has me easing off again. She responds by tightening her grasp. With her pressed against my chest, I can feel the rapid thump from her heart mirroring the fast beat from mine.

When I find the courage to open my eyes, Rune is sitting beside our joined form. His tongue lolls out in a happy display. I imagine he's all too pleased seeing his two favorite people united together.

Silence envelops us in shared tranquility. The lazy tide splashes the shore to serenade this intimate moment. It's a welcome reprieve from the storm raging in my thoughts. If only I truly deserved what she so willingly offers. This morning has been a rude awakening and it's barely eleven o'clock. But I'm going to savor her while I can. She's a pillar of unconditional warmth against me. Maybe I can be the same for her someday.

I take a liberty and bury my nose in the crook of her neck. My inhale is loud and bold, pulling her deep into me without remorse. That visceral ingestion is a primitive entity with its own agenda. Vanilla and lavender fill my lungs, along with the unmistakable scent of paradise.

If I'm not careful, this safe indulgence will take an indecent dip.

My palms rest on her hips. There's much for me to explore while she's dressed in little more than strings, but I restrain the urge. That doesn't stop my fingers from toying with the knots maintaining her modesty. Penny shivers with a muffled whimper as goosebumps erupt on her flesh.

My answering groan is pure satisfaction. "I've never done this."

She takes several seconds to mull that over. "Hugged someone?"

A bullish snort jostles our position. I can't even fault her for that comment. The idea isn't too farfetched considering my behavior.

"Just held a woman close for the sake of comfort." The confession is exhaled across her neck.

"Oh." Penny sags against me, trusting me to keep her upright.

That's precisely what I do, and plan to whenever she needs support. I already dread the moment we'll part. As if agreeing with me, her shoulders wobble with a hitched inhale.

I smooth a palm along the column of her spine. "Don't cry."

She sniffles. "I'm not."

"Don't lie either."

Her tear-streaked cheek sears into my chest as a brand of my own making. "But you hate me."

A scoff is my knee-jerk reply. I should let her believe it. Hell, I've gone out of my way to prove that exact point. It had the opposite effect, if anything. Such a waste. In all honesty, I'd be more likely to forgive those who wronged me beyond repair rather than dredge up an ounce of hate for this woman.

"Nah, Darlin'. I don't." Or *can't*, for that matter.

"If you say so," she hums. "I'm glad. This is really nice. We should do it more often."

"Yeah?" My posture puffs with premature pride.

She rests her chin on my sternum. The honesty shining in her eyes steals my breath. "Uh-huh. As a hugger, I give your execution a perfect score."

Not sure how much I like thinking about who she's been wrapped around. I'll have to make it better than the rest. "That doesn't give much room for improvement."

Penny wiggles against me to test the limits of my control. "You don't need it."

I suck straight desire between clenched teeth. "Giving me too much credit."

In more ways than one. Arousal threatens to punch a hole through my shorts. I'm only human, and extremely deprived of physical contact. She taunts my restraint without touching me. Pressed this close is game over.

"We'll see, huh?" She'll be quick to change her mind once those threads break.

"Wanna go for a swim?" I widen my stance, but there's not far to move. This hug will need to end soon or I'm likely to pass out.

Her brow quirks. "The water is too cold. Besides, you have some explaining to do."

"Me?" Gravel coats my tongue.

"Why did you come back?"

"Couldn't listen to you cry." That reminder serves to deflate the insistent lust directed at her.

Those hazel depths try to bore through my jaded layers. "Is that the only reason?"

No, but the truth requires more explanation than I'm willing to admit. I avert my gaze like a fucking coward. The shrug I offer is salt in the wound.

She pokes my chest. "Don't go quiet on me."

"I'm a dick."

She rolls her eyes. "What else is new?"

"That's the gist." And provides a logical escape from this embrace. It's extended well beyond even the most romantic standards. I groan as our bodies break apart. Pretty sure my flesh is steaming from where we touched.

"Typical," she mumbles.

There are multiple interpretations of such a simple utterance. Most of them—especially in my case—aren't good.

I drag my eyes to hers, hoping to reflect the sincerity that demands to be heard. "Forgive me?"

Her lips twist to one side. "I'll think about it."

"Better than I deserve," I mutter.

"Are you going to be nice?"

"I can't promise that." Nice isn't a term that will ever describe me. But for her, I'll try to be decent.

A natural lull sweeps in with a light breeze. The lake ripples, its glittering surface winking at us. Her attention remains stuck on me, though. My skin gets itchy under her scrutiny. I can feel the questions preparing to pepper me into a seasoned buffet.

"You're not a bad guy, Thorn."

"Definitely not a good one," I retort.

"Well, for what it's worth, I'm glad you came back." Her gaze cuts a suggestive path down my torso.

A fresh burst of lust spears me. Just when I forgot the ache in my balls. "Are you really?"

"Well, duh. I would've missed you."

I scrub over my mouth. "You wanted me to stay away."

"Not really," she admits in a whisper. "It was in the heat of the moment. Summer would suck without you."

That sparks an ugly reminder I can't seem to shake. I hate to ruin our established progress, but it's vital to me that we clear the air of poison. My eyes naturally seek the unbiased comfort of the lake in front of us.

At the last second, I return my focus to her. "Are you just using me as a cure for loneliness?"

Her sputtering disbelief whizzes through a slack jaw. "What?"

"Do you have ulterior motives?"

Penny is still gaping at me. "How can you even think that?"

"I can't let history repeat itself." I'm quick to borrow her line from earlier. There's no better justification.

Now it's her turn to understand why I lack trust and have a severe loss of tact. "Want to tell me about it?"

"Not even a little bit." I'm not ready to delve into the heavy stuff.

It's a topic I don't even like to think about. Ever. Secrets might be a hard limit for her. I sleep beside them. That's something she has to accept, or not. She barely tolerates me as it is. Finally, her lips part with the verdict.

"I see you," she mumbles.

The knot in my gut wrenches tight. "That's what I'm most afraid of."

"I don't need to know what haunts you, Thorn. Just tell me we can move forward without demons chasing us."

"Why do you think I'm out here?"

Her nod is slow. "Fair enough."

"Turns out I'm not just a dick, huh?" I drag a hand through my hair. "I'm also extremely fucked-up."

"Aren't we all?" She gestures to her face that's still puffy from shedding tears. "I gave myself emotional whiplash over memories that can't hurt me."

"Wanna tell me about it?"

Penny gasps in exaggerated offense. "Quit stealing my lines."

"I just like to watch you squirm, Darlin'." For once, I'm trying to lighten the mood.

"You're good at that." Her voice drops to a sultry octave.

Soon, there will be a noticeable tent pitched in my trunks. "Careful, or I'll make you cool off in the lake with me."

She visibly shudders. "Don't you dare. Not until I've adequately cooked in the sun first."

"Just fucking with you. But for real, you can always talk to me." I might be a broody bastard, but I still have broad shoulders to lean on.

She seems to arrive at a decision. "We're friends, right?"

"If that's what you'd like."

"For now," she hedges.

"Makes sense. I'm convenient, and can't seem to stay away from you."

"That's not what I meant."

I hold up a pacifying hand. "Hey, it's all right. I can be a not-so-memorable item on your wilderness bucket list, or whatever this trip is for you."

Penny frowns. "Selling yourself short again."

"It's what I do." Other than my furniture. That's high-quality shit.

"Who broke you, *Nash Hudson?*" She emphasizes my name like a fake persona.

I have a sneaking suspension she has personal experience with that. "That falls under the 'we're not discussing it' category, *Penny Blaire.*"

Her name gets the same treatment, which earns me a scoff.

"Fine, whatever. But by the way, this wilderness bucket list"—she grimaces, not bothering to mask her disdain for that term—"is one of the first things I've ever done for myself. I'm far from my comfort zone, but that's the point. True adventure is found in the unknown, right? I'm trying to find a little slice for myself."

I widen my eyes while digesting that unbelievable tidbit. "Wait, hold on. Of all the destinations to choose from, you picked a secluded cabin in Hacken, Minnesota?"

Her bland expression doesn't match my shock in the slightest. "Sure, why not?"

"It's not luxurious, or even on the map."

That's not me being an ass. Hacken is barely a speck when searching for towns in Minnesota. Not worthy of mention other than Excel Entertainment, which is nothing to go wild about. I can't recall the last time I laughed, but this might do it.

Penny ignores my barb with a swat. "I've had enough luxury to last me three lifetimes. It's overrated in my book. What I need is adventure. Cheap thrills. The unexpected. Big city excitement need not apply."

Almost sounds too good to be true…

"I can provide that, Darlin'." The possibilities are endless without leaving my property.

She nibbles her bottom lip. "You already are."

Our gazes latch and hold. The unspoken tension boomerangs from her to me, waiting for one of us to snatch the inevitable. I'm stepping forward before I realize my feet are moving. Penny mirrors my approach, her bare toes digging into the sand. Static energy zaps along my skin. The air becomes dense and stagnant. It takes great effort to draw a decent breath. Only a foot separates us, maybe less. Her fingers tremble in anticipation.

Rune barks just as I'm about to reach for her.

I shake off the trance and blink reality into focus. Penny looks to be struggling to do the same. We cough in unison, the cloying desire dissipating for another day.

She laughs, cheeks a dark crimson. "Uh, I guess I should go."

"Big plans?"

Her head tilts as she assesses the nature of my interest. "Are you trying to keep tabs on me?"

Always. But she doesn't need to hear that. "Can't I care about my friend? Or ask out of pure curiosity?"

She tips her head skyward with an overdone cackle. "That's a good one. You're funny, Thorn."

"Never been called that before."

"Shocker." Her breathy comeback drips with sarcasm.

I narrow my eyes. "Thought we had a truce?"

"Until you blew right through it," she fires back.

"We don't need to rehash that, huh?" My ego is bruised enough.

Penny is quick to drop the subject. "Just admit you're keeping tabs, in case you need to do a random inspection or something."

When she repeats my bullshit excuses back to me, it smells even worse. "Or something."

"That's what I thought." She winks. "I'm meeting Lydia for lunch in Thymouth. Is that right?"

I'm nodding. "Yeah, it's just west of here."

"Did you want to join us? I can drive."

"Tempting," I drawl. The outing holds promise, mostly being near Penny. "But no. Go have fun."

The pinch at her lips looks like she wants to argue. "Then I'm off."

"Be safe."

"That might as well be my middle name. Thanks for the hug, Thorn." Her smile is timid, but brighter than the sun.

My brain goes haywire and I'm transfixed all over again. "Don't mention it."

Penny lowers her gaze, long lashes forming a fan. "I just, uh, really needed that."

"Whenever you need another one, I'm at your service." Next time, after properly taking the edge off, I'll be content to hold her for as long as she allows.

"I'll hold you to that." She begins backing toward the path.

The potential pulls a genuine grin from me. "I hope you do."

CHAPTER SEVENTEEN

Penny

THE FINAL SONG ON MY PLAYLIST WHISPERS TO AN END. I pluck the buds from my ears and slow to a stop. My thighs burn from that last lap. The fire in my lungs matches. I pushed myself harder than normal. The pace I set was brutal, meant to chase a freedom I've yet to obtain. For several blissful moments, the music and woods were my only companions.

But trying to run from her—*them*—is a futile attempt.

I fold in half, my clammy palms slippery on my legs. Heavy breaths saw in and out at a labored pace. Sticky sweat cools on my skin, but the fury in my blood remains. Even with endorphins fueling me, my mind still fixates on the rude awakening from Mother Dearest. Her critical slander plays on repeat until darkness shrouds my vision.

"Hey."

I startle at the gruff greeting appearing from thin air. My palm lands on my racing heart, which has little to do with the three miles I just covered. Then I whirl on exhausted feet to face my intruder.

"Holy crap," I pant. "You scared me."

"Sorry, Darlin'." Nash lifts his arms in a stretch, exposing the lowest region of his torso.

I slouch with a dramatic sigh. All thoughts of my mother scatter with the tumbling leaves. The ultimate distraction just entered the scene from stage left. This is good timing. Too good. Suspicion lifts my brow.

"What're you doing sneaking up on me?"

He shrugs, unapologetic. "I heard you talking to someone. Well, kind of shouting. Didn't sound good. Figured I should check on you."

The fact that he's being considerate—genuine or not—thaws my bristly armor. I pause for a few seconds to calm the feisty jets ready to fire in my belly. He doesn't deserve a bitch fit for simply being nearby. But that reminds me.

"You just so happened to be in the same area?" The call with my mom ended at least ten minutes ago.

He strokes the stubble on his square chin. "Yep, I was passing by on a hike with Rune."

Who's nowhere to be seen. I do a diligent scan for argument's sake. "That's... interesting."

Nash must catch the skeptical dip in my voice. "He's off chasing a rabbit or something."

"I'm sure he is." I narrow my gaze to a fine point directly at his bogus story. It wouldn't surprise me if Nash sent him on a scavenger hunt to give us privacy. His dog is worthy of jealousy, though. "Are you reverting back to being a semi-stalker?"

"But is it stalking if you're aware that I'm doing it?"

"I'm not aware at the time," I clarify.

He shoots me a flat look. "Sure about that?"

"Not always," I grumble.

"It's for your safety, remember? What if a bear attacked you? Or you got lost? It's never been reported in these parts, but you could be ambushed." His smug expression isn't appreciated.

"Very funny." I roll my eyes, but he gets extra credit for recalling those ridiculous excuses used against him not so long ago. "Is that how you justify spying on me?"

"Not spying."

"Whatever makes you feel better. Is this so-called not spying a habit for you?" Because damn, I was starting to feel special.

Nash's eyes snare me into a daze as those blue depths swirl with hypnotic smoke. "I've never had the slightest urge to protect anyone except you."

"Awww," I coo while trying to gather my bearings. "That's sweet. Even if I should be a little creeped out."

"You're welcome." His focus shifts to feast on my outfit.

My gaze drops to do the same. I haven't paid much attention to the stylish appeal of active gear until now. Although, he seems to be more interested in the skin left uncovered. The sports bra might as well be a parka compared to my bikini. Same goes for the shorts, clingy as they might be.

But enough about me.

Despite my earlier reservations, Nash's casual attire is suitable for a hike. My lashes flutter at him with theatrical flair. It's a blessing to get my thoughts trained elsewhere. I'm only slightly disappointed that he's wearing a shirt.

The view is still glorious. My virginal loins get flustered when he turns his hat backward. A moan damn near escapes. I blame my weakened state. Besides, he should know better. Unless he made the switch on purpose. It must be some sort of trade secret.

"So, who was on the phone?"

I silently curse the cold bucket of water that reminder douses me with. "How much did you hear?"

"Plenty." The sheen in his soulful gaze reflects compassion. There's not an ounce of pity.

Maybe if I confide in him, he'll feel comfortable doing the same. If he wants to. Either way, I have the opportunity to put faith in him. One of us has to go first. Just a pinch to begin.

"I was talking to my mother."

More like defending myself against an ambush. Turns out that bears aren't the only risk in these woods. Very dangerous, especially against a person's character. Nash can add her direct hit to the record books. Not that anyone else will suffer from her vicious attacks.

"And she upset you." There's no doubt in his statement.

I choose a random tree to glare at. "She makes me feel… really bad about myself."

And that's paying her far more grace than she's ever given me.

Nash crosses his arms, brows pinching into tight disapproval. "Why did you answer?"

The memory of our final family meal together mocks me. "I promised her I would."

Like a good girl.

But it's not my mother's voice praising me. She would never, and I no longer need her approval. The man in front of me is an entirely different story, though. I squirm as that phrase resonates in his growly timbre. Nash must read my signals with an innate intuition reserved for long-standing couples.

"Do you always do as you're told?" His tone drops to lace that seemingly innocent curiosity with seduction.

"That depends."

"On what, Darlin'?"

"Who's giving the order." I'm not sure where this sultry vixen has been hiding, but I love her.

With him watching me, it's easy to take on a provocative role. There's a woman buried inside me with specific demands to be met. She has no need for caution. I want to expose that daring side, but don't know where to start. Behind my phone screen, I could be braver. I could pretend my experience isn't nonexistent. Now? That confidence wanes. But my mind is made up. I want this man, and I'll have him. So long as he wants me in return.

In truth, Nash could take charge and I'd willingly accept his fervor. My pulse skitters at the trust I'm surrendering. I'm usually dodging sexual advances rather than diving in with untapped gusto. He's once again proving to be everything I've been waiting for.

My not-so-subtle hint still hangs in the balance separating us. Nash has been alarmingly still while I've been so preoccupied with my internal debate. His steely gaze hasn't moved from me, probably on alert for foul play. Uncertainty strains from his broad frame. Maybe he thinks I'll bolt. My muscles twitch to suggest as much. I force my jitters to freeze while fighting the fire desperate for release.

Without noticeable warning, Nash's deliberation period slams to a close. He prowls forward with an obvious mission. When he stops, the space between us has shrunk to a slight foot.

His throat bobs with a thick swallow. "Want me to make you feel better?"

I gulp on reflex. "Okay."

That's all I need to say. Nash's fingers begin a slow, tantalizing trail from my inner wrist to my elbow. A shiver racks my entire body, and goosebumps quickly follow. He exhales dry amusement, almost a chuckle. I don't even get a chance to appreciate that arousing sound before his touch moves to my upper arm. A coarse rasp leads to my shoulder, aiming higher still. Eventually, his palm fastens in a delicate hold on the side of my neck. Heat is already brewing in my belly from what I assume is a tame prelude.

Nash leans in until our noses almost bump. He smells like hard work and bad decisions. Two things I love dearly. "You like to be teased?"

Once again, my lack of experience screeches to the surface. It's sad to admit the most I've done is avoid unwanted groping. That's precisely why I don't.

"Maybe," I offer as a compromise.

He dips his head to the side, lips brushing my cheek. "Should we find out?"

"Yes." My disjointed nod is too enthusiastic, but I'm concentrating on his exhale ruffling my hair. That's the only explanation for why I tack on a garbled, "Please."

His nose traces the shell of my ear. I feel his inhale just as much as I hear it. Prickles erupt on my scalp as his tongue darts out to flick my lobe. The piercings there are suddenly too sensitive. As if tuned into my senses, he sucks that soft skin into his mouth. It's completely natural for me to stretch my neck and grant him better access. A groan of approval rumbles from him, then he releases me with a nip.

"What do you want, Darlin'?"

You.

But that's not precisely what he's looking for.

Come on, brain. Be logical.

"Umm," I mumble dumbly.

"Too hot? I can offer a solution." Minty breath breezes across my face as he straightens.

"I might consider it after the preview you just gave me." And there's plenty more agreement where that came from.

Nash's eyes flash, and I want to weep. Those baby blues will be my undoing. "Did I make you feel better?"

I squint at his tense expression. "Getting there."

"Do you want me to kiss you?" His breath coasts along my lips.

It's pure instinct that has me tilting to receive what he's offering. I allow my eyes to flutter shut. "Yes."

A pause, then cool air filters in. "Too bad."

I come to my senses in the next second to find him at full height, an arrogant gleam in those cloudless sky eyes. "Huh?"

He slips his fingers down the slope of my neck. "I'm only returning the favor."

Thunderbolts crackle in my veins. Outrage quickly rolls

into the fight. If leaving me in limbo is his revenge ploy, he's going to be sorely disappointed with the results.

"A few spicy texts don't compare to this." I wave at his mouth, which is responsible for denying me. Or maybe his brain is doing the talking. Probably both.

"No?"

"No," I insist.

"Better complain to management." The bastard winks. Freaking. Winks.

Now my jaw hangs slack. "You're not nice."

"Never claimed otherwise, Darlin'."

Then he's backing away, a cocky smirk in plain sight. His mouth is sinful to stare at. It's not fair for a man to have lips like that, teasing the female population with more than just envy. And it gets worse. The ass has a dimple denting his left cheek. As if he needs more sex appeal. Maybe he's in isolation to stave off the hordes of women who surely throw themselves at him.

Or maybe he just hasn't met his match.

"Yeah, I don't think so." I lunge forward to fist his shirt and yank him against me.

Our lips crash just right, as if I'm an expert at this spontaneous move. On the contrary, Nash is the first guy I've kissed. Well, that's not completely true. The first kiss I've actually wanted is more accurate. This is definitely the first time I've taken the initiative. Others were platonic or staged. Thankfully not forced, although Nathaniel got close to dismantling that boundary.

These combative blunders steal my focus, which causes me to miss Nash's reaction. Or lack thereof. His lips are firm and unmoving against mine. I peel one eyelid open to peek at him. Dilated pupils clash with stormy blue. Horrifying nausea immediately churns in my belly. Nash might feel like I stole this kiss from him.

The comparison to Nathaniel and this moment is a devastating blow.

I pluck off him with a gasp. "Oh, this is wrong."

His stare lowers from mine to latch onto my mouth. He doesn't move otherwise, appearing stuck somewhere I can't access. The pained expression pinching his handsome features is an added slap to my foolish pride. I can only imagine the worst. This is probably dredging up awful memories.

There's no excuse for my careless behavior.

Nash didn't reciprocate my permission when I freely gave it. Instead, he was preparing to walk away. I figured he was being an arrogant ass by denying me. Taking the win he didn't get the other morning. It didn't occur to me that he might not want this. Talk about conceited.

My throat swells with too many apologies. There's nothing I can say that will make this better. But I have to try something.

His stance is still rigid and restrained. I see the force to remain steady tremble through him. A noise that can only be described as pissed-off-predator rumbles from him.

Damage control rushes through me. "I'm really sorry—"

Nash is on me before I can finish. Whatever shock held him hostage vanishes as he clutches me to his chest. He swoops in like a hunter but cups my jaw in a tender caress. I sink into him without hesitation. Our mouths fuse in a fiery embrace that makes me melt. My knees wobble from the impact. His grip is steady and solid, allowing me to collapse into him.

Fingers tunnel in my hair until a palm cradles the back of my head. Nash is in control, steering me wherever his desire leads. His tongue swipes along my bottom lip and I part for him automatically. The pleased noise he emits tells me that's the right choice.

I'm sloppy and unprepared, but we find a rhythm easily

enough. Tongues swipe while teeth gnash. Our lust grows hotter with every shared groan. That hunger growls in my stomach and begs to be fed. Lucky for me, he tastes better than dessert after a decadent meal.

Nash surrounds me with his towering presence. I feel delicate and precious under his care. He wasn't lying about wanting to protect me. That fierce desire streams from him with each lavish swipe. It's energized and overwhelming and I want more.

Every lackluster fumble evaporates in an instant. That's what Nash does to me. His lips on mine make me lose everything before him and this kiss. I'm a floating cloud in the sky, drawn to the atmosphere by his gravity.

Screw sweet nothings. These are filthy seductions. Crude staples piercing my flesh. In short—this is a *claiming*. He burrows under the surface in search of truth. I part my lips under his with the next stroke, opening wider for him to see everything.

He tugs me closer, as if by sheer effort we could join into one. Our movements turn frenzied to add friction between us. Smoky need wafts in the air. This crazed demand to take more and go faster.

I've never felt passion. It's impossible to predict this level of core-clenching yearning. I've never known chaste pecks and accidental grazes to incite sparks. Well, maybe with Nash. That's a theory to test later. But this, pressed near enough to feel the grooves from his abs? I might as well be the grand finale at a fireworks show.

And we're only kissing.

That entices me to reach higher. I rise on the balls of my feet and wrap my arms around his shoulders. Soft hair tickles my fingertips while I explore. Nails scratching along his scalp deliver a groan straight into my mouth. When I lick his bottom lip, he nibbles on mine. Give and take, switch and repeat. The cycle is fluid, seamless, and seems well-practiced.

Nash takes us one step further and hoists me up. My legs circle his waist on instinct, ankles crossed against his ass. The man is strong to lift me without any additional support. He moves up another notch on the impressive scale by holding me with only one arm banded under my butt.

In this position, I can feel him hard and wanting against me. It's pure instinct that has me rocking into him. His palm squeezes my ass while I grip onto him. Our mouths continue feasting without pause. I'm dizzy with arousal at this point, unable to think straight or logically.

That's when Nash begins to slow the pace. Tenderness replaces the desperation to connect. His lips worship mine with lazy strokes. A palm smooths along my back. With a groan, he severs the kiss. Almost immediately, he dives in for one more as if he can't resist. My toes curl as I prepare for round two. His chuckle gives me pause. The rusty sound is deep and gruff, but it's incredibly erotic.

His balmy forehead rests against mine. "We should stop, or I won't be able to."

I blink him into focus, my vision still hazy. "Yeah?"

He drops a peck on my nose. "Yeah."

This might've been a bit too fast, but I sure as shit don't regret it.

"Wow, that was some kiss." I lift trembling fingers to cover the tingles on my lips.

"Perfect score?" Nash cocks his brow.

"Thorn, you just exceeded all expectations."

"Doesn't get better than that." Pride swells his chest. Then he seems to recall something. "Did you honestly think I was upset you kissed me?"

Fire blazes across my cheeks. "Um, kinda?"

"Never doubt my interest, Darlin'. It's all you." His guard

is officially down. I have a sneaking sense that raw exposure is rare for him. He's choosing to let me in.

My brain is thoroughly kneaded mush. All I manage is a murmured, "Okay."

"Ready?" Nash gives my thighs a squeeze, then slowly lowers me to my feet.

I'm unsteady and sway on wet noodle legs. "Apparently not."

He hauls me right back in. "Did I wreck you?"

"Just swooned me. Real good." I snuggle against him without thought. "I think I like you, Thorn."

"That's good, Darlin." Nash traces the curve of my jaw with his thumb. "Because I know I like you."

CHAPTER EIGHTEEN

I CUT THROUGH THE GLASSY SURFACE WITH EVEN STROKES. Water sluices off my arms as I make a seamless rotation for another lap. A familiar ache slices into me, but the burn only makes me push harder. My breathing is timed and precise, not skipping a beat in the smooth cycle. I propel my legs faster as some sort of punishment. There's not much left in the tank. The flames spreading in my chest warn me to quit while I can.

When I catch sight of the large oak in my periphery, I ease off the speed. The current I've generated with my own motions splashes against me. The reprieve is instant, but strikes deeper when I duck under the waves. I float in the soundless vacuum for a minute, just long enough to calm the sizzle in my veins. Then my legs are launching me upright.

The trapped air expels from me with a whoosh. I stand, feet sinking into the sandy floor, with the lake hitting me at waist-level. It takes a few seconds to find solid ground. Energy wanes as I tuck my chin. Droplets stream from my hair, sliding downward in a cascade. I comb the damp strands back while clenching my eyes shut to fight the distorted blur. My vision clears a moment later.

"Hey, Thorn."

I whip sideways to face the shore, heart leaping straight to my throat. Penny is standing on the beach, openly staring. Her pink bikini—if those skimpy strings can pass as such—is straight from my dirty fantasies. The sight is too damn sweet to be true. My mouth pools with saliva at the view that barely-there suit gives me. The vision is such a wonder that I'm half-convinced my mind is playing tricks on me thanks to oxygen deprivation. Several blinks for clarity deliver the same all-too-real result.

As if hearing my thoughts, she wiggles her fingers in my direction. A smirk automatically slants my lips. I force a scowl to replace it on principle alone. It's completely asinine how crazy I am about her.

"The fuck, Darlin'?"

She bites her bottom lip. Blatant desire swirls in her gaze as she gives me a thorough appraisal. "Talk about an afternoon delight."

Muscles flex and preen under her appreciation before I can control them. "Didn't see you there."

"You weren't supposed to. That's the point, right?"

"Spying on me?"

Penny shrugs, feigning indifference. The sparkle in her eyes reflects the truth. "Figured I'd give it a try. See what all the fuss was about."

A satisfied rumble rolls up my throat.

This woman. Hot fucking damn. She slays me with that sass. When her naughty tongue drips with dirty suggestions, I forget my own name.

My girl might have a kinky side. The few hints she's casually dropped sent me reeling. I'm harder than concrete just picturing us exploring those secret whims. She'll beg for more, but I'll be the one pleading for mercy.

I almost fear the day she allows me to see all of her. It's sure to cause irreparable damage. Not that I have much that isn't already broken.

At any rate, steam is probably about to rise from the cool water. I curl my fingers into tight fists, needing the pressure to ground me. "What's the verdict?"

"It's not bad, but I don't care for that term. I prefer watching," Penny states. "Very closely."

"Do you like what you see?" The urge to posture slams into me again.

"Very much. You're a good swimmer." Her fingers form the okay symbol as she mouths *well done*.

I almost laugh, which continues to shock me. She's changed me so quickly and I'm not sure whether I like it. "How long have you been standing there?"

Her sigh is wistful. "It's tough to say. I seem to have lost track of time."

"And why might that be?" Even I hear the tease in my gruff timbre.

"If I had to guess, it's probably your biceps. Wait. That's not right. Maybe your pecs are responsible for getting me hot and bothered. Or maybe even that whole face of yours. Well… that's not very specific." Penny taps her lips. "Nope, it's definitely your dimple. I just want to lick that cute little divot."

"Cute?" That's straight trash. I'm sure my expression reveals utter disdain.

"Sexy," she corrects. "I mean, super sexy. Not cute."

"That's what I thought." Yet my tone is still affronted.

"Mhmm, super sexy." Her dreamy tone curls around my dick with a playful tug.

"Maybe you should come a little closer."

Penny digs her toes in the sand. "Why should I do that?"

"The view is even better." I allow the smirk to linger.

Her jaw hangs loose, gaze turning glassy. "That's a convincing argument, but Rune is the one who herded me over here. It would be rude to ditch him."

Only then do I notice my dog glued to her side. I'd been too focused on her to even consider where he ran off to. Fuck, I need to get a grip.

"Don't worry about him. He's a big boy."

"What? No. This pup is just a sugar puff sweetie pie. Aren't you, Runey-boy?" The baby voice she aims at him is emasculating as fuck, but he eats it up.

I feel secondhand shame as he licks the air. Guess he did lose his balls a few years back. Still, that's no excuse. We need to stand united, dammit.

My scowl is set for both of us. "Pretty sure you tried to call me something similar."

"Correction," she coos. "That was a failed attempt at a joke."

"Not important." I crave her touch, our blended heat. "C'mere, Darlin'."

"But—"

"Rune will follow." Unless he decides to chase a random scent again. His strategy is becoming transparent. I shouldn't be surprised. Hell, the mutt has been putty in her palms ever since she arrived.

Penny wades in with caution, slowing her stride. Once the water hits her knees, she gains more courage and trudges onward. "Oh, it's warm."

"Surprised?" The mild temperature barely registers compared to the sauna brewing in my blood. I squat until my shoulders are submerged to stave off the onslaught.

She watches me with lifted brows. "Extremely. Usually I'm freezing my tits off."

And what a shame that would be. She has a mighty fine pair that are currently pebbled for me. I'm nearly dizzy with want. This must be my long-awaited reward.

Or my untimely demise.

But for her, I might go down willingly.

Penny hovers within reach. If I held out my hand, she could grab it. Why I'm hesitating to do just that is anyone's guess.

I straighten and extend an open palm to her, fingers spread in invitation. "Want me to warm you up?"

"That sounds divine." Her damp skin slides against mine as she gets a grip on me.

If anything is divine, it's our flesh joining. Just our hands are connected, but the soothing pleasure pummels me all the same. The groan that rips from me is humiliating. A simple touch from her unravels me. I want to yank her forward until no space exists between us. It's a feat that requires me to grind that burning lust to ash. An impossible one considering that pleasurable zap has a direct link to my cock.

She must notice my fraying control when her thumb rubs along mine. "Is this okay?"

Biggest understatement in history. I'm one second from mauling her, my stance too rigid. "It's fine."

"No goggles?" She motions around my eyes in a fig-ure-eight pattern.

I grunt. "Don't need 'em."

"Oh, you're such a badass."

I recognize the fluff in her praise. "Is that all it takes to impress you?"

"Yes, I appreciate a man with eyeballs made of steel." She flutters her lashes for emphasis.

"It's not saltwater."

Penny takes a second to consider that. "Oh, right. Duh. I forgot."

"Didn't you notice?"

"Sure, I'm just used to the ocean." She shrugs it off. "You're still pretty badass."

I squint at her, long enough that she squirms. "What's your story, Darlin'?"

She drifts a step closer, hazel depths searching me for something I can't quite comprehend. "I'll tell you mine if you tell me yours."

The gate to my previous life is concealed behind grizzled scars I've allowed to define me. That protective shield keeps the suffocating guilt from pulling me under. But it's also become a crutch. One I'm not prepared to move forward without. There's no easy—or painless—route to take here. The only way out is through.

My gaze shifts to the shore, where Rune's disappointed expression mocks me. "I don't have much to tell."

Penny sniffs, her nose tipping to a haughty angle. "Then neither do I."

Not sure what I was expecting. "Guess that makes us even, and dull."

She searches my guarded expression. "We could make it a game."

"Or we could be mature and just talk about our shit."

"Rude," she mutters.

Her wounded tone clenches my heart in a firm vise. Somewhere in the past month, she crept in there and made a tidy space for herself.

I can't find the strength to deny her. Fucking hell. "Dammit, Darlin'."

"What'd I do now?"

"Everything," I growl.

Her face crumples, and I feel like a dick. Again. "That's a shitty thing to say."

"I'm aware," I grit. Poise and tact aren't my specialties.

"Message received, Thorn." She tries to tug her hand free.

Stark resignation settles in my gut. If I let her go, that will be the end for us.

"What kind of game?" I didn't expect the balm of relief to soothe me when admitting defeat.

Renewed joy sparks in her features. "Really?"

"Sure," I mutter. Maybe I should regret this decision.

"Truth or Dare?"

Like it matters. The results will be the same. My dignity is hers to fondle. "Whatever blows your skirt up."

Heat flairs in her gaze. "I'm not wearing a skirt."

And we're off to a wicked start. I can already tell this game is hers to win. "You don't have to remind me."

I'm already fighting this erection as if my next breath depends on it. A downward glance exposes my failure. The obvious bulge has me backtracking until I'm waist-deep. Now any signs pointing up could be misconstrued as a weird reflection.

Penny dutifully follows. "Should we set rules?"

"If you think that's necessary."

She grins at my snarky remark. "How about nothing too personal?"

"That's vague." But safe. I don't particularly prefer to pass the time by visiting all the skeletons in my closet.

And it turns out Penny has similar reservations. "We don't have to get crazy invasive. I don't want to dredge up the ugly past right now. Let's keep it light, but still informative."

"Good enough for me," I agree easily.

"Unless you choose a dare." She lets that option hang in the balance for me to snatch.

"We'll see how it goes."

"Who goes first?" She looks positively giddy bouncing on her feet.

I nod at her. "The lady, of course."

"Such a gentleman."

My snort calls bullshit. "Yeah, okay."

She rolls her eyes. "It's not a curse to be a good guy, Thorn."

"Didn't say it was. I'm just not claiming to be good."

"You wouldn't."

Mulish heels dig into the wet sand. "We gonna play or argue?"

"Someone's swim trunks are in a twist."

I pinch the bridge of my nose. "Haven't heard that before."

"Ugh," she huffs. "You're so combative."

"I've been saving it all up for you."

"Should I be honored?" She lifts her free hand from the water, showing off crossed fingers.

"Probably. You're the only one I talk to."

Which is completely by choice, but I've proved to be a stubborn asshole. This woman worked her way in. It's no lie that she wields monumental power over me. A snap from her fingers would go a long way.

Penny looks starry-eyed for a moment. "That's sweet, and makes me feel special."

And now I feel foolish. "Don't get a big head over it."

"Too late," she whispers. Red stains her cheeks in a pattern designed uniquely for me.

I use our clasped palms to draw her into me. Our hands forgo their hold as we cling to more of each other. She fits against my chest in a seamless curve, as if we were built from the same mold. Warmth blooms wherever we touch. My arms wrap around her to seal in the heat. An insistent throb rushes under my skin and I bite off a groan.

Penny finds a sliver of space to nuzzle closer, clinging to me like a suction cup. The sound she releases is my new definition of contentedness. There's no reason for me to verbalize my feelings. But she doesn't comment about how my body responds to her.

"Thorn," she purrs. "I have a question for you."

The sultry dip in her voice floats between us in a come-hither tone. My imagination spins straight to filthy possibilities. If she's about to suggest...

Her jaw drops when she peers up at me. "Oh, my gosh. Your face is pure smolder right now. What do you think I'm going to ask?"

"Doesn't matter," I mutter dumbly.

A telltale twinkle enters her gaze. "Truth or Dare?"

I almost smack my forehead. The game. Right. "If you're going first, I'm supposed to ask you."

"Really?"

"Haven't you played before?" I release her from my hold in an attempt to think clearly.

She unglues herself from me but doesn't go far. "No…"

Shocks rattle me again, but I'm learning to expect those responses. "Me either. We can create our own version."

"Okay," she chirps.

"Truth."

Penny sticks out her tongue. "That's the easy choice."

"Are you calling me easy?" I reclaim her hand in mine, dropping a kiss on her inner wrist.

Her lips part with a breathy exhale. "No, you're the furthest thing from easy."

"Damn straight, Darlin'. And that's not gonna change." Unless she insists on something. I fold for her faster than a deck of cards.

"Where did you learn to work with wood?" She pauses to consider something. "Is there a proper term for your job?"

"That's two questions."

Her expression deflates into thinly veiled exasperation. "They're a set, stickler. Didn't know you cared so much for rules."

"Only so I can break them."

"Good line," Penny praises. Then she frowns. "We're not getting any answers at this rate."

"Are you in a hurry?"

"Not really." That flippant retort carries a lot more than the desire for answers.

"Carpentry is probably most accurate," I explain. "And I taught myself."

She fans her face. "There you go impressing me again."

"This is nothing, Darlin'." I gesture in the general direction of my cabin.

"I disagree," she mumbles.

Before she can fuss at me again, I get us on track. "Truth or Dare?"

"Truth."

I quirk a brow but don't comment further. "Where are you from?"

"Florida." No hesitation or fumble.

But I flinch from the impact. The state is large, yet too small. My earlier regret finds me. Only one down, and my questions reveal too much.

"Dare," I choose before she can ask.

Penny almost seems surprised by my choice. "Oh, shoot. Now I have to think of something for you to do."

"That's how the game works." Or so I assume. I'm a newbie as well.

"I might've confused this with Twenty Questions."

That sounds like my worst nightmare. "Too late now."

She nods. "Should we create rules for these too?"

"You want limitations? Otherwise, I might send you streaking through the woods."

Her mouth opens wide enough to catch flies. "You wouldn't dare."

"That's the entire point." I wink at her.

"No stripping." She slaps the stipulation down with a huff.

"I'm just fucking with you. We don't have to play."

"Oh, we're playing." She goes quiet for a moment. "I dare you to find me a rock from the bottom of the lake."

My feet are already on a preliminary hunt, bumping several options. I could grab one with my toes and avoid going under, but there's no fun in that. "Add to your collection?"

"Exactly."

I squeeze her palm in mine before letting go. "Be right back."

Then I dive below the surface. The water is a crisp reprieve from the midday sun. My upper half rehydrates as I reach a hand out to search the sand.

Contrary to what I let Penny assume, it's not the healthiest habit to open my eyes in lake water. A short spurt won't hurt, though. I do a quick peek when my fingers brush a smooth surface. It's definitely a rock.

Once I've returned to breathing oxygen, I open my palm to reveal her prize. "Dare accomplished."

She snatches the plain stone eagerly as if it's worth millions. "I love it."

I wipe stray droplets from my eyes. "Your turn."

Penny's eyes carve a molten path across my wet torso. Her attraction might as well be a magnet. "Dare."

The urge to meld our bodies ripples through me. "Kiss me."

"Where?" Her smoky voice billows around slackened inhibitions.

My eyes nearly cross at the free rein she just lobbed over. This game suddenly requires my full concentration, or I might drown. I stare at her while she waits for my decision. There's a place I long to feel her mark on me, consequences be damned.

I tap the center of my chest. "Here."

Penny makes a pleased hum while branding me with her lips. It could be a chaste peck, but she lingers. Rabid hunger rips into me while her mouth drifts to cover more area. Her tongue sneaks out to taste me before she pulls back. "Did I hit the spot?"

The rumble from me is satisfaction finally being reached. "Uh-huh."

When the fog clears, I refocus on her. A knowing smile curls that sinfully sweet pout. She tilts her neck, exposing the slender column for my taking. No further instructions are needed.

I latch one hand on her hip with the other curving around her nape for support. Then my lips are descending to her up-turned throat. I feel her gulp and pay extra attention to that sensitive lump. Blunt nails dig into my shoulders while I suckle at her. Slippery skin glides together as we silently demand more. The slick friction is nothing but a tease. When the lust pounds too hard in my dick, I break apart from her.

"Um, wow." Her husky tone reflects the fire in my gut.

"Just remember. This was your idea."

"And I wouldn't change my mind." But her voice lacks conviction.

If I was a decent man, I'd pump the brakes. It's obvious she isn't very experienced with this shit. Not that I have much to brag about. My sexual urges have been on sabbatical for the better part of a decade. But Penny didn't purposefully isolate herself in the woods. She isn't shying away from me either.

Quite the opposite as she breathes, "Dare."

I smirk at her bold choice. "Is it your turn?"

"Does it matter?" She obliterates another blockade with that taunt.

Our bodies rock into a seesaw motion even though the lake is still. We move forward to touch and separate when the burn gets too intense. It's almost as if we're connected on an instinctual level. I scoff at my own stupidity. The poetic drivel this woman wrenches from me is pathetic.

"What do you like?" I asked an equally sexualized question the other morning when we were locked in a similar embrace.

"Is that a dare?"

I forgot that's what she chose. "Are we still playing?"

Her fingers trace the flexed grooves in my abs. "Yes, with our own version."

"Does that mean you're going to tell me what you like?"

She licks her bottom lip. "Whatever you want to do to me."

"Giving me too much leeway, Darlin'."

"Depends on how you choose to use it."

I bite my fist against the raging lust boiling in my blood. "The things I want would probably send you running."

She steps into me again, peaked nipples brushing my chest. "Try me."

That's all the encouragement I require. My lips return to her skin, beginning with the delicate curve at her shoulder. I sip at her, quenching my thirst from every stray drop. Her unique flavor is better than sugar. Toasted vanilla and wanton seduction bathe my mouth.

Penny is my indulgence. A temptation I can't resist. The change I didn't think existed, much less that I wanted this desperately. I haul her closer as that last thought penetrates. Driving need controls my motions when she arches into me. Her pliable form molds to fit my every filthy whim.

The ridge at her collarbone beckons me. My tongue drags along the endless expanse her bikini offers. I can feast on almost all of her without lifting the strings. That's a dare of my own making that I plan to meet.

My lips lift just enough for me to speak. "I normally wouldn't drink from the lake, but you purify it."

"What a line." But the wide grin splitting her face says she enjoys it.

With my teeth, I tug at the stretchy fabric barely confining her tits. "More?"

She nods. "Please."

I scoop water into my cupped palm and pour it over her breasts. My mouth is quick to drink from the funnel her cleavage makes. The cool relief spreads to my throat and I repeat the process. I'm mindless with the cravings she fuels in me. My cock pulses and twerks in an attempt to join the fray. How fucking consumed I'd be buried balls deep. I might never find a way out of her clutches.

Slender fingers circle my wrist and pull. I straighten just enough to discover her intentions. Pillowy lips and a wicked tongue are the target destination. That's all the warning I get before Penny licks along my index finger. A fever spikes in my veins as she swirls around the tip. Then she sucks the entire digit in with a single pull. Her suction is too strong for me to resist.

Black spots dance across my vision. "Jesus, Darlin'. What're you doing to me?"

She toys with my finger for several labored breaths. Tongue and teeth work together to drive my arousal to dangerous levels. The warm seduction of her mouth makes my dick weep in envy. My balls tighten when her hips nudge against me. When she finally pops off my finger, I'm ready to burst.

"Good?"

There isn't an adequate response I'm able to provide. Instead, I refocus on my previous task. Returning the favor should do the trick. Moisture pools in the notch at the base of her throat. I'm homed in and slurping until the sustenance that patch gracious gives is fully consumed. The raw flavor registers a moment later.

"Salty," I groan into her flesh.

"I thought lake water isn't."

"This is all you." The proof is in the actions.

I crush my mouth to hers to share. On reflex, my hand cradles her cheek as if she'll pull away. Combined flavor bursts between us, but it's not enough. I rub my thumb along her jaw, and she opens for me. Our tongues are quick to greet one another. The slippery glide grips me firmly. That's all it takes for me to be submerged in her again. Another minute and I'll blow my load in Timbered Lake.

Somehow, I find the strength to stumble back from the ledge. My forehead rests against hers as I gather the tatters of my control.

When the dust clears, Penny shivers and licks her bottom lip. "Oh, that's hot."

I replay our first kiss. The conversation I overheard sounded ugly, and reminded me of dark days I don't care to recall. Even I could see that Penny needed a distraction. I'm all too familiar with the tactic. It turned into a test of willpower. She didn't disappoint when the pressure turned on.

This little game might end with a similar result.

My gaze fastens on her hardened nipple. Her erotic flavor already lingers on my lips longer than it should. What a taste that would be. Maybe I'll try—

"Are we going to have sex?"

I jolt at her blurted interruption. It shouldn't come across as a shock, but the suggestion douses my furious desire with lukewarm water. Reality crashes down seconds later. She deserves far better than the rough fuck I'd provide.

The reality of our situation doesn't stop me from replying. "Is that a truth?"

"Sure." Her swallow is audible. "Or dare."

"Which one, Darlin'?" It makes all the difference.

"Truth." Then she adds a whispered, "For now."

My gut sinks at the hopeful leap in her voice. "I'll leave that decision up to you."

But in all honesty, I can't see myself willing to defile her in such filth. A little foreplay is much different than going all the way. It takes the edge off well enough, along with providing fresh footage for my spank bank. There's no reason to take more from her beyond that. My dwindling requirements in that department have been adequately handled by Rosy Palmer for years.

"What about your needs?" Her gaze makes a noticeable dip downward.

"Don't worry about me, Darlin'." Sex isn't on my radar. It might as well be a foreign concept. Besides, my previous attempts left me feeling more broken than before. I prefer blissful ignorance. The knowledge that Penny's warmth punctures my frozen exterior is plenty.

She clears her throat, cheeks bursting with a familiar flush. "But Little Thorn seems pretty… excited."

"Little?" All traces of lust are officially snuffed from my system. There's no stronger hit to a man's ego than minimizing his dick.

"Compared to the rest of you." She completes a thorough inspection for emphasis.

"Let me tell you a little something," I murmur against her lips. "There's nothing little about me."

Her gaze gets unfocused. "Uh-huh."

I stand to my full height with a grunt. "Glad that's settled."

"So, about the sex…" She dangles the forbidden fruit without fear that I'll steal a bite.

My head gives a harsh jerk. "Forget about it. I don't want you to regret anything."

"Regret?" She makes the word sound like a foul curse. "How could I regret you?"

Her innocent disbelief is almost amusing. Penny Blaire is many things. In the end, she will become my greatest regret. I don't plan for her to feel the same about me.

"We're not gonna find out, Darlin'. That's what I'm trying to avoid."

"But I want you, Thorn. The entire package." It's apparent she doesn't accept no for an answer. Or maybe she's reserved the stubborn sass for me. I'm okay thinking she'll walk away with permanent reminders of our months together.

The damage I'll carry from her is already taking root. That doesn't scare me, though.

Just the opposite, in fact. I never thought I'd find someone to fill in the empty void my existence has become. It's invigorating and terrifying… and she's from a land far, far away.

I'm choosing to enjoy her while I can.

The expiration date looms one beat closer. "I'm not rushing you. Don't ask me to do that. There's plenty of time for us."

"Yeah, okay." Her throat bobs with another slow gulp. "No need to rush."

I'm satisfied by her surrender. Temporary as it might be. "That's right, Darlin'. Nice and slow. We'll take our time."

Until she's forced to accept that the only choice left is goodbye.

CHAPTER NINETEEN

LYDIA BLINDLY STABS AT HER LUNCH WITH A FORK. HER GAZE is glued on me, and has been since we were seated thirty minutes ago. I can practically feel the questions burning on her tongue. Just as she's about to take the bite of pasta into her mouth, the floodgates burst open.

"So, has Mr. Surly Silence slipped you the dick yet?"

I shouldn't have taken a sip of my iced tea. She probably planned the attack accordingly. Laughter bubbles while I try to keep my mouth shut. It's a valiant effort, but liquid dribbles from my pinched lips. An entire stream soon follows.

"Classy." She has the gall to call me out while openly chewing her food.

I scoff and begin sopping up my mess. "Hypocrite."

"Whoa," she spews. "Low blow, newbie. Not to mention totally false."

"Is it, though?"

"Yes, prissy pants. I already told you that Hacken doesn't raise classy bitches. That's exactly how I spotted you so fast across the bar. Your lifted pinky might as well be a beaming spotlight in these parts."

"Hey! I take offense to that." Mostly the prissy pants part. Her pinky comment is accurate. My fingers curl into chastised fists. "It's a habit that's tough to break. Besides, it keeps the bones straight. Do you want gnarled knuckles when you're older?"

Lydia blinks at me. "Are those the lies they teach you in finishing school?"

"I didn't go to finishing school," I mutter. Only because I had private tutors for those lessons. That admission certainly won't help my case, though.

"And my broke ass lives in a castle fit for a queen." Then she gives me a penetrating once-over that I feel in my soul. "I singled you out for a reason. You stood out like a polished turd in a pile of moldy crap. Smelling the same old shit gets old."

I gag at the visual. "Thank you?"

She points at me with her fork. "Although, you're not overly polished either. I appreciate that about you. Very humble."

My parents would be outraged by her observation. Me? I smile in gracious delight. "That's the nicest thing you've ever said to me."

Lydia rolls her eyes in a dramatic fashion. "You should probably get out more."

"What do you think I'm trying to do?" I gesture at our surroundings. We're occupying one of the five tables. It makes no difference that the other four are empty.

"The patio at Timbered Tavern doesn't count."

"Does for me," I grumble. "This bar is my main food source."

She cringes. "That's nothing to brag about. Also, you should be concerned for your health."

"It's hard to screw up a salad." I gesture to my empty bowl.

"The fact you refuse to try anything else on the menu is very telling."

"Whatever. I like it here. We're having fun." I tip my face to the sky, taking in the sunny rays.

Lydia spears more noodles. "You and I have very different definitions of fun."

"Compared to what I'm used to, this is paradise."

Her chewing slows as she digests that nugget. "How's that possible?"

"You wouldn't understand." Not many can, other than girls trapped in privileged oppression. It's hard to complain about a life of luxury without sounding like a spoiled brat.

Larsen Belle is the only one I felt truly comfortable venting to. That makes me wonder if she ever patched up the problems with her man. She never called me after I went to thank her. I scoff at myself. Not like she's super swamped at the hospital or anything.

"Hello?" My friend waves her hand an inch from my face.

I blink back to the here and now. "Sorry."

Concern creases her brow. "Where'd you go?"

"Just to Bayside Regional for a visit." As if that means anything to anyone except me.

She responds accordingly. "Huh?"

"Never mind." I swat at the not-so-distant memories. "What were we talking about?"

"Your obsession with Hacken," she deadpans.

I laugh. "Maybe you need a vacation."

"There's no maybe about it." Lydia snaps her fingers. "Have you decided where you're going next? I can tag along for a week or forty."

My smile slips into a grimace. I get queasy whenever I think about leaving. "No clue."

"What's this about?" She motions to the frown undoubtedly splashed on my face.

"I don't want to leave." Traitorous heat pricks my eyes. Thankfully, the emotion is hidden behind my sunglasses.

"Not yet, no. The new-town-shine is still blinding you. Give it another month and you'll be bored." She sounds so confident that I almost believe her.

But July starts tomorrow, which means August is that much closer. I try to fake it for her. "Probably."

"Ugh, you're such a bad liar." Either her intuition is above average, or I'm just transparent. Probably both. "You're never going to leave, and I'll be stuck in this hole forever."

"I wouldn't go that far."

She squints at me until I'm ready to squirm. Her assessing gaze isn't shielded by shades. "Which part?"

"Both?" I can hear the dirt piling up as I dig myself into a rut.

"Uh-huh, that's what I thought." Another theatrical eye roll. "Speaking of getting cozy, don't think I forgot about Mr. Surly Silence's dick."

"What?"

Lydia laughs at the jealous whip in my tone. "Are you getting it or not?"

"No." And it will probably stay that way, based on his evasive comments the other day.

She takes a long pull from her lemonade. "Just as I suspected, you're totally smitten."

Fire erupts in an upward rush along my neck. "Not totally."

"You don't get to split hairs with me. Is the feeling mutual?"

"Tough to say," I mumble. And not for lack of trying.

Nash is many things, but open with his feelings isn't one of them. I can tell he likes me to a certain extent. If only I had more experience to determine where the line begins. Then I'll figure out how to cross it. Or more like dismantle it entirely.

There's nothing sexy about still clutching my cherry at twenty-two simply because my father kept me under such strict rule. I should've ditched the sexist, elitist dictatorship a lot sooner. Then I wouldn't stumble at every interaction like a pre-teen with her first crush. How lame.

Lydia's shrill whistle cracks into my reverie. "Oh, hot damn. This afternoon is about to get interesting."

I just gape at her overreaction to absolutely nothing. We're still the sole patrons on this patio. "Are you seeing things?"

"Trouble approaching at five o'clock." Her focus settles on the far corner near the entrance gate.

I choke on my iced tea—again—when catching sight of the trouble in mention. The broody figure stalks directly to our table. Blue flames are locked and loaded, ready to incinerate me.

"Nash," I wheeze. Catching sight of him in public is astounding. "Uh, what're you doing here?"

Thunder crashes in his features as he towers over me. The height difference in this position is stark. "You invited me."

"But you declined," I counter.

Much like every other occasion I've offered before vacating the premises. He has yet to accept. But Mama didn't raise a quitter. That argument lacks authenticity. She didn't raise me either.

"Can't change my mind?"

"I suppose." It's just very uncharacteristic. Speaking of that. "Where's Rune?"

"Back at the cabin."

"Why?"

"You'll see." The ominous hint clings to the space between us.

"Do you want a chair?" Lydia points to the open spot on my left.

He ignores her completely, glare fixed firmly on me. "You done?"

I blink at his brutish behavior. "No."

His glare moves to the printed bill tucked under a silverware roll. "How much longer?"

"Why?"

"Wanna take you somewhere."

"Now?" I jab my finger into the table as if that's going to alter the outcome.

"When you're done." He grunts. "And willing to admit it."

Nice burn. *Not.*

My internal roasting is stellar. "I'll stop by your place in a bit then."

A tense hush falls over us once I volley that compromise to him. He can't honestly expect me to just obediently follow like a Golden Retriever. Even Rune would shoot him a scowl before trotting behind him.

From the corner of my eye, I notice Lydia is too still. Her fork is frozen in mid-air, inches from her mouth. She prefers to digest my spat with Mr. Surly Silence. I can only imagine how she'll react to this doozy.

Nash doesn't move either. In fact, he's become a statuesque presence beside me. Then his reaction finally hits. Blatant re-fusal flattens his features into an impenetrable mask. He even clucks his tongue for good measure.

"I'll be in my truck out front."

"You have a car?" I want to smack some sense into my-self for that one.

"Truck," he corrects. "Can't miss it."

Before I gather my wits to respond, he's already halfway gone. I scoop my jaw off the ground with an affronted snort. He can wait all damn afternoon before I pry my ass off this chair.

"Wow," Lydia drawls. "That was better than I expected."

"I know," I'm quick to agree. Then her words register. I turn my gape to her. "Wait, what?"

"If you're not sleeping with that man, you really should be. He's probably a beast in the sack." Her tone is too dreamy for my liking.

I cross my arms as heat sizzles in my cheeks. "Find your own caveman to drool over."

"Oh, babe. I'm trying. Especially after that sizzler of a scene. Talk about foreplay. Yum." She fans her face. "Break me off a piece, yeah?"

"Knock it off." I push her shoulder.

Lydia's giggle ends with a snort. "Territorial. I respect that."

"Whatever," I mutter. Chasing my only friend within thousands of miles off Nash's scent wasn't on my list to get done today. But here we are.

"You better go get him, or I will." She makes a shooing motion.

The ultimatum does nothing to unglue my butt from this uncomfortable plastic. That doesn't mean I have to sit here and take it. "You're a hussy."

"Well, duh." Her smile is too smug for my liking. "I've never claimed otherwise."

But classy isn't a trait she'll accept. Amusement tips my mouth until I remember the bossy conditions slapped on me. "I'm not going anywhere. You're still eating."

"And I'll finish every bite while picturing something much more… meaty." Lydia smacks her lips.

"Are you serious right now?" I squint at her, not that she can tell.

"Stick around and find out, or listen to your kitty purr. Let her lead. She's waited long enough."

"My… kitty?" I fight the urge to cower, but there's no hiding my cringe.

She sighs. "I was trying a classier approach for your sensitive ears. Would you prefer I use pussy?"

"I can't believe you just said that." There's no doubt my skin is redder than the marinara sauce coating her pasta.

"Who's gonna hear me?" She forks another bite, slowly dragging the prongs between her teeth. "Besides, I'm a hussy."

"Trying to make me one too," I complain.

Lydia winks. "Welcome to the club, newbie."

CHAPTER TWENTY

Nash

THE DIGITAL CLOCK ON MY DASH SWITCHES TO TACK ON another minute. That makes four. Pressure lodges in my chest. I wonder how long Penny will make me wait. Little does she realize I'll stay here all damn day if that's what it takes.

My idling appearance on this curb is startling on its own. The drive to Timbered Tavern didn't seem like a choice. Fury thrashes in my veins whenever I think about her near Greg. The bastard doesn't deserve her smiles, polite and plastic as they might be.

Maybe I should've been gentler with my approach. It's not her fault I've become an obsessive freak.

That almost gets a laugh from me, but a dry scoff is more appropriate. Gentle isn't a term that owns real estate in my vocabulary.

All of the raging conflict suddenly fades to a muted gray. The blonde bombshell from my most illicit fantasies turns the corner. I take my first decent breath since stalking away from her table. A smirk creeps across my lips as appreciation for this moment strikes. And not a second too soon.

She listened to me. That's what counts.

Penny appears on the sidewalk like an angry cyclone that gains momentum with each sassy sway from her hips. I can sense the impending crash from each hostile stomp she takes. She whips off her sunglasses like they've offended her. Barely restrained chaos swirls in her light eyes, demanding retribution.

Fucking divine.

The door flings open fast enough to expel a gust of air. Static crackles in the suddenly tense cab as she slides onto the leather seat. A quiet click ricochets off the brewing strain when she buckles in.

I don't waste a breath before shifting the truck into gear and merging into nonexistent traffic. Rubber meets asphalt with a steady thump. My thumb taps the steering wheel to match the beat. Music might ease the burden bouncing between us. Or she'll use it as a way to avoid me longer.

Silence has never betrayed me until now.

One mile becomes two. There are only seven left until we'll arrive at our destination. My surprise will be spoiled if her mood remains rotten. But the necessary finesse to fix this evades me.

"That was rude." Penny once again has the social knack I struggle to find. Even a grumpy greeting is better than none.

The lead balloon in my stomach deflates. "Forgive me?"

"I'm here, aren't I?" Physically, yes. But her emotional and mental presence feels stunted.

"You didn't have to come." But I didn't provide an alternative.

"Yes, I did." Penny has her face averted, but the hurt in her voice is plain to hear. "Otherwise, Lydia was going to jump your bones."

The last part is mostly an unintelligible jumble, but I catch the gist. "She was, huh?"

"Would you let her?" She's still turned toward the window, hiding her vulnerability.

"Nah, there's only one girl I want jumping on my bone." The slight change in script earns me a twitch from her lips.

"Oh?" She chances a fast peek at me.

"That's an honor reserved for you."

Penny scoffs. "How romantic."

I wince. That's another word not found in my vocabulary.

But I've surprised myself once or twice where she's involved. "Doesn't make you feel special?"

She had mentioned something similar in the lake. That was before I interrupted her lunch and forced her choice. The response she shoots at me screams as much.

"You should feel special," she mutters.

"Trust me, Darlin'. I know exactly how fortunate I am. You could've rented a cabin from any poor shmuck. Somehow, you chose me." Which is why I'm not letting this small miracle too far from sight.

Her rigid posture softens around the edges. "Okay, good."

I see the small crack in her fury for the advantage it is. This is my chance to make a move, regardless of how small. Besides, not touching her is beginning to grate on me.

Penny's fists are clenched into tight balls. I reach over and blindly pry her fingers loose. She fights me for all of two seconds before allowing my hand to slide into hers. The relief is instant.

"That's better." I slouch in my seat as the pressure fades.

"Where are you taking me?" Her gaze feasts on the sprawling landscape stretching far and wide.

"Surprised you didn't ask sooner."

"I was preoccupied."

Yes, by my far-from-romantic persuasion tactics. "Guess I could've waited until you got home."

Or stolen her before she leaves this town for good.

"Too late now. So…?" She makes a rolling motion with her free wrist.

"There's a natural treasure I want to share with you."

"That sounds awfully nice of you, Thorn."

"Thought you'd appreciate it," I grumble.

"Oh, you're being thoughtful too." She wiggles her brows. "But you won't tell me more?"

"We're almost there." I flick at the road winding ahead of us.

"Secrets, secrets." The faintest hint of a smile quirks her mouth.

Not a shock she takes pleasure in that. Penny is well-versed on the topic.

Although the more I think about it, she's probably trying to carve a fresh path for herself. Create an existence that's her own. She practically told me as much when describing her travel plans. The adventure she seeks led her straight to me.

That doesn't explain her faulty address, though. Maybe she doesn't have a permanent one to claim, which could work well in my favor. But that's a crock of optimistic shit I have no business wishing for. I don't know her well, but I know enough. She's the type that can't be contained to a tiny hole such as Hacken, Minnesota. That just means I'll use our time wisely.

I give her palm a squeeze. "How old are you, Penny Blaire?"

She finally swivels until our eyes clash. "How old do you think I am?"

"Ah, that's a slippery slope." But I'm not scared of sliding down. "Twenty-one?"

"Twenty-two," she corrects.

"Just graduated from college in May?"

Her lips part with a gasp. "How'd you know?"

"Took a shot in the dark." I flip on the blinker to hang a left. Five more miles. "So, this really is your road to self-discovery."

"Did you think I was lying?" The offended pang in her voice sends me twelve paces backward.

"You'll have to forgive me, Darlin'. My faith in people is nonexistent. It's nothing personal."

Her brand of sunshine makes me question an entire existence spent in solitude, though. Each day with her brings forward different complications with my once foolproof plan.

Penny wrinkles her nose. "Was that meant to be an apology?"

"Sure, something like that." My thoughts don't translate to a meaning she can comprehend.

"Well, for what it's worth, I like your truck." Her bland tone makes it hard to tell.

"You're still mad?"

"Frustrated, yes."

I glance over at her sitting pretty in the passenger seat. "You're the only person to ride shotgun."

"Really?" Disbelief doesn't accent the request for reassurance. It's more like awe.

I nod. "Rune usually sits there, but no one else."

"Why'd you leave him behind?"

"He hates being on a leash."

Penny shakes her head as if to clear it. "Okay…?"

"It's required where we're going," I explain.

"Out here in the middle of nowhere?" She flails her hand at the open fields and zero civilization.

"You think I'm lying?"

"Stealing my lines again," she gripes.

I'm still not forgiven. The desire to get us on even ground is causing more problems than it's solving. My brain struggles to find a solution.

Maybe a history lesson will soothe her animosity toward me. It might even get me further than where we're already headed.

"This truck is the first thing I bought when I came to town." My fingers curl around a worn patch on the steering wheel.

She chews on that information for a minute. "It must've been brand new then."

I smirk at the faded memory, but she might not see it. "Yeah."

A curious gaze peeks over at me. Progress. "How did you afford it?"

The immediate stab in my gut is a pain I've carried with me all these years. "Inheritance. At least, what was left of it."

"Who did you get it from?" Penny mumbles something

under her breath. "I'm sorry if that's insensitive. You don't have to tell me."

The genuine sympathy in her voice suggests she has experience on the subject. Wading into her past can wait. If I don't keep talking, I'll gladly let their story remain buried.

I pin a fierce glare out the windshield. "My parents."

"Plural?" Her blurt is loud. "As in both of them?"

I tighten my grip on the wheel until the leather creaks. "They're dead."

Penny gasps. "What?"

Bile churns in my gut as I recall the detailed police reports. "My dad hadn't been himself in months before the accident. His behavior was more reckless than usual. Between not paying attention and going too fast, he was asking for trouble. That Maserati was like his second child, and he trusted it as such. He spun on the wet pavement. The precious car hit a tree head-on."

Trembling fingers lift to cover her slack jaw. "No."

"They died on impact."

She leans over the center console to wrap me in a half hug. "I know we aren't supposed to say sorry for your loss in the thick of it, but I'm really freaking sorry. That's awful, Nash."

It's a challenge to remain in the present. My mind begs to disconnect, to reclaim my former cold and detached shell. "It's okay. Your comfort helps. A lot. I like to think it's for the best that they were together in the end."

"But you were left alone, right?" Unshed tears shimmer in her eyes as she settles back in the seat.

"Don't cry for me, Darlin'." The sight of her crying could shred what's left of my heart.

Penny wipes at the streaks racing down her cheeks. "How can I not?"

I lift her palm that's still clasped with mine, kissing her knuckles. "It was a long time ago."

"But you were so young."

"Not really. Twenty very much crosses the line into adulthood. I just had to grow up faster than expected."

"Is that why you choose to stay isolated?"

"Yeah, mostly." I scrub at my face as the bitter truth beats at me. "There's more to the story, but it's ugly and doesn't really matter anymore. After their funeral, I learned just how powerful and detrimental a voice can be. It's freedom or demise. People can use what you say against you. So, I decided not to say anything at all. It's been over seven years of near silence. Other than Rune, and the conversations I can count on one hand. Until you arrived. We know how that turned out."

Her sniffles fill the silted silence for several beats. "Who broke you, Thorn?"

It's a question she's asked before, but I still don't have the power to answer. Not completely. "A horrible decision that wasn't even mine."

I can sense she wants to pry deeper, but also notices I've hit my limit. Conveniently, the park entrance just so happens to appear on our right. It's the perfect excuse I need to escape this conversation.

But a bit of closure won't hurt much more.

I park the truck in the empty lot and kill the engine. My exhale is weary with the pain I just shed. With a somewhat smooth transition, I have Penny clutched against my side. She rests her head against me as I press a kiss to her temple. The stress bleeds out, replaced by that strange calm I'm getting accustomed to. Similar to having this girl within reach.

My pulse thumps under her ear while I gather courage. "I didn't mean to dump so much on you."

Penny's honest gaze searches mine. "I'm glad you did. It makes me feel closer to you."

"Didn't think of it that way," I mumble.

She snuggles into me. "You're welcome."

The chuckle that rises from me is rusty and unexpected. "Still was more than I planned to purge. It felt good, though. Almost... I don't even know how to describe it."

"Therapeutic?"

"Better than what I could come up with." I avert my gaze as prickles needle me from the inside. "Thanks for listening. I've, uh, never talked to anyone about that."

"It was my pleasure. Your trust in me means a lot, Thorn. Thanks for that."

"That's nothing."

"Not to me." She pats my chest. "I'm always here for you. We're friends, right?"

I snort. "I think we're a lot more than that."

"Well, yeah." When a blush stains Penny's cheeks, she tries to break free from our embrace. "I didn't want to assume and be awkward in this fragile bubble."

"Don't hide from me, Darlin'." I grip her chin between my thumb and forefinger, tugging until our lips brush. She smiles against my mouth, far too pleased with crushing me. Just goes to show she's clueless about how far I've already fallen. "You make me believe there's still good out there."

Her hitched inhale sputters between us. "I feel the same about you."

"All right," I breathe. "Enough heavy shit. Let's get out of this hot box."

Penny blinks the lingering emotion from her eyes. Then she's searching our surroundings. A large sign gives a fairly big hint.

"Timbered Falls Park?"

"I'll show you the main attraction." I exit the truck without another word.

She joins me in front of the hood. Her gaze is quick to focus on the rough terrain straight ahead. "I'm not really dressed for a hike."

That's not what we're here for, but she doesn't know that yet. For argument's sake, I give her outfit a thorough inspection. Summer is the best season for no other reason than what's on glorious display mere feet from me. I admire the generous amount of golden skin she has exposed far longer than necessary. Tough job, but I've been assigned to do it.

Penny's frilly skirt hits mid-thigh and leaves the rest of her legs deliciously bare. The sandals strapped to her feet are a bigger problem. Their soles appear almost nonexistent.

I lower to one knee and pat my back. "Hop on."

"You want me to get on?" She shuffles toward me.

More like off, with some help from my fingers or tongue. Lust is fast to surge through my veins. But we're not here for that either. I force myself to croak, "Yep."

She clambers on with less grace than a newborn fawn. Her limbs cinch around me in a vacuum seal. I struggle to breathe as she finishes getting situated.

"Ready?"

"Uh-huh." Her warm exhale fans my neck.

Before arousal can take root, my legs propel me upright in a fluid motion. She squeaks at the abrupt movement. Her arms somehow manage to tighten their choking grip. My fingers work on unblocking my airway. Then she crosses her ankles over my lower torso, and I nearly tumble sideways.

"You okay up there?" Protective instincts rush to the surface.

"Um, sure. Just a tad unstable." Her fear is mine, but she has nothing to be afraid of.

My palms clamp around her knees while I start walking. "I've got you, Darlin'. It's not far."

"I trust you." But she still sounds hesitant.

That makes me laugh. Twice in one afternoon. "Haven't you ever ridden piggyback?"

"No?" The question in her tone makes me pause on the trail.

"You sure?"

"Yes." Her confidence returns for that answer.

I rub my palm along her smooth shin. "Guess that makes me your first."

Penny's lips brush my ear when she leans in. "We'll see about that."

The sultry tease in her voice has me seeing smoke. Or maybe it's steam spewing from my pores. I keep my gaze trained on the dirt to avoid the wreckage. The risk of stumbling throbs in my cock. Her accidental nudges only entice the beast. Damn horny bastard will never rest at this rate.

"This looks awful familiar," she comments as we travel along the wooded path.

"Patience." I squeeze her calf.

She wiggles against me. "That tickles."

"Shouldn't have told me that."

"What're you going to do, Thorn?" Her teeth nip at my jaw.

This reminds me of some of the conversations we had over text. I'm finally in a position to retaliate. After securing my grip on her, I extend my stride until she's practically bucking against me.

Penny giggles at my bouncing gait. "My skirt is flapping in the breeze. If anyone passes us, they're going to get a juicy shot of my ass."

A possessive noise rumbles from me. I'm quick to whip an arm behind us to capture the fluttering material. "Not gonna happen."

Her responding hum is pleased. "I like when you get growly."

That's when the telltale flow of rushing water provides a preview for us. Penny freezes for a second, but I don't pause. The crashing volume rises while the trees begin to thin.

She digs her nails into my shoulders as if they're some sort of brake pedal. "What's that?"

"Almost there," I say.

The postcard-worthy view appears a moment later. Penny's

breath sputters as I step onto the large rock slab framing the western side of Timbered Falls. I remember my first visit to this exact location. An upward glance reveals that overwhelming awe in her gaze. Fresh wonder filters through me as I experience the natural escape for the umpteenth time. It never gets old.

After crouching to the ground, I release Penny from my clutches. She's strolling toward the edge the instant her feet touch the ground. It's almost like she's in a trance. I follow behind, maintaining the illusion of space to give her free rein to explore. An hour could pass before she's able to soak it all in.

Her wide eyes scour the cascading streams and rapids. Three waterfalls pour a continuous flood into the bay below, and shadows dance from the steep cliffs above, creating a furtive play. The spray of mist before us shoots up a tiny rainbow, so close we could reach out and take the colors in our palms. Sunlight streaks across the surface, highlighting the sandy bottom in calmer sections.

When the urge gets too strong, I erase the short distance separating us. My arms encircle her from behind, crushing her back to my chest. The thrashing current provides a soothing song as we drift in silence. We're suspended in serenity while exchanging comfort. This moment, with her cradled against me, feels purer than the grand spectacle surrounding us.

Penny's voice carries over the roaring falls. "This totally makes up for your bossy display earlier."

I rest my chin on her shoulder. "Figured you'd like it."

"Love it," she corrects.

The abundant approval spreads warmth through my chest. "I used to come here a lot in the beginning."

She sighs in what can only be described as contentment. "I can see why. This is wonderful."

"This might make me sound crazier than I already am,

but I didn't feel quite so alone." There I go, exposing more of my damage to this woman.

"You're one with nature." She makes a wide arc with her arm.

"That's a bit too fluffy for me."

"Pfffft," she admonishes. "You're a total softie. Just needed a certain southern girl to shake the sweet stuff loose."

I can't deny her influence over me. After all, she might be healing me. "Being here brings me peace when there's none to find. Although, more recently, I've found a more reliable source."

Penny turns in my arms to face me. "Oh?"

When our gazes collide, all else ceases to exist. Timbered Falls might as well be a one-dimensional cutout compared to her mesmerizing features. Two equally stunning brown and green pools lull me into a sense of calm that I lost hope in achieving long ago—until she proved otherwise. She's the only one who can mend the wounds that previously refused to even scab over.

We have much left to uncover, but what I see is plenty to reveal the truth. I can't see myself without her, in whatever context. Not sure when that happened, but here we are. She's mine for now.

Beneath the soothing comfort, feverish embers build and demand to be stoked.

"There's a fire between us, Darlin'. Do you feel it?" Gravelly need roughens my voice.

She nods, our foreheads bumping together with the jerky movement. "Yes."

I drift my nose along the slope of hers. "When did it start for you?"

"The first time I saw you enter the clearing," she breaths. "While you were chasing Rune."

A gruff noise scrapes from the back of my throat. "And I didn't talk to you."

Her eyes flash at the memory. "No, you didn't."

"But we're well past that now, huh?" My thumb traces lazy circles on her hipbone.

"Better be," she mutters.

Leave it to me to snuff out the spark. I won't let this moment be wasted. "Wanna know when I could feel you were different for me?"

Warmth returns in her tone when she says, "Tell me."

"You were playing music so damn loud that I had to investigate. When I saw you through the window, I couldn't look away."

Surprise registers in her features. "You were watching me?"

"Does that bother you?"

Her deliberation only requires a brief pause. "No. Maybe I was secretly hoping someone was out there."

The way she justifies my obscure need for her strikes at my armored heart. "Where have you been hiding?"

"The past doesn't matter. I'm here now."

Which circles us back to the beginning. "What're we gonna do about these flames? The heat isn't dying down."

"No," she whispers her agreement.

"Only getting hotter," I continue.

"Uh-huh."

"What do you wanna do, Darlin'?" I'm not sure how much more I can withstand.

Penny's lashes flutter until those hazel depths clash with mine. "Let it burn."

CHAPTER TWENTY-ONE

W ITH MY PLEASE-PROCEED-RIGHT-NOW SIGNAL, NASH swoops in for a stealthy kiss. We share a mutual groan as our mouths crash together. The furious rapids below us have nothing on the thunderous beat in my pulse. I can hear his breath increase while our tongues glide in a sensual caress. Then teeth nibble and gnash, prodding away at the final vestiges of control.

My fingers explore the contours of his biceps on the upward path to his broad shoulders. With his palms on my ass, he reels me in until not even a splinter comes between us. We form a seamless bond that makes my soul sing. Comforts I've only recently discovered swim to the surface.

In his unrelenting clutches, I'm cherished.

Protected.

Craved.

Even ducked down, Nash is so much taller than my petite frame. I could climb him like a tree without worry that he'd stumble. Everywhere I touch is a solid force against me. Not just his flexed muscles and impressive stature. When I lift my arms to lock at his nape, that steely bulge greets me again.

Nash is very aroused—and very eager to gain entry, if the hard inches at my belly are any indication. That's a necessary ingredient for what I'm assuming happens next. His lips work me into a frenzy while I try to rise on the balls of my feet. It's a challenge to stay rooted in place when my body becomes fixated on finding relief. That one-track motivation fuels me to open wider for his kiss.

Our passion is fluid and effortless, yet rough and untamed. I love to think that we drive each other wild. This intense drive boils hotter with each swipe from our dueling tongues. The coarse scruff on his jaw scratches my skin. That abrasion zips downward to settle in the very depths of my core. The resulting shiver pebbles my skin, but I'm far from chilled between my legs.

Nash rips his mouth from mine with a tortured snarl. "Maybe we should slow down."

I pepper his chiseled jaw with spicy pecks. "What about the fire between us?"

"We can put it on ice." His lips crook ever so slightly.

"That sounds unpleasant. And cold." I exaggerate a shudder.

He dips to press our foreheads together. "I'm not good for you."

"That's true." My quick agreement makes him flinch. I hurry to ease the sting with a kiss. "You're a bad boy, Thorn. So bad."

"Quit, Darlin'." But amusement brightens his shadowed expression.

"Not a chance." There's a distinct heat between my legs that only he can soothe.

Nash releases me, arms falling limp at his sides. "I'm not a good man."

"I disagree." There's iron and grit in my voice. "You're the best decision I've made for myself."

"There are far better than me. I shouldn't be a consideration."

My hand rests flat over his pounding heart. "You're the only contender I'm willing to consider."

His envy-inducing lips flatten into a firm line. But he doesn't argue. Yet.

Nash Hudson is an entire mood, darkening the sunny

sky with his mere presence. I lounge in the storm without fear. The undeniable destruction is far from view. All I feel is the promise of carnal rapture gaining traction. This man has the ability to either make me soar—or crash and burn. Although, either option could be quite rewarding. I won't complain about a bit of pain to receive pleasure. That seductive fire billows in my belly with each breath. Only from his command will I shatter and be rebuilt.

If he's gloomy skies with streaks of lightning, then I'll be the rainbows that accompany each break from the chaos. Without his initial turmoil, I wouldn't get the chance to shine for him. I'd still be a muted blur in the background. Nash gives me a voice, much like he claims I do for him. There's beauty in the combination we create.

And I refuse to surrender our possibility to change each other.

"Trust me." I curl my fingers into a fist, bunching his shirt in my grip. "You don't realize how little choice I've had."

His eyes narrow into slits. "I find that hard to believe."

I pin him with a look just as fierce. "Please don't make assumptions about me. You'll fail."

Appreciation flashes over his expression. "Likewise."

"Don't give up on what we could have," I whisper.

Nash hesitates, his hands regaining purchase on my hips as if I'm keeping him grounded. I'll gladly give him the support he refuses to accept. Even with the green light on maximum power, he doesn't deem himself worthy. I'm brimming with positive encouragement to convince him otherwise. Screw looking desperate. This man needs someone in his corner. A friend, if nothing else.

But as he said, we're far past that.

"I won't be able to take you on dates." Nash's broken edges try to repel me, but I'm trained in the art of deflection.

"That's not true. We're on one right now."

His hardness rocks into me as we sway in the breeze. "I'll never be comfortable sitting in a crowded restaurant."

"Fine with me. I've been to enough to last a lifetime."

"You want to settle for less?" The vulnerability in his voice pierces my heart.

"Never," I retort. "That's precisely why my sights are set on you."

Nash kisses me, soft and sweet. It feels like his stubborn spikes are submitting. "What're you doing to me, Darlin'?"

"Everything you've been missing." My hand is still fisted in his shirt, which acts as an anchor. "I'm the havoc to your storm."

"That doesn't make sense."

"Neither do we, yet we're here together." I tug until he's flush against me. "I want you, Thorn."

"You want me?" The slight tremble in his tone reveals disbelief.

"Only you. Badly." It feels like I've been waiting twenty-two years for him.

"That I can handle." Nash's throat bobs with a heavy swallow. "You're gonna let me corrupt you?"

Tingles spread through my lower half at those words. I bite off a moan. "Please."

We're barreling down an uncharted path, but I trust him to steer.

"What do you like?" At this point, he's asked at least twice without getting a decent response.

I still don't have details to share. Maybe I will after he provides me with some experience. "Surprise me."

"Giving me all the control?"

"Uh-huh."

"I won't be gentle," he grinds through clenched teeth.

"That's okay." It's probably not, but it's also too late. I'm already waist-deep and lost in this man.

"Must you push me this far?" He's back to crowding my space, caging me against him. "Until I snap and lose all decency?"

"By all means," I exhale. "Give me your worst."

With that challenge carelessly tossed down, his restraint is finally put to rest. "Just remember, you asked for it."

Then Nash transforms into the beastly warrior my favorite erotic novels are famous for. A furious rumble wrenches free while his eyelids droop to become hooded. Blue smoke smolders in that hungry stare. Wide palms grip my shirt, tugging the material down to expose my breasts. With an arm banded around my lower back, he dips me to feast on the pillowy flesh. That wicked tongue drags down the ample cleavage my push-up bra oh-so-generously provides.

He yanks me upright seconds later, lips wet from tasting my skin. The unleashed visual he presents sends all rational thoughts into a tailspin. I've never seen a sexual deviant, but he just became mine. His touch wanders down my sides in the direction of my upper thighs. Flared nostrils drag in a noisy breath. I absently wonder if he can smell the desire seeping from me. It's shameful how turned on I am, but I suppose that's the entire point.

As if hearing my filthy musings, Nash steals my mouth in a savage kiss. I blindly grasp his hair while tangling our tongues together. His teeth tug at my bottom lip until I'm dizzy with want. I'd probably allow him to do just about anything to me without protest.

Nash flexes his muscles to haul me off my feet. His movements are a blur of domination and an insatiable appetite. My belly growls with the same demanding need. I'm hoisted in a hasty fashion, but the motion is fluid. My back bumps into a tree while I'm still gathering my bearings, legs struggling to cinch around his waist. The fabric of my skirt pools just right around my hips. Turns out I was dressed for the occasion after all. He hitches me higher, a sound of primal male satisfaction accosting our natural surroundings.

But I suppose he belongs with the raw elements in this frenzied state. We both do.

My thong is shredded with a single yank of brute strength. I hear a zipper lower as he undoes his jeans. A downward peek reveals the denim pooled around his splayed thighs. That's when clarity attempts to swipe at the lusty fog in my brain. I should probably warn him, or prepare myself. Probably the latter, considering this isn't going to be vanilla missionary. I've provoked the beast and he's set to deliver a harsh fuck-ing. Serves me right.

"You ready for me?" Blunt fingers drag along my slick slit.

"Yep," I squeak.

He circles my clit with expert pressure. "I'll take my time next round. We'll take the edge off first."

That's one way of putting it.

All I can manage is a jerky nod. Nash doesn't question me further. Whatever wetness he finds must be adequate. Then he's prodding at my untried entrance. The words climb my throat, but it's too late. He slams into me with a brutal thrust. A scream rips from me as my innocence is torn straight through.

His invasion is fast and true. A direct hit to my hymen. The crippling pain immediately follows. Pins and needles prickle along my entire lower half. It's a small relief that the searing ache is somewhat confined.

My mouth hangs open in delayed shock. He's big and I'm too tight. At least I'm properly turned on. Unprepared and snug I might be, but the slick arousal certainly made that ini-tial acceptance easier. Even so, it feels like I've been sliced in half. My eyes sting in pathetic pity of what's happening down below. I try to absorb the moisture with rapid blinks before he can see. But a few traitorous drops slip free.

Nash's startled gaze leaps to mine. "No, Darlin'. Are you a—"

"Virgin?" My gasp is rattled. "Yes, I was. Past tense, thank you very much."

His face seeks solace in the crook of my neck. "I can't believe this."

Another slash of agony knifes me. "Is it that bad?"

Nash lifts from his hiding space to face me. Raw emotion glitters in his blue eyes. "Nah, Darlin'. It's incredible."

"Well, that doesn't sound bad at all."

"I just would've done things differently." He gingerly leans in to stamp my lips with his. "Why didn't you tell me?"

Raw emotion throttles me, and I cough. "I was afraid."

"That I wouldn't want you?" He makes it sound like the mere possibility is absurd.

"I didn't want my lack of experience to scare you off. Being a virgin at twenty-two isn't what it used to be."

Nash just blinks at me. "How did it used to be?"

The fact we're carrying on a conversation while he's buried inside me isn't all that glamorous. The cherry-popping moment is rarely one to brag about, or so I've heard. This awkward exchange definitely fits with the rumors floating around happy hour.

"Never mind," I huff. "The deed is done. We can move on."

I watch a vast array of emotions flicker across his features. Regret is the last to register. The fact he might want to hit the undo button nearly crushes me. If I wasn't already doused in extreme discomfort, that would tip me over the hump.

Then he cradles my jaw in his large palm. The action is tender, and not at all what I expected from him. His crooked smile damn near makes my head spin. "I should've prepared you, Penny."

"It's fine."

"It's really not." He begins to withdraw very slowly. That safe pace gives me precious moments to realize he's trying to vacate the premises of my vagina.

"What're you doing?" Alarm is shrill in my tone.

"Taking care of you." As if that explains everything.

My pulse spikes at the unlimited options. I do a quick scan of our joined forms. "How?"

"I'm, um, going to make you feel better." The fact that he's already started lowering to his knees clues me in.

"Absolutely not." I tighten my legs around him, which sends an angry throb through my center.

"But—"

I reinforce my grip on his shoulders. "No way. I'm gross down there."

Nash winces. "Which is my fault."

"And mine. Mostly mine," I correct. "Please don't go down there with your mouth."

He wants to argue. His mouth is parted with the words. Then resignation sets in. Maybe he realizes this is my first time and I should get the final say. Or that's wishful thinking.

"Okay, Darlin'. But we don't have to go further. I'll clean you up the best I can—"

"Stop being so sweet," I blurt.

His stricken gaze collides with mine. "The fuck?"

"This is just a lot to take in," I rush to explain.

He glances down with a cringe. "Sorry about that."

"Okay, stop. Don't apologize about your size." I lift a palm to cover my face. "You're going to make me cry."

He pries my fingers away. "You've got some explaining to do."

Oh, that's a new one. *Wait.* I pause for dramatic effect. Then realize I have nothing all that shocking to share. It seems I'm always digging myself from a rut when it comes to him. "I saved myself for someone special, Thorn."

"That makes me feel worse," he deadpans.

"Don't you see? I'm saying *you're* special. There's nothing to feel bad about."

That slice of honesty carves from my chest to drop in his lap. Or cinched around his dick that just broke through my virginity.

"But how is this possible?" He bumps forward, sending himself deeper along my untried walls.

I glare at the trees swaying above. If nothing else, our little chat is giving me ample time to adjust. The sharp stabbing has lessened into a dull throb. "Do you really want to discuss this right now?"

"Later," he concedes.

"Glad that's settled," I mutter.

"It won't be good for you, though. Fuck. I already had doubts about getting you off in the time my two-pump-chump status would allow." This considerate version could pay me a visit more often.

I kiss his dimple. "Don't worry. I'm really sensitive."

"After what I just did? I can only imagine."

"No," I roll my eyes. "My clit. I can orgasm super quick."

A very welcome heat enters Nash's gaze. That need to please me twitches his cock. "Is that so?"

"Sometimes less than thirty seconds." Now that's worth bragging about.

"You're finally gonna tell me what you like." There's no question in his tone.

"Want me to show you?" I begin threading my hand between us.

He swats my fingers away. "For fuck's sake, Darlin'. I can manage."

"Well, if you insist." A thrill shoots through me at his disgruntled frown. *Welcome back, Thorn.*

His thumb is quick to zero in on the promised land.

Tingles erupt and spread as he begins a swirling motion. When he presses down, my muscles jolt and I clench around him. "You're very sensitive."

"Wasn't lying." I knock my head against the tree behind me. "Oh, yeah. Just like that."

He hums low in his throat. "So fucking wet."

A delicious buzz thrums under my skin. I allow my lashes to fan shut as the flames spread outward in a fiery rush. My hips begin to rock on their own, chasing the relief already sprouting through the depths. That's when I notice Nash isn't moving.

With a pleased sigh, I open my eyes to find him watching me. "I want to feel you too."

"This doesn't count?" He speeds up the spirals on my clit.

Apparently, he's still waiting for permission to continue. I don't want him to hold back. Quite the opposite. If I'm being catapulted over the ledge, he better be tumbling with me.

I buck my hips. "Get going, Thorn."

His smirk is extra cocky in this moment. "You're so fucking sexy."

"Prove it," I taunt.

Nash nips at me, his tongue probing mine in lavish strokes. The lewd action better be a preview for what's about to come. Just as he begins a gentle retreat, a fresh wave of guilt enters his expression. "Shit."

"What's wrong?"

His forehead thumps against my sternum. "I'm not wearing a condom."

I squint at him. "Have you done this before?"

His eyes roll. "Yeah, but it's been a long time. Might as well be a virgin too."

That makes me feel marginally better. Then I remember what he forgot. "Don't worry, I have an implant."

His gaze locks on my chest. "For what?"

"Birth control," I laugh.

The bouncy humor shifts his cock inside of me. Our groans are an erotic announcement. He's not going to leave me hanging in limbo. We've already started.

I use my hold on him as leverage to slide up and down on his length. The small test delivers no pain. "Finish us."

Nash palms my ass, adding a squeeze for good measure. "This is going to be embarrassingly short."

"It's good practice." I wiggle my brows.

As it turns out, a promise for more is all the further encouragement he requires. Nash resumes his attentions to my clit while feeding me his girthy length. The man is definitely blessed in the penis department. I stretch around him with each shallow pump.

His eyes are crazed while searching mine, muscles flexed tighter than a drawn bow. "What do you think about Little Thorn now?"

"Not so little," I whimper.

He punches his hips into me. "That's right, Darlin'. Take all of me."

And I do just that. He's buried to the hilt before slowly pulling out. His tip teases my entrance, then he's sliding deep again. The rhythm is slow, but hypnotic. With the pressure from his thumb, I easily relax into the galloping tempo. It doesn't take more than a few strokes for pleasure to filter in. There's still a lingering ache, but each thrust alleviates more of the discomfort.

Bark scrapes along my spine with each forward push from him. I hardly notice. My body is too attuned to the insistent flutters he's stirring with each plunge. When I chance a look at him, his full concentration is trained between my legs. His jaw is locked so tight that a twitch leaps at the joint. It almost looks like he's suffering. Sympathy plucks at me.

"You can go faster," I wheeze.

"That's not necessary." He peers up at me with soft warmth in his gaze.

"But—"

"Trust me, Darlin'. I'm barely hanging on as it is." The strain in his voice matches the expanding force tugging at me.

I cup his cheek, stubble rough under my fingers. "Then let go."

Nash closes his eyes and leans into my touch. Then he's a man on a mission to completion. The lax pace finds another gear on his next grind. I suck in a sharp breath when he strikes a certain spot. The consistent glide provokes my climax until I'm climbing to the peak. Sweat dots his brow as he works me faster. The squelching noise is obscene. My blush threatens to give me a fever.

He doesn't falter as I begin to tremble. I'm lost in the throes with stars dancing in my vision. The spasms that rack me are far more intense than when I'm alone. His shaft provides the missing piece to send me higher. Just as I'm cresting into euphoric bliss, a clumsy hand searches for mine. He entwines our fingers in a tender embrace. That intimate connection, how we first came together, sends me shooting over the cliff. I fracture in his arms as the fire engulfs me. With a gruff shout, Nash follows me into the abyss.

We float in our mutual relief for several minutes. The rushing rapids provide a soothing playlist for our afterglow. I'm limp and sweaty and extremely satisfied.

My contented sigh says it all. "Is it always like that?"

His labored exhales puff across my clammy skin. "I barely remember, but no. Definitely not."

"Good." I like that what we shared is special. Maybe he'll think of me every now and then once I'm gone.

And that's a serious downer.

He must catch my inconvenient grimace. "What's wrong?"

I chase the premature sorrow away with a forced smile. "Nothing. I'm great, thanks to you."

Nash slowly untangles our bodies, guiding me down to stand on wobbly legs. His palm remains glued to the base of my spine in unconditional support. Just in case.

I twirl my ankles in an attempt to resume circulation. "Well, we can add sexual awakening to the list I'm accomplishing with this trip."

He grunts while scrubbing at his chin. "Can't believe I just popped your cherry against a damn tree."

"Wouldn't have it any other way, big guy." I give his bicep a loving pat.

"Not sure how your virginity survived twenty-two years." His smolder gives me a tantalizing once-over.

"I was sheltered. Very sheltered." I rub my temples. "You were my first real kiss too."

His dropped jaw swings my way. "The fuck?"

"I mean, there were a few others—"

He gathers me in a fierce hug, tucking my head against his chest. "Stop talking about guys who aren't me. Especially after we just had sex."

"Noted," I mumble into his shirt.

Nash strokes a palm along my back. "Can I take you somewhere else?"

I lift my dreamy gaze to meet his. "Another surprise?"

He nods. "Something like that. "

"If it's anything like your last one, you don't even need to ask."

"And if it's not?"

My shrug is all for show. "I'll still let you sweep me away."

CHAPTER TWENTY-TWO

I TURN OFF THE FAUCET AND STRAIGHTEN FROM MY STOOPED position over the tub. A grin surfaces as I observe my handiwork. It's an expression I'm becoming more familiar with lately, all thanks to the woman waiting not so patiently in the hallway.

Speaking of, there's still a noticeable calm pumping through my veins. Our bumbled fuck in Timbered Falls was unexpected, yet long overdue. That gives me pause. Degrading what we shared to a simple fuck doesn't sit right. No, there's nothing simple about what we have brewing between us. I almost fear the repercussions. My carnal appetite has returned with very specific tastes. Flames whisper filthy suggestions that are far from sated. That hunger grips my dick in a fiery hold. A deep inhale smacks me with lavender and renewed control, reminding me just what the fuck I've been doing for the past thirty minutes.

And the semi in my jeans doesn't have an invite to this occasion.

Before granting Penny entry, I scan the room for a final inspection. The candles are lit. Steam fogs the mirror, divulging the sauna-like conditions. There are enough floral-scented products scattered about to keep an entire boutique in business. Soft music croons from a wireless speaker. Rose petals litter the tiles and bath water. Last, but definitely not least, are the overflowing bubbles.

It's official. My bathroom has been transformed into a woman's relaxation sanctuary.

Maybe manipulating wood isn't all I'm good at.

A grunt gets paired with a sharp eye roll. Penny is definitely rubbing off on me. I might just let her keep it up. Only one way to find out if she's interested.

With a twist, I turn the knob to face her critique. I don't have to look far. She's standing just outside the door with a beaming grin aimed at me. Rune's tail thumps on the floor as he sits dutifully beside her. He sniffs the air and immediately sneezes. I don't blame him. Our man cave is being infiltrated by perfume and frills. Fucking hell. But the warmth spreading through my chest betrays me. It doesn't bother me.

On the contrary, I'm the one responsible for it.

Eager enthusiasm bounces Penny's feet. "Can I come in now?"

I sweep an arm across the threshold. "Your palace awaits, Darlin'."

Did someone order cheese? Damn.

She hops forward once free rein is handed over. Her rushed gait slams to a halt after she crosses the threshold. Wide eyes bounce from floor to ceiling and everything in between. She spins in a circle for a visual sweep of the full display. Her fingers tremble as she lifts them to cover her mouth.

I can't look away while Penny completes a thorough assessment of how far I've fallen. She belongs here, surrounded by girly shit… and me. The dim lighting illuminates her features in a soft glow. Rosy cheeks and shy glances beckon me to shadow her.

My masculinity might be heavily in question by most who already dare to ridicule me. Too fucking bad none of their judgmental asses will ever step foot in this cabin. She deserves to be pampered after the gift she gave me. Her opinion is all that matters, which is currently in deliberation over the fruits of my labor.

"Um, wow."

This is girly shit, but I couldn't care less. "Don't think I missed your silent appreciation for my tub."

"What did you do, Thorn?" Shock and awe quake in her voice. There are other emotions too.

I'm too chicken shit to recognize them. "Nothing much."

"This isn't nothing." Her watery gaze latches onto mine. "This is incredible."

I grip the back of my neck. "It's my first attempt, so don't judge me too harshly."

Penny scoffs. "I'd never guess based on the… wait, are those essential oils?"

Amusement trickles from me as she stumbles closer to inspect the small bottles. "That's what the label said."

"How… why… I mean, you did this on purpose?" She appraises the scene I've set with unshed tears floating in her eyes. "You went shopping for bath supplies?

"Online," I confirm.

"When?"

The insinuation almost makes me snarl. "Do you actually think I bought all this girly shit with someone else in mind?"

She smiles at my growly tone. "No. I just like to rile you up sometimes. Thorn in beast-mode is very sexy."

Renewed guilt crashes into me. "Didn't learn your lesson earlier?"

"Nope, not even a smidge."

"I'll never take you for granted again." I reach for her hand, lacing our fingers together.

Her focus drops to our clasped palms. "No, you won't."

"You gave me something special. Now I want to return the favor." Not that a bubble bath compares. I'll have to prepare dozens of luxuries before I'll be even remotely deemed deserving to stand beside her.

The glee shining in her gaze dims when she shoots me a sidelong glare. "My virginity isn't a trophy, or an achievement that deserves recognition. You don't owe me anything, Thorn. There isn't a debt you have to repay."

I step behind her, wrapping her in what's meant to be re-assurance. My lips create a scorching path along her shoulder. "No, it's an honor that you chose me. One I'll never be worthy of. But let me try."

Penny sags into me. "Well, you did go through a lot of trouble."

And that's my cue. With regret already weighing down my limbs, I break apart from her warmth. I'm about to make a less-than-graceful exit until I notice Rune is purposely maintaining his distance. He didn't go far, choosing to curl up on the wooden floor. Seems we both can't stray far from her.

I bend to scratch him between the ears. "Afraid to come in, boy?"

His mismatched eyes seem to narrow at my patronizing tone.

Penny's giggle chimes from behind me. "You talk to him too?"

"Of course." I turn to face her again. "How else do you explain my snappy wit and exceptional conversation skills?"

She blinks at me. The delayed pause says it all. "Having a dog as your only source of social interaction would do it."

With lightning-fast reflexes, I snag her around the waist and reel her to me. My nose is buried in her hair a second later. "Very funny, Darlin'."

Penny rises on her feet and treats me to a juicy kiss. "You're not the only one with a shining personality."

I give her ass a soft smack. "Get this beautiful butt in the tub before the water gets cold."

"Is that an order?" She flutters those long lashes at me.

"Do you want it to be?"

Her bottom lip gets tortured between her teeth. "Maybe?"

"Fuck, Darlin'. The things you do to me." I release

her—*again*—and begin a hasty retreat, otherwise her time to relax will be ruined. "Let me know if you need anything else."

"Where are you going?" Affronted fists are parked on her curvy hips.

"To the kitchen?" I hitch a thumb in that general direction.

Penny's pout could make hardened criminals go legit. "You're going to leave me alone?"

"Isn't that how this usually works?"

"Yes," she huffs. "I usually soak by myself. This is different."

"How?" My voice holds all the uncertainty lodged in my gut.

"You deserve to reap some rewards for your efforts." Her fingers flick through the frothy water.

"I'm not getting in there."

"Scared of the bubbles?" Her tone is pure delight.

"Sure, let's go with that." I'm not interested in reeking like a flower factory well after she's gone.

"You could still lend a hand."

There's another phase to this process, but I wasn't sure she would welcome it. "I can manage that."

"That's what I thought." Penny hooks her thumbs in the waistband of her skirt. The stretchy material lowers to expose her bare pussy.

I choke on the excessive saliva that my mouth has been busy pooling. It takes gallant effort I wasn't even aware I possessed to avert my eyes. "Do you want some privacy to get undressed?"

She snorts. "Your footlong meat baton just about wrecked me earlier. I think it's okay if you catch a glimpse of the ladies."

This time I cough into my fist. "My what?"

"You heard me." Penny doesn't bother to shield her blatant interest, slicing a downward journey to my cock.

Heat flairs behind my zipper while her concentration remains acutely narrowed in. "Footlong?"

"Sure felt like it," she murmurs.

"I appreciate the generosity." Although, she's fairly accurate in her measurements.

A pleased noise purrs from her lush lips. "I appreciate a lot more than that."

One solid dicking is all it took for this woman to become a sultry siren. Good Lord, I'm screwed.

"Get your ass in the tub, Darlin'." I scrub over my eyes to erase the mental image of her deepthroating me.

"I don't have clean clothes for after." She glances over at me. "And *someone* ripped my panties."

The reminder provokes the caveman she's unleashed. He yawns with a stretch, ready for another solo performance. Before I can descend into too dirty of a spiral, I jut my chin to the chair in the corner. "Grabbed you a shirt and boxers."

"Such a gentleman." If she only knew the thoughts plaguing my mind.

Without further fuss or flirtation, Penny whips off her shirt and bra. I only get a short peek at her perky tits before she's sinking into the bath. A decadent moan echoes off the tiles. This is proving to be a test of willpower more than simple pleasures.

"Oh, this is paradise." She rests her head on the inflatable pillow I attached.

"Yeah?" Pride squares my stance.

"Uh-huh. You did so good." Her eyes slide shut with another groan. "You're never getting rid of me after this."

If only that were the truth.

I prop an elbow on the wall while openly indulging in my favorite hobby. The main difference is that she's well aware I'm watching every exaggerated move she makes. I get a little harder with each slosh and splash. Between the bubbles and water level, her body is mostly concealed from view. My hammering arousal sighs in relief. Until she sits forward and crooks her finger at me.

"C'mere, Thorn. Keep me company."

I'm already moving before my feet get the memo. By some miracle, I don't crack my skull on the porcelain lip. My fingers blindly reach for the large sponge I stashed from sight. "Can I scrub you clean?"

She nods. "But only if you get me dirty again."

"That can be arranged."

As in while she's still soaking wet. No point in delaying any further. I dip the sponge into the tub, letting the excess water dribble down her chest. The sight satisfies some innate, primal part of me.

"Is this what after-sex care feels like?"

"After the way I brutalized you? Yes." I wipe across her collarbones, paying special attention to the dip between. "But we can make it a regular thing."

Penny's heavy-lidded eyes train on me. "I enjoyed your crash course on getting banged against a tree."

"Not sure how. Your first time should've been better." I claimed her innocence like a savage but can't find the strength to regret it.

She grips my wrist to pause the soothing motions. "Didn't you hear me? I wouldn't change a thing. You exceeded my expectations."

"What a low bar you set. I'll make things right." With my tongue on her clit until she begs me to stop.

Her sigh is a soft surrender. "You won't hear me protest."

I drag my hand under the surface to wash between her legs. She hisses when I reach the juncture. My eyes fling to her. "Hurts?"

Penny squirms under my touch. "Just sensitive."

A sinkhole forms in my stomach. "I'm such a bastard for taking you that way."

"You didn't know."

"Even if you weren't a virgin, it was rough and brutal."

"I like you untamed. You gave me the wurst." She makes a stroking motion with her curled fingers.

A strangled laugh rips from me. We both startle at the sound, pausing for a moment. Even Rune rouses from his snooze to glance at me. Penny just gawks while I shrug off the rare expression. The force of her heated stare is too much.

I dunk the sponge harder than necessary, making a splash. "What's gotten into you, Darlin'?"

"I think we both know."

"No longer prim and proper, huh?"

"Nope, you saw to that." She winks.

"Stop forgiving me."

Penny toys with my fingers, linking us in a loose hold. "Then how will we make amends?"

That's a better segue than I could wish for. I reach for the shampoo. "Wet your hair."

She eyes the bottle in my grip. "You're spoiling me."

A blob splats on my palm. "Just to warn you, I've never done this."

"It's hard to mess up." She turns to give me better access to her head.

The vanilla-scented gel is quick to lather in her golden strands. Suds fizzle and pop as I massage her scalp. I notice Penny's lashes fluttering, which seems like a good sign.

"This seems a bit out of your wheelhouse, Thorn." She moans when I add more pressure.

"Are you complaining?"

"Nope. Just making an observation."

"Figured I'd add extra comfort and consoling while pampering you."

"I approve," she breathes. "Can I get used to this treatment?"

With a cupped palm, I begin the rinse cycle. "Until you leave."

She goes quiet. Painfully so. "Right."

"What's running through that bombshell brain, Darlin'?"

"I'm not sure yet." Then she giggles, ending on a snort. "I still can't believe I let you bang me in public."

It's my turn to grunt at her description. "I wouldn't call Timbered Falls public."

She peers over her shoulder to catch my gaze. "Anyone can stop by."

"But they don't."

Penny resituates herself after I get all the shampoo out. Her cheek rests on a bent knee while she studies me too closely. "Just admit we were lucky."

I trace the slippery slope down her throat. "I've already admitted as much."

Her exhale is a comfort. "I'm lucky too. It wasn't easy finding you in the middle of nowhere."

"No, I bet it wasn't."

And I'm damn fortunate she chose this random location. My lips seek hers to stave off the incessant need for contact. I swipe out my tongue for more. Hers is there to tussle, always ready for me. She tastes clean and pure again, but there's a hint of filthy intentions waiting to be unveiled.

She brushes her nose along mine when I pull away. "What happens next, Thorn?"

"You tell me."

"Are you going to escort me home?"

I gulp at the unknown clogging my windpipe. "Or you could sleep here."

"On the couch?"

"In my bed." Where she belongs, and no other woman has been.

Penny walks her fingers up my chest. "That depends."

Fiery lust reignites in my blood. "Don't tease me, Darlin'."

"Then you better join me between the sheets."

CHAPTER TWENTY-THREE

Penny

I ROUSE FROM THE CLUTCHES OF SLUMBER SWADDLED IN AN unfamiliar, yet toasty, warmth. That foreign feeling has me jolting alert. Clunky weight restricts my impulsive reaction from leaping too far. Those bulky arms flex and go rigid around me. Even with fog muddling my brain, the message is received. I'm not going anywhere without my human blanket knowing.

Ah, shucks. I guess I'll just stay here and bask in Nash's body heat. His naked skin is like a furnace against mine. Fresh pine and spicy musk surround me. *Freaking yum.* I bury my nose in the sheets. A gritty moan trips from me and I scrub at the dried drool on my chin. Real sexy.

A backward peek reveals that Nash is awake, but maybe just cresting into consciousness. My jerky movements probably got an early rise from him. He's wedged behind me without a sliver of space between us. With his front plastered to my back, every inch of him is giving me an enthusiastic greeting. A recognizable bulge prods at my rear. *Well, hello.* Someone is very excited to see me... or my ass.

I feel the moment he becomes aware of the disco stick offering me a ride. He stiffens—all over, not just his cock—before reaching some conclusion and returning to his slack position. Flutters attack my belly when a lazy smirk slants his mouth. Apparently, he's perfectly fine sharing the tight quarters with his third leg. I suppose it's a compliment, or I'm choosing to accept it as such.

There's a sluggish lag to his blinks. Cloudless blue skies

have never appeared quite so serene. Drowsiness clings to his droopy eyelids. His hair is mussed in that shameless style only guys can pull off. There's an endearing quality about him in this unguarded state. A cramp in my neck complains about the awkward ogling. When I roll to my back, Nash instantly cuddles me against his chest.

I don't hesitate to nuzzle into his warmth. "You make a fabulous pillow."

"Are you calling me soft?"

"Yep." I poke his bare pec. My finger might as well bounce off the firm muscle. "Super squishy."

"Glad to be of service." His laughter is a gruff rumble, rusty from disuse more than sleep. But I've heard him let loose more often lately. Nash looks almost peaceful. The usual pinch between is brows is lax.

I trace the smooth plane, drifting my fingers along the curve of his brow. "Looks like you slept well."

His pulse kicks faster under my ear. "Best night I can re-member. Usually I just toss and turn until I give up."

My heart sings. "Wow, I bet you're refreshed."

"Guess I needed the right bed partner." His wide palm curls around my hip, as if he's afraid to let me go. "And proper motivation. You wore me out, Darlin'."

"Me? That"—I wave a sloppy palm to my nether re-gion—"was your doing."

Nash didn't just tuck me in after my bath. His mouth did magical things to alleviate the soreness from our vigorous fuck. I wrinkle my nose at the term. Sex is fine with me, and beside the point. This very talented guy gave me five orgasms without coming up for air. My clit is still numb.

When I tried to return the favor, he snuggled behind me as the big spoon. It's safe to conclude he's a giver. He's also proving to be a serious swoon magnet. Nash's fingers are ab-sently running through the ends of my hair. I doubt he even notices. This entire scene is just so… normal. I love it, and want many more to follow.

A traitorous crater sinks in my stomach. Truth is a bitter pill that I'm not interested in swallowing. I won't let my looming departure spoil our fun.

"Want coffee?" It's as if he knew I needed a distraction. Again.

I do. A steamy mug is a vital part of my wake-up routine. But I'm in the mood for something a bit more organic first. "Is that the only item on your menu?"

"The fridge is stocked. What do you like for breakfast?"

"What do you like, Thorn?" I tease his nipple with my lips, giving the flat disk a flick.

He jerks underneath me. "That felt good."

"How about this?" I drift my nails down his torso.

An erotic groan is my answer. "Where are you headed?"

"I'm interested in what you have there." My finger makes a swirling motion to the noticeable lump protruding from his lap.

Nash shifts in an attempt to hide the evidence under the blanket. "Fucking dick never listens. You can ignore that."

"I'd rather not."

"Just morning wood, Darlin'."

"Maybe that's some wood I can get my hands on." I whip off the covers to expose his tented boxer briefs. "I think Footlong Thorn wants to play hide the salami in my mouth."

He flings an arm over his eyes, his brawny chest shaking with amusement. "You're ridiculous."

"That might be true, but you're the one with a boner. I should at least say hello. It would be rude not to." I continue tracing his torso with soft touches.

Goosebumps pebble his flesh. "Very tempting."

"Why are you resisting?"

"Good fucking question." His stare is steeped with reckless abandon. "But I've taken enough from you already."

"Taken?" I cluck my tongue. "More like accepted—after much persuasion—what was very willingly handed over."

The hand on my hip lifts to cinch me into a half hug. "Don't feel pressured just because I can't control my cock."

"Trust me," I purr against his stubbled jaw. "This is something I've been thinking about."

Nash fists the comforter, veins bulging in his forearm. "Fuck."

"Maybe later." I snap the elastic band between his hips. "Can I kiss you there first?"

"That doesn't require permission." His voice holds that growly edge I melt for.

I grow bold and palm him through the stretched material. "Pretty sure it does. That's how lawsuits and prison sentences happen."

"Not when it comes to you sucking my cock. Footlong Thorn is all yours."

"Oh, I like that claim of ownership. Is he mine for keeps?"

"Yes." Zero hesitation.

That gets me slinking downward in what I hope is an alluring descent. The flames in Nash's eyes are encouraging. I hook my thumbs in his boxers and shuck the fabric off in a seemingly effortless maneuver, allowing his cock to bob free from the cotton confines. My breath stalls for a shuddered beat when I see his entire package within reach.

Nerves cause a prickly jumble in my throat. "I should probably warn you."

He waits for me to finish, but my confidence stumbles. "About what, Darlin'?"

I'm kneeling near his thigh, gaze locked at my Everest. "I, uh, don't know what I'm doing."

The tension in Nash's features softens with perceived

compassion. "There's not much you can do wrong. Just don't drag your teeth along my shaft. So long as you avoid that, I'll be in heaven."

With those simple instructions, I'm properly fluffed for the task. And I'm not the only one. I haven't touched his dick, but there's a pearly drop already leaking out. That's all the further encouragement I need.

Instinct kicks in while I decide where to start. It's humiliating to expose my lack of talents in all things sexual. But that doesn't stop me from fisting him in a tentative grip. My thumb and middle finger barely brush when I try to form a firm grasp. He groans through clenched teeth as I give him a cursory stroke. His arousal almost looks painful and angry based on the crimson hue.

I'm mesmerized by his sheer size in my control. How I'm supposed to fit him in my mouth is a mystery. This process is going to require some trial and error.

"Just the tip first," I mumble under my breath.

Nash props himself up on bent elbows. "Huh?"

"I'm exchanging a few kind words with Footlong Thorn. It's none of your concern."

He collapses to the mattress with a grunt. "Fucking killing me, Darlin'."

"That's what I'm trying to prevent," I retort. "You're so big. I'm going to choke."

"Just stick near the head. It won't take long." His conviction delivers warmth to my chest.

"Please be nice." I brush him with my lips. "I'm going to slobber on your knob. That's supposed to happen. Do we have an understanding?"

"I can't believe you're talking to my dick."

"Jealous?"

"Extremely." The smolder he pins on me is an explosion set to detonate in my core.

"Now you know how it feels," I drawl.

"And how's that?" The amusement in his tone makes me grin.

"You were reciting sweet everythings to my vagina for hours." A thrum zips through the well-loved area at the mention.

"Sweet everythings?"

"Yep, screw the nothings." I motion between us. "This is everything."

"Everything," he exhales in agreement.

That only entices me. "Sounds good, right?"

"So good," Nash groans. "Keep talking."

"I think he wants us to get along," I murmur to the underside of his shaft.

A gravelly chuckle provides confirmation. This little detour is leading to the main event. I'm just getting acquainted. There are no rules, not that we set. That means I don't have to rush. Along the same lines, Nash seems perfectly content to let me explore. A peek at his face is proof enough. Well, the sweat dotting his forehead might suggest he's expending a large amount of control.

Another bead of fluid appears when I squeeze his tip. I swipe at the liquid with my thumb and Nash bucks his hips. When I pump my hand, his abs flex and tense with a shuddered exhale. These experimental touches arrive at the same result. He likes what I'm doing.

I delve deep to summon my inner sex kitten. Although, Nash did a fine job of that on his own.

"You want this?" I hover my tongue inches from his rigid length.

His blink is slow. "You're asking me?"

"Well, it's only polite." And delaying his gratification. Apparently, that makes his pleasure even better.

"By all means, Darlin'. Go ahead."

"Okay." Determination settles into me. "I'm ready."

A full body laugh jostles his dick in my grip. "You sure about that?"

"Yes," I snip. "Nothing a penis pep-talk can't fix."

"A what now?"

"Shhh," I admonish. "Mind your business. Just relax and take the blowjob like a man."

"Damn, baby." Blunt teeth gnaw on his bottom lip. "Keep talking like that and I'll never let you leave the room."

"Promise?" I rotate my wrist while adding more pressure. His pupils blow wide. "Uh-huh."

"Good." Then I'm sucking him into my mouth.

A string of dirty expletives spills from him, as if he's already on the cusp. I smile while lowering farther on his dick. My lips stretch around him as I pay special care to shield my teeth. He's hardened steel encased in slick desire. His blurted profanity gives me courage to unhinge my jaw and accept more of him. He's going off the rails for me. As I'm finding a shallow rhythm, I realize this is kind of like savoring a phallic-shaped treat. Just like a popsicle. I begin bobbing with extra effort.

"You're so fucking sexy," he rasps.

I moan in response, and he shudders. A peek at his face is the definition of carnal ecstasy. Nash thrusts ever so slightly, bumping the back of my throat. The nonsense he spits in response spurs me. On the next dive, I push too far and gag. My eyes begin to water, but I'm determined to make this good for him. A yank on my hair slams on the brakes. I release his tip with a wet slurp.

His eyes are wild. "Don't take me so deep."

"It's fine." I try to lunge in for more.

"Darlin'." His rough tone sounds like a warning.

"I've got this, Thorn. Leave it to me."

And he does. With renewed vigor, I hollow my cheeks. I

keep my hand fisted at his base for leverage. As it turns out, my prior buildup got him more prepared than expected. The grunts he makes are pure sex. I'm getting turned on just by hearing his pleasure. That heat brews into brave motions. I'm about to make another attempt at taking him into my throat when he stops me. Again.

"Just use your hand. I'm gonna come."

I scoff. "That's cheating. I want the real deal."

It seems like a rite of passage for my sexual awakening.

He gapes at me. "Where have you been, Darlin'?"

"In your fantasies," I coo.

My tongue gets back to work delivering swipes and licks. The slippery noises from my suction are crude. His muffled curses and strained posture are incentives to move faster. He needs the orgasm bliss just beyond reach. I want him to fall apart from my doing. Unintelligible murmurs mouth silent encouragement. Almost there.

That's when he goes still. With a final plunge, Nash erupts with a loud bellow. I swallow everything he gives me in two gulps. Salty zing and long-awaited relief stain my tastebuds. Two of my favorite things.

I sit on my heels to catch him in the post-blowjob glow. Nash is panting with labored breaths. His body is sprawled wide across the bed without any indication of moving.

"That was kinda fun." I smack my puffy lips.

He appears dazed. "I'm here for a repeat whenever the mood strikes."

"And I'll be happy to provide the sweet everythings."

CHAPTER TWENTY-FOUR

Nash

P ENNY BENDS SIDEWAYS TO DIP HER FINGERS INTO THE LAKE, dragging along a rippled trail from our leisurely pace. Her arm drapes lower, her palm creating a scoop. The oar in my right hand hits a rock that jars my grip. I falter to regain control, resume a steady flow, and stay on course. Oh, and not tip us over. That's when a generous splatter douses my face and shirt. Victorious giggles soon follow.

"Real mature." But the cool splash soothes my sweaty skin.

"I'm flirting with you." Penny blows me a kiss.

"Does that mean you like me, Darlin'?"

"Thought that was obvious by now."

"Never hurts to hear it," I drawl.

She rests her chin on a closed fist. The intense eye contact she serves packs a punch. "I'm crazy about you, Thorn. It's maddening. Sometimes I wonder what I'm going to do with all these feelings."

"Give them to me." My voice is meant to seduce her.

The shiver rolling down her arms is my own victory. "Don't you have your own?"

"Yeah, but I'll take the brunt for both of us." That's what I'll use to fill the hole once she's gone.

I can't hold on to her. Penny is steam on the surface just before sunset. The heat from the day that refuses to quit, even when darkness swoops in. Soon, this anomaly will be whisked away to lands far brighter.

"Or we could share the load," she counters. "Isn't that how this works?"

"And what is *this* exactly?" The emphasis on our unknown widens her stare.

"I'm not sure."

"Me either," I admit. "But you're just visiting. I'll be stuck clutching the wind."

Penny frowns. "Where do you think I'm going?"

"It doesn't matter. You're still going." The hollow pang in my chest is one I've learned to survive with.

"Maybe I won't go too far."

"It doesn't matter," I repeat.

Hurt spikes in her features. "Enlighten me, Thorn."

"Just forget it. Let's not ruin what we have left."

And I've officially dumped gloomy precipitation on our sunny afternoon.

The pressure we continue to ignore expands until we can't look at each other. Penny focuses on the passing trees, a breeze kicking her golden hair. I steer us along the shore, far enough to avoid weeds. We've been cruising for a mile or two. Even though I've upset her, she still spoils me with blatant appreciation. Those heated glances push me harder. She'll need to pay me the same motivations on the return trip, or we'll never get home.

"You really built this canoe?" She pets the glossy wood with open affection.

"Yeah, sure did." That's not the first confirmation. Probably won't be the last.

"With your bare hands?"

I wrench the oars with more force than necessary. "Giving me a complex, Darlin'."

"I don't mean to," she's quick to blurt. "It's just really impressive. The seams are so smooth. I can't feel any nails or screws or whatever you used."

"I own a tool for that." More like a dozen.

"You're rich, huh? People must shell out the big bucks for a Nash Hudson piece." She rubs her fingers together in the universal symbol for cash.

"Remember when I told you about building entire cabins by myself?"

She scoffs and rolls her eyes. "Yeah, yeah. You're inhuman, but I still don't understand how that's possible."

"When I moved to Hacken, I had… quite a bit of anger and resentment to burn through. Construction seemed like a better outlet than most." And that's exactly how I've spent the last seven years.

Then I wonder what would've happened if I'd stumbled upon Penny all those years ago, rather than the hardware store. She's breathed fresh purpose into me. A touch from her erases scars I've sentenced myself to carry. The warmth in her eyes suggests I'm more than damaged goods. But that's not the most startling.

With her in my arms, I can actually sleep. Fucking hell, I'm screwed.

"What's that look for?" She acknowledges my pain even when I try to hide in the shadows.

I refuse to use her as a crutch, though. "Is a canoe more impressive?"

If so, I've been busting my ass for the wrong rewards.

"Well, no." Penny takes a breath to scrutinize me. "Now that we're back on the subject—and you're more chatty— how did you get all the electrical and plumbing stuff done?"

"I hired a few contractors." It dings my pride to admit it, but those guys were vital cogs in the system.

Her grin is smug satisfaction. "Oh, the truth comes out."

"Does that muddy your opinion of me?"

She squints while holding a pinch of space between her

fingers. "You had my unconditional adoration under false pretenses. I'm not sure how to repair the deceit."

An idea—impulsive and reckless, of course—springs to mind. "Want me to build you a place of your own?"

"Or I can share yours."

My heart leaps, nearly shedding its jaded armor. "That would solve several problems."

"Precisely," she purrs.

That's a fantasy I'm afraid to believe. We have weeks left before any decisions have to be made. She can stay at Monroe permanently, but I'd prefer her much closer. Much like now.

The distance separating us needs to disappear. "Want to paddle?"

Penny studies my movements. "It looks difficult."

"I'll help you."

"If I don't fall into the water." She wobbles toward me on unsteady legs.

I'm quick to position her between my outstretched thighs. "Grip here."

Her fingers curl over mine and we pull together on the next glide. She follows my lead—and guiding motions—for several rounds. My dutiful darling parks her ass on my lap with a huff.

"It's hard."

I bump my hips upward. "Sure is."

She wiggles against my arousal, earning a throaty groan from me. "Are you always raring to go?"

Smoky lust throbs in my veins. "Whenever you're around."

"Ohhhh, that's almost romantic." Penny rests her head on me.

"Do what I can." I nuzzle into the curve at her neck.

"Is rowing something you do often?"

I nod. "The repetitive motions calm me."

She hums while watching my even strokes. "I can see that."

"Swimming and splitting wood are similar." The endorphin release doesn't hurt either. "What's something you like to do?"

"Repetitive motions," she repeats. Penny bites her lip, and I can sense where this conversation is going.

"Other than me, Darlin'." The woman is proving to be insatiable. I'm not one to complain.

"Damn." She mulls the question over as I slow our strokes. "Well, I love romance novels."

"Never read one," I admit. I'm not one for reading, period.

"Maybe you should."

"Or you could read one to me," I suggest on a breeze.

Penny gasps. "That's a sexy idea."

That gives me pause, the canoe gliding to a stop. "Really?"

She turns slightly to face me. "Oh, yeah. The books I love are very spicy."

I squeeze her hips. "Can't wait, Darlin'."

Her thoughts drift for a quiet moment while absorbing our surroundings. "Are you from Minnesota originally?"

I follow her lead, gazing at the multitude of trees on the bank. "Nah, not even close. I was born and raised in South Carolina, but we moved to Florida before I started high school."

"What?" She clambers upright. Her abrupt motions rock the canoe.

"Shit." I brace to stop an unfortunate capsize.

Penny notices me fighting to secure our dry position and stills instantly. Her wince is dripping with guilt. "Whoops. Sorry, Thorn."

"We're good. You didn't tip us."

"Almost did." She shakes her head, recalling our previous topic. "You lived in Florida?"

"For a short while."

"That's where I'm from." She doesn't sound too pleased about it.

"Small world, eh?" Sometimes I think our demons got lonely and sent us to the same place.

"Kindred spirits," she murmurs. Then she seems to get lost in her thoughts again, taking several moments to gather a response. "Have you adjusted to the cold?"

I grunt and shudder for emphasis. "Fuck no. The winters are brutal for a southern boy."

"Yeah, I'm worried about that."

That traitorous jump in my chest is bound to destroy me. "Sticking around for the snow?"

"Thinking about it."

A cool bite in the air distracts me. I hold a hand out upright to feel the wind gaining speed. Without hesitation, she presses her palm flat against mine.

Her sigh is soft and sweet, wrapping me in hope I abandoned long ago. "Do you believe in fate, Thorn?"

My eyes feast on every spot she's connected to me. "Nah, Darlin'. But I believe in you."

A furious gust tilts us to the far right. I glance upward to find fury and destruction rolling in. Clouds are coming in fast. An early drizzle warns us that a downpour is in our future.

"We're about to get caught in the rain."

"No, no, no." Her chanted protest is followed with a squeal as she tries to take shelter under my shirt.

My chuckle is heated. "Afraid you'll melt, Darlin'?"

"Our moment is ruined. Freaking storm," she gripes to the darkening sky.

I hug her against me. "It's what brought us together."

"That was a power outage."

"Caused by a storm," I remind her with a smirk.

"Okay," she relents. Her arms thrust straight out. That's

when a torrent erupts from the heavens in pelting sheets. "Kiss me, Thorn. Kiss me like you're the hero in my fairy tale romance."

I squint into the steam that soaks us within seconds. "That's a lot of pressure."

"Give me your best," Penny murmurs. "Your worst. Your lackluster attempts. Your dreams and nightmares. Successes and failures. I want it all, Thorn."

"Everything," I breathe against her lips.

CHAPTER TWENTY-FIVE

I SPEAR MY HANDS INTO HIS HAIR AND TUG HIM CLOSER. BRANCE responds by pushing forward until we're plastered together. In a rare show of concern, he cradles the back of my head so it doesn't ram into the shelf. The move makes me want to straddle his lap.

Before I can suggest it, Brance doubles his efforts on my clit. He adds another finger into the mix and my brain turns to mush.

"Oh, f-fuck," I wheeze. "I'm g-gonna—"

Penny abruptly slams the book closed. Her flushed cheeks are hidden behind the cover. I glare at the male model now blocking her from view. His appearance—fictional or not—is an offensive invasion of this intimate exchange. The stark design elements only serve to embellish his ripped physique. But the guy was loving on his woman. I can't fault him for that.

"Why'd you stop?"

"Isn't it obvious?" She fans her face with the pages.

"Too spicy?"

Her breathing is labored from a few scandalous lines. "I'd meant to choose something saucy, but not this explicit."

"It wasn't that graphic." I snort at the absurd notion, then steal the book from her wandering hands. Another minute in her possession and she'll be stroking his fake abs. The title is a fuckery in itself.

Ask Me Why.

Another scoff rips from me. It would be better to ask me why this dude is setting such shitty expectations for real men. What a crock. I crack the spine open with purpose.

Penny yelps and snatches her precious book away from me. "What do you think you're doing? That's criminal."

"I'm gonna read the next part."

She narrows her eyes. "Why?"

"You didn't let the lady finish."

A snarky brow quirks. "Want to know how she reaches completion?"

"He better not leave her hanging."

"Never," Penny states with conviction. "Brance knows the right buttons to push."

"Brance?" I roll my eyes. "What kind of name is that?"

Her eyes narrow at my snide tone. "Are you jealous?"

"That you're drooling over another man? Yes, Darlin'."

"He's not real." And she seems rather upset about that.

"Looks real enough in that picture."

"You're silly."

If only it were that easy. "You mispronounced 'manly and very secure in his masculinity.'"

"Isn't that what I said?" Penny stretches out on the canopy beneath us. "I'm comfy, Thorn. This might be one of your best builds."

"Not too bad, huh?" I tug at the snug cotton fastened to the nearest trunk.

We're suspended off the ground by a few feet in my latest creation. I'm no slouch and tested my design limits for this deluxe version. The fabric is pulled taut between four trees. There's still a bit of a sag to maintain the cocoon vibe, but it's just an illusion. This is as sturdy as a hammock comes. If I can even call it such. The hybrid might as well be a floating mattress or some shit.

Our heads are resting in opposite directions to face each other. Her feet are secure in my hands while mine are angled a safe distance from her nose. I press my thumb along her arch. She moans and tilts her heel for more. My fingers dig into her sole with enough pressure to make her mouth drop open in soundless ecstasy. She's a fucking vision, and I'm the lucky bastard with a front row seat.

Penny's relaxed pose allows the dress she's wearing to bunch near her hips. Only a lacy thong hides her pretty pussy from me. I'm biding my time before ripping that scrap off with my teeth.

"Want to hear a secret?" Her whisper tongues the arousal lying in wait.

I adjust the throb behind my zipper. "Always."

She walks her fingers along my shin. "I picture you while reading these books. Well, ever since I met you."

"And what happens while you're reading these books alone in bed, thinking of me?"

"I dunno." The fire staining her cheeks says she very much knows.

"Are you embarrassed?" I skim a palm along the curve of her calf.

"No," she says. Her averted gaze suggests a fib.

"Then tell me," I urge her.

"I changed my mind. You should read the next part." She tries to pry her feet from my grip.

"What are you doing?" I hold on tight to her ankles, which are crossed over my sternum.

"Just getting more comfortable. It's too… hot."

"Where, Darlin'?" I have a sneaking suspicion she's not discussing the weather. The leafy branches overhead shade us from the July heat.

Her hips shift in an agitated motion. "Down there. Inside."

My girl still clings to her shy roots, yet seems ready to unleash a naughty side. The raunchy paperback glued to her side suggests as much.

I circle her straightened knee. "Are you wet?"

Penny squirms harder under my heated stare. "Maybe."

"Should I check?" My touch wanders to her inner thigh.

She chews on the inside of her cheek. "Or I can show you."

Blood rushes to my groin at a dizzying rate. "Gonna spread your legs for me?"

"If you let go," she teases.

I relent on the assumed condition that she's about to put on a show. My hold loosens and she slips free. Penny contorts her lower half into a sexual masterpiece. Her bent knees point to the sky and freshly massaged heels almost kiss her ass. This splayed position puts her on open display for me. There's a noticeable wet spot in the center of her panties.

"Damn, Darlin'." I rest a palm over the foot she parked by my hip. "Is that just from thinking about me?"

"Yes," she admits with a breathy exhale. "While I was reading, I pictured your face buried here. You were staring at me while I rolled my hips to get that extra friction. The stubble on your jaw makes all the difference."

I'm stuck in a trance as she slides a hand under the frilly elastic that's shielding her slit. She taps at her clit, jerking from the sensation. A moan drips from her parted lips. My dick is an iron rod ready to bust at the seams, but this isn't about me.

Penny just relayed a fantasy. The request is in those specific details. She wants this to play out just as described. I've gone down on her at least a dozen times in the past week, but it seems that she's asking for a special favor this time around.

I drift a soft touch along her parted thigh. "Are we gonna reenact what you just told me?"

"Yes." No sign of her timid cloak from earlier.

"How does it start?"

"I can't believe I'm considering this," she mumbles.

"What's that?" My voice is little more than a gritty rasp.

"Touching myself in front of you." Penny's cheeks are

on fire again. "This I can do well and often. Practice makes perfect, just not with an audience."

Just listening to her sets the fever in my veins to near boiling. I'm not sure if she realizes how fucking erotic her words are. It puts the passage she read to shame.

"How can I put you more at ease?" While forcing myself not to interfere.

"You like to watch." She shimmies to remove her panties, tossing the scrap at me.

"Only when it comes to you." I catch the lace midair, then bury my nose in her proffered preview. "Fucking divine."

Penny gawks at my filthy action. "That was really… um, wow."

"Couldn't even help it. I love your scent." Especially when it's blended with mine.

Her fingers make a downward path through the glistening treasure she just exposed. "You're my adventure, Thorn. I don't want this to end."

That dreaded topic doesn't belong in this scene. "Who says it has to?"

"Even I have orgasm limits." Her clarification calms the itching beneath my skin.

I turn on my side, propped on a bent elbow. "Maybe we should find out how many it takes."

"Starting now?" Her hips buck as she circles her clit. She's using a very soft hand most likely meant to taunt me. There's not a chance she'll get off that way.

"You need some relief?"

She nods. "Please."

"Show me where."

Penny scoots toward me, fingers still petting in leisurely strokes. "Here."

I'm about to be served her pussy on a platinum platter. "You smell like dessert."

"Good enough to eat?"

"Last time I checked." I gulp down the saliva that's rapidly pooling in my mouth.

"Want a refresher to make sure?"

"Fuck yes. C'mere, Darlin'." I roll to my back and pull at her leg.

"We're doing this in the hammock?" She bounces slightly for emphasis.

"Sure, why not?"

"What if we fall?"

I frown at her. "Do you think I would allow that to happen?"

The mere idea is an insult. I can't fault her concern, though. We've been caught in unconventional situations more often than not when the mood strikes.

Her silence is revealing. She confirms with a muted, "No."

"That's what I thought. Now ride my face."

She sits up to gape at me. "You want me to sit on you?"

Her eyes leave mine to glance around the woods. I release a gruff scoff. As if anyone is within range to see or hear what I'm about to do. Rune is the only one who might witness my feasting, but he's off chasing tail of his own.

I motion to her when she delays. "Very much so."

Penny crawls over to me. Her movements are awkward as she kneels to straddle my mouth. "Like hover?"

I chuckle. "Like grind down until you're all I smell and taste. Feed me the entire meal, Darlin'."

She still hesitates. "That sounds… suffocating."

My palms curve around her hips. "Exactly. Drown me, or come all over my face trying."

A moan that's pure sex glides up her throat. "Okay, I can do that."

"So responsive."

Hazel eyes peek down at me. "I haven't done anything yet."

"It's just what you do without question." I'm lost for a moment with her spread in such a generous position over me. This woman is about to wreck me. Hell, she already has. I trace the tantalizing dip at her waist. "If this continues, I won't let you leave."

"Then ask me to stay."

"Would you?"

Her voice is drenched in surrender when she confesses, "It doesn't feel like a choice anymore."

"Fucking right it's not." I wrench her onto my mouth, the next curse muffled in her heat.

Penny lurches forward from the abrupt motion, but rights herself with a punishing grip in my hair. Within seconds, I'm bathed in her arousal. My eyes want to roll back at the on-slaught of tangy sweetness. Her rich flavor could sate my appetite, but I'm always hungry for more. She's silk and sugar along my tongue. I'll never get enough.

This is forever on my tongue. It tastes better than happiness served medium-rare in my wildest dreams. My lips buzz along her slickness. She wheezes strings of random nonsense that encourage me to create more vibrations.

"Oh, shit. You're way too good at this." She begins rocking against me, just as described. "This won't take long, Thorn."

That's a stroke to my ego, as her delicate fingers yank and grab. In return, her fantasy is mine to deliver. I never drop my gaze. If she wants my stare, it's all hers. Conviction plunges my tongue into her wanton heat. I'll watch her for as long as she'll allow. Fierce possession bores from my focus. She can see just what this does to me.

As if hearing my thoughts, Penny lowers her gaze to clash with mine. Desire swirls in those depths, matching the tempo I'm swiping at her center. Golden hair glitters in the sun when she tosses her head back. Penny looks like a goddess wielding her power without abandon. Desperation spreads through my chest. Her passion fuels my own.

I feed her my middle finger, stroking in and out at a lazy pace. Her inner walls clench around me. It's not enough. One becomes two as I finger her tightness. The nails against my scalp dig in for leverage. She's not shy about rolling her slippery core across my lips. With each forward motion, her confidence grows. I find her clit and latch on with a harsh pull. Her responding wail shakes through the trees.

"Tell me to come," she breathes.

My lips drop from her, but my fingers continue their assault. "What?"

Penny's gaze is hazy with the need for relief. "I can't stop thinking about it."

Understanding dawns in my lust-fueled thoughts. I smirk against her pussy. "Want me to call you a good girl too?"

A shudder trembles her limbs. She bites back an indecent mewl. "Maybe."

I groan into her slick flesh. "My good girl is kinky."

"I'm beginning to think so."

"Be a good girl and come for me, Darlin'."

Any response from her dies off with a whimper as I double my efforts to finish her off. The suction around her clit is paired with rapid flicks from my tongue. Her pleasure is mine to gain. She snaps her hips once, twice, then goes still. I'm drinking her down in the next beat. My throat works to swallow every drop.

"Holy shit." She's still quaking from her climax when I pull my mouth away.

I kiss her thigh, dragging my lips along her soft skin. "Again?"

Penny trembles with a moan. "Again."

CHAPTER TWENTY-SIX

Penny

THE PAPER BAG SLIPS OFF MY KNEE WHEN WE HIT A BUMP IN the gravel. Nash swerves to avoid another. This curvy road makes the trek home an adventure. The five-mile stretch is the only way in or out, so we're forced to accept whatever conditions set before us.

I had to brake for a pack of turtles the other day. That was interesting. And speaking of oddities, the man behind the wheel keeps me on my toes.

Giddy flutters take flight in my belly when I glance at the wide palm interlocked with mine. "I can't believe you willingly went into town."

He peeks over at me. "You act like I never go."

My gaze narrows on his sharp profile—so strong and stoic. "Do you?"

Nash's smirk is telling. "Not really."

"That's what I thought."

"You needed stuff." He nods at the purchases in my lap.

Feminine products, to be exact. A great test to any budding relationship is a trip down the tampon aisle. The way his shadow loomed behind me as I scanned the limited selection haunts me.

Heat prickles along my nape at the reminder. "I could've gone alone."

"Nah, I had a few things to get. Plus, I don't mind spending time with you." Cue the swoon.

The dip in my stomach is paired with a goofy grin. Then I roll my eyes at his can of soda. "Yeah, real essential."

But having his company is never a reason to complain. I just like to keep him on his toes too. The wink he shoots over totally calls me out.

Nash pulls into the dirt drive in front of his cabin. His forearm flexes when he shifts the truck into park. A breathy sigh escapes me as I treat myself to a complete Nash Hudson perusal. A random—and very strange—thought occurs to me.

"Who cuts your hair?"

He appears thoroughly caught off guard, cheeks puffing with hot air. "Me. Why?"

"Looks great. Very even." I toss a chef's kiss into the air between us.

"I don't even know how to respond," he mutters.

Lucky for him, that's never a problem for me. "When I tried to cut my own, I lost scissor privileges for months."

"That must've been awful for you." His deadpan tone alerts me to how he really feels.

"It actually was. Thanks for caring." Which provides me a straight path to a subject I've been too afraid to address. Thunder kicks in my chest as I stockpile courage. "Have you ever been in love, Thorn?"

He shakes his head slowly, almost sad. "No. It wasn't possible."

"Past tense?"

"Things change," he murmurs.

"Like your heart?"

"Maybe." His stare is locked on our linked fingers. "How about you?"

The butterfly wings revive in my belly to flap with added enthusiasm. "Ditto."

"You would say that." Amusement glitters in his baby blues.

"Maybe I'm scared to say more."

"Me too." After a stilted pause, he opens his door and steps out.

I follow suit, meeting him by the hood. "Love is a foreign concept. Or was. It didn't exist in my previous life."

Nash reclaims my hand in his. "Were you reincarnated?"

"Maybe," I muse. "But I'm definitely reinvented. Same as you."

He chews on that for several beats. "Have you talked to your parents lately?"

My smile droops with that unfortunate transition. "Not since early last week."

Only because my mother needed a verbal punching bag after hosting her most recent charity event. I'm convinced my father and brothers can't be bothered to care, and she insists on torturing me.

"Don't your parents worry about you?"

I tip my head back with a manic cackle. "You'd think so, but no. Our relationship isn't like that. I was always more of a pawn."

"The fuck?"

"My family isn't normal." And that's putting it mildly. "Things have been really strained since they tried to marry me off to the highest bidder. It almost worked too."

Nash recoils. "You were engaged?"

"For all of thirty seconds, and not by choice." Bile collects in my throat. I struggle to choke down the putrid lump.

"It was an arrangement?"

"With all the fixings. My unlawfully betrothed was Nathaniel Hollingsworth," I recite with a haughty accent. It takes me a few seconds to realize Nash is still as stone beside me. When I look over, his complexion is ashen. "Are you okay?"

"Did you just say Nathaniel Hollingsworth?" His tone is wooden and brittle.

"Um, yeah." It's unnatural to hear his name this often. Repeating it in my head is bad enough.

"As in Hollingsworth Enterprises?"

I snort. "What a sham that turned out to be. How do you know him?"

"He killed my dad."

My jaw drops with a pop. "What? I thought your parents were in an accident."

He curses under his breath. "Nathaniel didn't directly kill him, but he destroyed his life. My mother went down right beside him."

I muffle a gasp with my palm. "No."

It's public record that Nathaniel's victims numbered well into the hundreds, but I didn't personally know any of them. That's how con artists earn their keep. He didn't get caught for over a decade. I guess that's how successful embezzlement schemes are pulled off. Not sure how, since I don't speak criminal. He kept his operation running for over a decade without getting caught, and it's sweet karma to know that he's rotting in jail for just as long.

"Yes." Nash's harsh retort startles me, especially when he rips his hand from mine. Then the floodgates open with a deafening rush. "Nathaniel weaseled his way into my father's inner circle. It only took a year. Maybe less. That piece of shit bankrupted my dad's company. He conned him, stole almost every cent, and ruined his reputation as a parting gift."

"Holy shit," I mumble. "How did it happen?"

"The fuck if I know. I had just left home for college when the deal started. Clueless and distant. My dad had a small computer engineering business. He wanted to expand, turn it into an empire. To provide for me and my mom. But he was a guppy trying to swim with sharks. His growing fortune caught the attention of the wrong people. It didn't help that his lack of social awareness made him an easy target."

Waves crash in my ears, the sound of our past catching up to us. "That's awful."

Nash is the picture of rage and wrath. His balled fists tremble as he begins pacing. "It's fucking disgusting. Nathaniel made the partnership investment look legit. My dad was leery about signing over so much control, but my mom only saw the potential for status and wealth. She wanted to bump elbows with the elite. Nathaniel had connections with all the richest, most influential types. And he played my father like a fiddle. Soon enough, my father's pride and joy was hemorrhaging. There was nothing he could do, and that obliterated him. By the time I found out, Nathaniel had already pulled the proverbial trigger."

I'm frozen in place as I digest this news. As someone who can always fill the silence, I find myself significantly inadequate in this moment. He doesn't need me to babble sympathies, though.

His restless motions become more frantic. Dust plumes behind him as he beats a track into the dirt. "My dad had to sell his assets, including the Maserati. He fucking loved that car. Maybe more than his business. His mind wasn't right when he took my mom out for a final drive. That's the night they died."

Hot misery blurs my vision. "Nash, I don't even know what to say."

Each stomp he makes rumbles the earth. "And on top of that, my parents' deaths weren't enough for that asshole. Days after their funeral, he claimed my father's debt wasn't paid. He knew there was money left in the pot and tried extorting me for an asinine amount. It's a miracle he couldn't touch my inheritance."

"What a nightmare. I had no idea how vile he truly is. This is just... I don't have the words." I gag on the sickening truth in that statement.

"That man is a monster." His eyes flash to me on his next agitated pass.

"I'm super sorry I mentioned him by name. He means less than nothing to me."

"But you're from that world. You were going to marry him." Nash's upper lip curls with blatant disdain.

"Hey," I snap. His snide tone isn't appreciated and raises my defenses. "You don't know the story, Thorn. I had no intention of going through with it."

He comes to an abrupt halt, glare pinning me in place. "Did he finally get caught in his conspiracy?"

I slump my shoulders under the weight of his imploring stare. "Yes, but that was after I got myself hospitalized and left home without a backward glance."

"Shit." His enraged mask cracks ever so slightly at the corners. "Are you okay?"

"You're asking me?"

Nash takes a step toward me. "I don't like imagining you in pain."

"My spirit was slowly breaking. I couldn't live like that anymore." Tears burn my eyes, but I swipe them away. "My hopes and dreams didn't matter. All they cared about was my ability to maintain the family name. Marrying for love doesn't exist where I come from. The only Winchester daughter was expected to obediently comply. Blindly accepting the union with Nathaniel was part of that. I never would've gone back if he hadn't gotten arrested."

The momentary apology in his expression vanishes. Familiar storm clouds roll in. A chill follows and I shiver.

"Hold the fuck on." He glares at me with such animosity that I feel dirty. "Are you Penelope Winchester?"

"That's me." Although, the way he spits my full name like a curse makes me want to deny the association.

Nash's wild pacing resumes. "I can't believe this."

"It's a bit… strange," I admit after floundering in the thrashing chaos swarming us.

"We were raised in similar circles. Too similar. The only difference is my family was cast out to sink. Everyone turned their backs. We weren't worth a scandal."

"I had no idea." The mumbled phrase feels like a weak excuse.

Sweat dots his brow while he prepares to sling more horrors at me. "The Winchester Foundation is what my mother was desperate to get involved in. My mom was obsessed with yours. She aspired to be submerged in that glam and glory."

My body attempts to curl in on itself. The feat to remain upright trembles through me. "I would've strongly suggested against that."

He scowls. "It doesn't matter. After Nathaniel's con job, my parents were disgraced. They all took his side. It wasn't worth a scandal. No one would even attend their funeral."

And these are the people who raised me. I feel sick all over again. Numb hopelessness slithers down my spine. "What can I do, Thorn?"

"You've done enough harm already." He's grieving and most likely in some state of shock, so I choose to let his misplaced blame slide. After all, he just found out that I had ties to the man responsible for ruining his life. The emotional turmoil is to be expected.

That doesn't mean I don't flinch from his verbal smack. I want to crawl under a rock and hide. "But I'm not that girl anymore."

"You can't just shed an identity like that."

"No? You seem to have done that just fine." I thrust a sloppy arm in his general direction. "Is Nash Hudson even your real name?"

Blue flames attempt to incinerate me. "That's not the point."

"How ironic," I mutter. "Not that you care in this moment, but I'm in the process of changing mine legally."

"That won't change who you are, *Penelope*."

I drag my tongue along my teeth to swipe away the gravel he's spitting. "Only if you insist on reviving the past."

He spreads his arms out wide, his chest heaving with mounting agony. "That's all I have to hold at night."

The breath in my lungs sputters to ice. I'm inadvertently stabbing at old wounds. His parents are gone. He chose solitude to escape, but our brief time together has proven he's not happy alone. Maybe I need to remind him that the brightest rainbows appear after the worst storms.

And that we're destined for more.

My fingers twitch with the urge to reach for him. "I think we were brought together for a reason, Thorn."

"To torment me?"

I nearly stumble from his jarring insinuation. "I'm not your enemy."

He scoffs. "No, but you're the next best thing."

That's a trap I'm not willingly stepping in. "I'd like to believe there were other powers in play when I randomly stumbled upon your rental site. What are the chances, right?"

"The coincidence isn't lost on me. You were sent here as a test."

"What?"

"Not sure how you figured me out."

"I'm lost." But this is beginning to feel like a personal attack.

"Don't play coy. Why else would you choose this exact location?"

"It's fate, Thorn. Nothing more than destiny."

"You expect me to believe that?" He's shredding my positive outlook into ribbons without concern.

I'm left to clutch the tattered remnants. "Why wouldn't you?"

"It reeks like deceit." The few feet separating us is cold and distant. Lightning might as well strike the ground to prove we're still here. "I'm not in the market for bullshit. Find some other unsuspecting shmuck to slum it with."

Now I do stumble back, a palm slapping to my chest. The shot he just fired carves deep. "Wait. Are you trying to turn this around on me?"

"Surprised I figured it out?" His snarled resentment punches me in the stomach. "Was this all a ruse? Entertainment for the rich girl? Did the mansion get boring? You needed a vacation from luxury?"

I jolt with each rapid-fire slam against my character. "Are you serious right now?"

Nash sets off in erratic motion again, not bothering to listen. "Did you find a faded tabloid? But reading that trash wasn't enough. You wanted a cheap thrill with the poor kid who lost his parents to a white-collar scandal."

My heart hurts. Physically aches in my chest. It feels like there's a hole being dug with a spoon. I'm willing to cut Nash some slack, but this is going too far. "What are you accusing me of?"

"Did I not speak clearly enough for you? Maybe I should send a text to get the message across." When he shakes his head, exasperation is heavy in the motion.

This man is hurting and lost to his memories, which guts me more than I can explain. I don't know how to reach him. Now probably isn't the best time to try. He's trying to push me away with these wildly ridiculous assumptions. I might just let him.

"You're being cruel."

"Welcome to my world, Darlin'. Fate and destiny don't belong here. Hell, those ridiculous notions aren't even on the map. That's why I chose this place. What's your excuse?"

"That's low, Nash." My voice is a pitiful whisper.

"Is this not the adventure you were wishing for? Sorry to disappoint."

"Why are you doing this?"

But he still isn't listening.

"How can you claim to be happy here?" He rips at his hair, eyes wounded. "I should've fucking listened to my gut. You were always too good to be true. This perfect woman dropped in my lap. How fucking cliché."

"You're a dick."

"I thought that was your favorite part of me." The zinger could be taken as a joke, but his callous tone is meant to leave a mark. "Maybe you'll finally listen. I'm not good for you."

Our conversation is on a teetering peak. If we aren't careful, our actions will force the fragile point to crumble. Only our mutual agreement can set us straight. This is a crossroads, and we're standing on opposite ends of the fork.

"Maybe we should finish this later."

"How typical," he sneers. "The damage is done, and you get to walk off unscathed."

I suck in a hitched breath. "Ouch."

"Did that hurt to hear?" His lazy drawl is rich in condescension. "I can't even be that upset with you. The second I invited you in, I signed away my sanity. It seems I fell into the same habits as my father. But you brought the demons to my door. Those scars on your soul will fester. You have to live with that."

The audible crack through my chest makes my eyes water. Each droplet that hits my cheeks is a betrayal against me. I hate the tears that dare to leak weakness. But there's strength in letting go too. Even so, he doesn't deserve to see me cry.

"Fuck you, Nash. You're going to regret those words, but I won't forget them. Congratulations are in order." I slow clap while backing toward the path leading to my cabin. "You just destroyed us."

"Nah, Darlin'." His smirk is mean, the final glimpse I get from him. "You're wrong. We were never an us to destroy."

CHAPTER TWENTY-SEVEN

Nash

I FUCKED UP.

It took all of one second after Penny stormed off to realize just how monumentally I'd blown shit to smithereens. Nope, scratch that. I figured out my grave mistake while I was making it. But that didn't stop me. I just kept on digging into a deeper pit.

The crater in my chest blows wide as I stare into the wooded fortress that used to be my comfort. There's no feasible or logical explanation for how I acted. In what universe would Penelope Winchester bother to track me down? None. Not even the most backward, upside-down version of a black hole. But I couldn't stop myself from assuming the opposite.

Once Penny's real identity fell at my feet, I couldn't see reason. I became a different person—one I don't recognize. That warped version was the closest thing to an out-of-body experience that I can imagine.

My gut sinks as a spotlight shines down on the obvious. I'd been fooling myself. That doesn't make the truth easier to swallow. I've been wallowing in self-pity ever since. Five or six days have passed. The minutes and hours blend with sunrise and sunset until I only see darkness.

I don't know how to fix this. My shortcomings are on display once again. In all honestly, it might've been a blessing in disguise. There's no chance a girl like Penelope Winchester would be happy here for the long haul. It was a stretch for Penny Blaire. A hollow grunt escapes me. I'm talking about her like she's two different people. And I've officially lost my mind. It walked out with her.

Silence hounds me. I never felt the need to fill the void until now. Penny has left a lasting impression that I fear I'll never escape. What's worse is that I don't want to. I'm all too willing to wallow in the misery her shadow left behind.

With each rustle of brush, she calls me Thorn. Her laugh coasts along every breeze. I hear her soft moans whenever the tide rolls in and smacks the shore. Those damn sweet everythings are the final nail.

It's devastating.

I tip my face to the trees above when a gust blows through and shakes the branches. My heart is sore. The traitorous bastard is exposed and bleeding out. Penny hasn't made any attempts to contact me. I've given her space to mend from my unwarranted attack. But it's more than that, of course. I'm ashamed of myself, and that's kept me away. August begins next week. Whether she stays or goes, I can't let her hate me. I need to make an effort, for her sake just as much as mine. Enough of this broken boy act.

A glance at my only companion shows more disappointment. Rune is pissed at me too. He just sits at the door. If I let him out, he goes straight to Penny's cabin.

"Yeah, yeah. Let's see what she says, huh?"

He doesn't bother to lift his head before snorting at me.

I send him a pacifying salute while digging out my phone.

Me: Can we talk?

The minutes that pass are excruciating. My impatience stomps into the wood floor as I pace. There are enough knots in my stomach to build a ropes course. I'm a wreck when the ping finally alerts me.

Penny: Go ahead.

Me: In person...

Penny: You know where to find me.

That's the best invite I'll receive.

I'm already halfway out the door when I remember her gift. Rune gets a head start as I snag the peace offering that's conveniently in reach. I carved my own version of an olive branch. It's cheesy as cheddar, but it might make her smile. I could really use one of those right about now.

The walk passes in a blur as I try to make sense of the mess in my brain. Overgrown branches snag my shirt, but I barely notice the rip. It feels like mere moments before I'm approaching the clearing. My steady stride lurches to a clumsy halt. The hollow pang in my chest throbs from the not-so-distant view. Not too long ago, I was leering at her from a similar spot.

Penny is already standing on her porch when I swerve off the path. Apparently, the invitation only extends to her lawn. It's still better than I deserve.

Rune is parked dutifully at her side as I stride across the grass. Her hand rubs through his fur, the motions almost robotic. I stop in front of the stairs. It doesn't seem wise to test the limits on this unstable ground between us. She quirks a brow at my inferior position. There's a gleam in her eyes that urges me to start this fragile situation.

"I need to apologize," I begin.

She crosses her arms. "Uh-huh."

The fiery agony in my throat triples in size. "I'm sorry. Really fucking sorry."

"Well, that's a relief. I didn't think you gave half a shit about my feelings. You were really convincing." Her flat tone slices at me.

The urge to comfort her trembles my knees. "No, Darlin'. Never. You mean everything to me."

"I don't believe you." Penny averts her gaze, unshed emotion pooling within the brown and green.

"That"—I blindly point toward the scene of the crime—"wasn't about you. I couldn't see beyond the grief and lashed out. None of my pain and suffering is yours to claim. What you give me is the total opposite, and I threw it back in your face. There's no excuse for how I acted. I was cruel to the only one who's shown me kindness in years. You're the last person I'd hurt intentionally."

"Yet you raged all over me." She's not spiteful. Just wary and disappointed, which is so much worse.

"I did." Guilt stoops my posture. "But I feel really fucking bad about it."

She snorts. "Really fucking bad, huh?"

Shame burns across my nape. I squeeze the inflicted area. "Not sure how to do this."

"What're you trying to do exactly?"

"Apologize?"

"You already did," she's quick to point out. "I'm not ready to forgive you."

"I'm not asking you for that."

"No?" She grins, but it's forced. The crinkles around her eyes are noticeably absent.

Resolve hardens in my gut. "I don't deserve it."

"Ah, the tough guy act." Penny twists her lips to one side. "What happens next then?"

The box in my grip suddenly feels like a bundle of dynamite. I dare to climb the first step that separates us. Penny's brows leap when she catches sight of my offering.

"Here." I pass her the wrapped package.

She rips at the tissue paper. "What's this?"

"Just a token."

"For?"

Love. But I don't say that. It would be counterproductive. "Just because."

Her gasp announces when the item has been revealed. "Nash, this is stunning."

"Glad you think so." Gaining her approval is very much the purpose.

She inspects the intricate carving with a squint. "Wait, this tree looks familiar."

"Really?" The smile in my voice betrays me.

Penny bends forward to swat my pec, mouth hanging open. "Is this *the tree* from Timbered Falls?"

I rise onto the next stair. Only one more separates us. "That's a very specific observation. Oaks don't have many distinguishing characteristics."

Her expression flattens into a scowl. "This seems wildly inappropriate under the current circumstances."

My chin dips at being properly scolded. "Something to remember me by."

"I have a lot more than this," she mumbles under her breath.

"What's that?" I scrub over my mouth to hide a smirk.

Her shrewd glare appraises my intentions. "Is this your attempt at groveling?"

"Maybe? Never tried before now." I cringe. "If it isn't obvious, I'm way out of my depth."

Penny glances at her gift with open affection. "This is a stellar maiden voyage."

Warmth spreads through my veins. "I'm hoping we can reestablish our truce."

"And why might we do that?" Her tone lifts with a teasing note.

"We're friends, right?"

The sparkle in her gaze snuffs out. "Right."

I inwardly curse at the gloomy clouds that overcast her sunny features. "Fuck, I'm already ruining it."

"Work in progress." Her smile is still brittle thanks to me. "Still think I'm out to get you?"

"No, I never did. That was the jaded gouge in my shoulder talking."

"That gouge is really mean."

I'm already nodding. "Yeah, not my finest moment. Probably the worst, honestly. But I also think this entire nightmare woke me up from an unrealistic dream."

A furrow creases her forehead. "What do you mean?"

There's a purge gaining momentum in my stomach. I don't have the strength to stop the mushy onslaught. On the contrary, I eliminate the remaining step keeping us apart.

I take another liberty and tuck some golden hair behind her ear. "Do you think I search for rocks shaped like hearts? Prepare a bubble bath more appropriate for a spa? Play truth or dare just to see you smile? Stomp into town like a man possessed? Carve you a tree from wood that's from the abrasive trunk where I took your virginity?"

She's blinking too fast, probably trying to digest the intensity of my confession. "Um, no?"

"Fuck, Penny." I snatch her hand and place it flat over my chest. "I love you. So fucking much it's wrecking me. More than enough to know I won't survive losing you. That's why you can't stay."

"What?" Her gasp is breathy with disbelief.

"I love you too much to watch your hopes and dreams be shelved again. You can't sacrifice your future for me. That means I won't have you at all." I let go of her wrist and step back.

"Wow," she breathes. "That's incredibly noble, but also extremely presumptuous."

"I'm trying to do the right thing."

She narrows her eyes. "Try harder."

The pressure in my chest threatens to decimate me. "I don't know how to interpret that."

"Well, lucky for you, there are three weeks left on my rental contract."

"And then what?"

There's fire in her stare. "That's up to you, and this so-called grand gesture to let me leave."

"It's for the best, Darlin'. You won't be happy here."

Penny clucks her tongue, dismissal heavy in the sound. "Whatever you say, noble knight. I'm not going to beg you to reconsider."

"As you shouldn't."

"Maybe I should finally listen, right? You're not good for me." She flings the harsh sentiment at me much like I did to her.

My flinch nearly makes me tumble down the stairs. "I deserve that."

"Sure do." She resumes her defensive pose, arms crossed tight over her chest. "Plus, you're sloppy in presentation. Did you get into a fight with a bear?"

"Huh?"

"Your shirt is torn, Thorn."

I chuckle, but the sound is empty. "That's fitting. I'm a torn thorn."

Her mouth curls into a grin—true and bright. "Now you're just feeling sorry for yourself."

"Someone has to," I mutter.

"Oh, puh-lease." Penny rolls her eyes, giving me a light shove. "Go home, Torn Thorn. I have nothing left to say."

CHAPTER TWENTY-EIGHT

"**S**URPRISE!"

I flail backward at the overly cheerful and un-expected greeting. Black spots speckle my vision as I try to realign my soul with my body. Talk about a jolt. Then I'm blinking at my best friend as if she has three heads. My eyeballs must be deceiving me. Not even in the most un-realistic plot twists would this prissy fashionista willingly shlep to Hacken, Minnesota.

"Holy shit, Lou." My palm smacks against the thunder-ing in my chest.

Her model-perfect features scrunch into exaggerated con-cern. "Umm, hi. What's wrong with your face?"

"You scared the shit out of me."

She wrinkles her nose. "That's one way to welcome me."

"What're you doing here?"

Elouise shoves past me to enter the cabin. "Did you not hear me? I said surprise."

"Yeah, I caught that. But why?"

"To visit you." Her snarky tone demands I don't further question her motives.

"I never thought you'd make the trip."

"And I thought you'd be more excited," she mutters.

I wake from the startled daze and lunge at her. Chanel per-fume and designer couture assault my nose. "Am I dreaming?"

She returns my hug, arms squeezing far too tight. "Does this feel real?"

"That sounds sexual."

Her hips thrust into mine. "You're welcome."

"Shameless," I laugh while prying our limbs apart. "You look great, Lou."

"Are you shocked?" She does a twirl fit for the runway. Her outfit probably cost more than the entire town of Hacken.

"Not even a little bit."

Lou gives me a slow once-over. Her perusal ends with a cringe. "What happened to you?"

I glance down at my tank top and cutoffs. "Am I missing a stain or something?"

"Fleet Farm called and wants you to return their clothes. Immediately."

A cackle spews from me. "Fleet Farm? How do you even know what that is?"

She inspects her manicure with a shrug. "Saw one on the drive up. Seems like a place you'd find that outfit."

I roll my eyes. "Glad you haven't changed, Lou."

"Can't say the same for you, country bumpkin."

So humble and kind, this one. "How long are you in town for?"

"Wait, before we get into all that, I need to tell you something."

I clap a palm over my mouth. "Are you pregnant?"

"Excuse you?" Her scowl could raze an entire forest. "Are you calling me fat?"

"Never. It's just the first thought that popped into my mind."

"That's demented. Anywho, I probably should've mentioned this sooner." Then she pauses to scrutinize me. "Don't freak out, okay?"

"You're freaking me out right now."

She flicks her wrist toward the window. "I saw a man hiding in the bushes. Pretty sure he's still there."

I hang my head with a snort. "He would."

Elouise gapes at me, jaw wide enough to catch flies. "Do you know this person?"

"Yes," I sigh. "That's my, uh… the property owner."

She sashays to the door that's still swung open. "This is his cabin?"

"One of them, yes."

"And he's hiding very poorly behind a tree because…?"

I shrug. "You're here?"

She gasps. "Should I be offended?"

"No, he doesn't people super well."

"I didn't want to assume, but it's not entirely normal to spy on people. Unless it's his job." She whirls to face me. "Is he undercover or something?"

"Or something," I mumble. Then I bat those thoughts away. "He's overly cautious. Just watching over the place."

She makes fake binoculars with her hands. "Wow, he's a scrumptious snack. Is he a stalker?"

"Maybe he thinks so, but his intentions are honorable and harmless. Mostly. He's more like a—"

"Bodyguard?" She clasps her palms together.

I tilt my head while mulling the job role over. "Sure, that works."

She bites her bottom lip with a purr. "Umm, his hotness just got hotter."

I nudge her out of the doorway. "Don't get any ideas."

"Dibs?"

"Total dibs," I confirm. "That man is all mine."

"Good for you." She touches my shoulder and hisses, as if I scalded her. "Please tell me he took your virginity."

I don't want to discuss this with her, but there's no point denying the truth. "He did."

"Oh. My. Gawd. You're living a fairy tale. That's adorable."

Her mouth squishes into a pucker. "Why is he cowering in the weeds?"

"We had a… misunderstanding." That's the gist. Besides, it doesn't feel right to share his sacred secrets. He probably would never have told me if I hadn't mentioned Nathaniel in the first place. But this way, we've aired out all the dirty laundry. Now the real healing can begin.

"How bad was the fight?" Elouise reads between the lines, of course.

"It was pretty brutal in the thick of it, but we're not beyond repair." I refuse to believe otherwise. Nash just needs to get on the happily ever after wagon. "He's a really good guy. I'm just waiting for him to realize it."

She nods in understanding. "One of those 'don't fuck with my woman, or I'll end you' types?"

"Yeah," I sigh.

"A diamond in the rough." She hovers over me to observe his dedicated protective habits. "Are you going out there to talk to him?"

"I probably should," I mumble.

"You're not moving," Elouise whispers in my ear. "When are you leaving? The clock is ticking."

"I'm not sure anymore," I hedge.

She moves to stand beside me, focus narrowing in on mine. "What do you mean, Pen?"

"I might stay."

"Back the fuck up." She thrusts a palm between us. "You'd stay here?"

"Yeah."

Her next exhale is a husky choke. "Willingly?"

"Yep."

"Permanently on purpose?"

Now I laugh. "Yes, and you're ridiculous."

"And I'm worried you're delusional. All this fresh air is

making you loopy. Maybe we should take a trip to Tahiti and recalibrate."

I bump her with my hip. "You're such a snob."

"Duh, and you are too."

"No," I spit. "Definitely not."

"Used to be," she sings.

"*Had* to be, or I would've been eaten alive." The vicious wenches in those elite circles are fierce and ruthless.

"That's fair. This is a huge risk, though." She scours the cabin for something. "And you didn't get a dog."

"Nope. Rune slid himself into that role." The mutt in mention is rolling in the grass just feet from us.

She wrinkles her brow at the unfamiliar name, but brushes it off. "So, there's hope for you yet."

"No, not really. I'm pretty set." Especially if the stubborn jackass in the bushes figures out he doesn't get the final say.

Lou taps her lips. "Okay, but does this mean you're free tonight?"

"For you? Absolutely."

She pumps a fist in the air. "Great! We'll go to the local watering hole and paint the town hot pink!"

"Just remember where we are."

"Oh, don't worry. My expectations are very low. I've been meaning to visit a real hole in the wall." She stomps her stiletto into the floor.

"That I can provide for you."

She wraps an arm around my neck to tug me close. "This is why we're friends."

"I keep you grounded and level?"

"More like squeaky and clean."

"Same thing."

Lou shoos me forward. "Go take care of your relationship business. Then we can get our small-town party pants on. These folks won't see us coming."

I don't even humor that with a response. "Just sit tight, okay? I'll be right back."

Her hum of agreement is steeped in thinly veiled impatience. "It's not like I can hang loose in this cramped cabin."

I'm almost across the porch when I glance at the driveway. "Where's your car, Lou?"

She tips her head back with a laugh. "You think I drove myself? That's hilarious."

My jaw drops as I peek back at her. "Did you seriously pay someone to haul your skinny ass this entire way?"

She doesn't appear berated in the least, whipping out her phone to pass the time. "They're not going to do it for free."

"Wow," I breathe. "That's something."

Whatever reply she provides is lost in the breeze. My focus is trained forward as I stomp down the stairs with flames at my heels. The impending confrontation twists me in a tangle. I just wish he could accept what I already have.

Nash must see me, or hear my agitation. In the next breath, he's materializing from the woods. The itchy frustration under my skin fizzles almost instantly. It's obvious he hasn't been sleeping. His movements are sluggish and there are dark circles under his sad eyes. He's standing in front of me broad and beastly, but appears to be a shell of his virile self.

Even in rough shape, he steals my breath. He also douses my spirits. A sinking suspicion tries to alert me. His rigid posture and guarded stare reveal-slash-warn that he's not here to make amends.

I clear my throat to regain a false sense of control. "Wasn't expecting you to drop by."

Nash's gaze is an unwavering smolder. "Me either."

"What's up, Thorn?"

"Just checking on… you." He stumbles on that last word. My belly flips. "Why?"

He curls his hands into fists, as if fighting the urge to reach out. "Isn't it obvious?"

"No," I murmur. "I'm not sure about anything at the moment."

"You're gonna make me say it?"

"Only if you want to."

"I'm crazy about you, Darlin'." He surrenders to his impulse, tracing the slope of my throat with a calloused thumb. "I can't stay gone for long."

Hope is a premature ball in my chest. "Are you still giving me the boot on August fifteenth?"

Nash drops his hand with a frown. "That's not a very nice way of putting it."

"Fine," I huff. "Are you still planning to steal my choice and make me leave?"

He tips his face to the sky with a groan. "That's even worse."

"You're not giving me an answer."

The sound he releases is pure torture. "I don't want you to be stuck here with me."

"And why not?" I choose to ignore his poor choice of phrasing. The last thing I feel is stuck. But I'm not about to mince his meaning.

"Do you forgive me, Darlin'?" He sounds exhausted.

"I'm getting there. That's not the only issue." I study his disheveled appearance with a keen eye. "Have you forgiven yourself?"

He shakes his head. "I don't des—"

I smush a finger over his lips. "Who says you don't?"

His jaw clenches as he chews on an answer. "I want better for you."

"In what way?"

"Everything," he supplies with a limp smirk.

My mouth droops at the edges in response. "This is a team effort. So far, you're playing solo."

"Huh?"

"You bulldozed me twice in one week. If you don't want me to stick around, I won't force myself on you. But I get a choice in this, Thorn."

Nash grimaces. "That's the only choice that matters, which is why you shouldn't stay. How you feel about me today will change. Eventually, you'll wish you'd left and chased those abandoned dreams. I'm not sure I can carry your regret once it settles in."

"And I'm not sure you're ready to listen," I sigh. "Why are you doing this to us?"

"I'm doing this for you." His defense is paired with a wounded groan.

Once again, I see beyond the sacrificial mechanisms he's armored himself with. This man has been alone for seven long years. I'll be damned if he spends another day by himself.

With a tilt to my chin, I let him see the stubborn honesty in my stare. "I forgot to tell you something yesterday."

"Yeah?"

"I love you." My palm lifts to cup his scruffy cheek. "I love you, Nash. That love isn't a consolation prize I just happened to stumble upon. It's everything I dreamed about in my previous cardboard existence. Don't you see? You're who I set out to find. I want to build a life with you here, if only you would let me."

He leans into my touch with a sigh. "I'm not the reason you left everything else behind. You can't convince me your big adventure starts and ends and grows roots in these woods."

"I can't?"

"Even if you can look past the misguided hate I slung at you, my shortcomings are covering this entire land." He spreads his arms wide. "This is all I'll ever be."

"Oh, Torn Thorn." My smile wobbles at the corners. "You're very sweet and swoony, but this tortured hero act is entirely unnecessary. I already chose you, and it breaks my heart that you'd believe otherwise."

Nash's exhale hitches. The unshed sorrow clinging to his lashes guts me. "Don't do this for me, Darlin'."

The troops rally in my chest, preparing for battle. "I'm doing this for *us*. Until you can prove my love for you is meaningless, I'm not going anywhere."

CHAPTER TWENTY-NINE

"LET ME GET THIS STRAIGHT," Elouise sputters. "You love him?"

My sigh is steeped in whimsical fantasy. "Yes."

She tosses me some serious side-eye. "And he loves you?"

"That's what he said." As in two hours ago when she started this interrogation.

Her gaze takes a meaningful glance backward. "Then why is he following us ten paces behind rather than joining our duo?"

The fact that Nash is tagging along at all is startling. My stomach cramps at the thought of him being uncomfortable. But I know the man well enough that he's not going to put himself in an awkward situation without just cause.

I settle for a shrug. "He has his methods, and I have mine."

Her salon chignon doesn't move when she shakes her head. "This is why I don't couple."

"And this is why you don't small town." I wrench open the door and usher her inside. "Ladies first."

"What're you calling yourself—?" Her stride and question come to a simultaneous halt. "Whoa, whoa. Where did you drag me?"

I move to stand beside her in what poses as a lobby. "Timbered Tavern."

She blinks her false lashes in a comical fashion. "Are you joking?"

"Nope, not even a little bit. You wanted a hole in the wall."

"This is a really deep hole," she mumbles.

"Come on, Lou. My friend is already here."

Elouise grips my elbow. "You know someone in this dive?"

"I sure do. You'll love her."

Hesitant steps follow me. "I'm afraid, Pen. People are staring, and they look hungry."

"Feel free to stick with Nash. He'll protect you."

She squeaks when a guy makes a lewd gesture at her. "Somehow, I highly doubt that."

I guide her through the meager crowd. "Then you better take the chance with me."

"Holy shit. Look what the Disney princesses dragged in." Lydia smacks the bar with a whistle. "This one's even fancier than you."

"Hey, I take offense to that." My exaggerated pout is all for show as I settle onto the stool beside her.

"You shouldn't," she stage-whispers to me.

A very unladylike snort spews from me. "Trust me, I don't."

Lou—in all her overpriced labels glory—deserves the title without an inkling of doubt. If I'm a polished turd, the poised model on my left is a diamond-encrusted nugget that smells like roses.

The woman in mention fluffs her hair. "Aww, aren't you a puddin' lump?"

Lydia squints at her. "A what now?"

"I appreciate the boost to my ego, sugar plum." Her southern accent is making a thick appearance tonight. It's one of her favorite party tricks, seeing as we were forced to adopt a neutral dialect.

"As if you need more hot air." I hold my hands wide over her head to signify how big it already is.

She swats at me with a scowl. "It's always nice to be complimented, Pen."

On cue, Greg struts his manwhore stuff toward my flashy friend. "Well, hello. Who might you be?"

Elouise wrinkles her pert nose. "Outta your league, butter biscuit."

His brow furrows. "Does that mean you don't wanna fuck me in the staff lounge when I go on break? We could use the trash room if you prefer."

Elouise turns her horrified expression on Lydia. "Is he serious?"

"Unfortunately," she mutters. "He chases tail faster than a Golden Retriever. Woof, woof."

"That's a disturbing visual," I remark.

"Oh, bless your heart. It's a no from me," Elouise drawls. "But thanks for the invite. I'll have a margarita on the house for the emotional trauma this has caused me."

Greg straightens from his hunter's stance. "Wanna double?"

She assesses his sincerity with a calculating glare. "Is that a sexual innuendo?"

"Only if you want it to be." He winks at her. That shameless quality might get him places.

Her nails drum on the counter to a salacious beat. "Make me a drink and we'll see where that leads."

Lydia leans into me as if she's about to solve a mystery. "While they're occupied, are we going to discuss the Mr. Surly Silence-shaped shadow lurking in the corner?"

I force myself not to look over my shoulder at Nash. It physically pains me, but I'm trying to stay strong. "No."

She does the honors, glancing in the direction I last saw him. "No?"

"There's nothing new to report."

Her blink is coated in confusion. "We just sat down ten minutes ago. What happened before that?"

"A conflict of opposing opinions." I frown. "He thinks I'm going to scurry off at the first sign of trouble. That couldn't be further from the truth."

"Okay, wow." She edges away while keeping her gaze trained on me. "That sounds complicated."

"Yeah, kinda. He put himself on a timeout." I hitch a thumb to where he's most likely still standing.

"Not sure I've heard that before."

The tangle in my belly pulls taut. "I hope he's coming to his senses as we speak."

"And if he doesn't?"

I cross my arms tight over my chest. "I'm not sticking around to find out."

Lydia drops her jaw. "Really? That's savage."

"No, I'm full of shit." My false bravado fades with a slouch. "I'm going to fight in that man's corner until he tells me to stop."

"You're not leaving?" Joy radiates from her tone.

"I don't think I can."

She nudges me with her elbow. "Well, you won't hear me complain."

"What about your grand travel plans?"

"Oh, we're still doing that. Stay tuned for details." Lydia bounces on her stool, looking uncharacteristically giddy.

"Here you go." Greg delivers a cocktail I didn't order.

I gawk at the overly embellished glass. Cherries, orange slices, and pineapple wedges explode from the rim. "What's this?"

"From the big guy."

I whip my head around to find Nash in the exact spot he's been since we walked in. The shadows under his eyes pummel my pride. It's almost enough to surrender, but that won't get us anywhere. Not truly. I'm willing to admit this man has found a permanent place in my heart. He's not leaving any faster than I intend to turn tail on this little town.

Then I recall his latest peace offering. "How—?"

"He sent a note." Greg dangles a napkin inches from my face. "See?"

"Tie me to the bedpost," I read aloud. "What kind of kinky shit is that?"

Greg points at the pink drink. "Try it and find out."

A fruity explosion erupts on my tastebuds. "Oh, that's delicious. He's playing dirty."

I turn to catch his unwavering stare. My fingers wiggle at him. Nash smirks, flashing me that devastating dimple. I just about topple sideways from the onslaught.

"So very dirty," I mumble.

Lydia plasters herself against me again. "There's an entire bar's worth of booze in that. Drink responsibly."

I quirk a brow. "Speaking from experience?"

"Greg and his fucking trash room," she mutters. "Or maybe it's trash room fucking. Either way, be careful."

My gaze returns to Nash. "You don't need to worry about me."

Lou is busy slurping her own drink. "I'm gonna bang the bartender."

I spit precious alcohol down my shirt. "Come again?"

She bites her straw. "If he's lucky."

"Totally called it," Lydia spouts. "Enjoy the ride, fancy pants."

My prim and proper friend gnashes her teeth in the air, seeming to have suddenly changed her mind about the man's appeal. "Oh, I plan to. He's about to add a sweet twist to my tart sour."

Laughter shakes my frame and I fight to remain upright. "Are you making a new cocktail recipe?"

"Yep, but there's no tail necessary." She strokes an imaginary object that's most likely phallic in nature. "Once I'm done with him, he'll only be chasing mine."

"I almost feel sorry for the guy," Lydia mutters. "But he totally deserves it."

Elouise polishes off her margarita and signals for a refill. "Don't they all?"

"Nah, it turns out they aren't all hounds. Right, newbie?" Lydia nods at a very specific point along the far wall.

I hold up my glass, the pressure in my stomach springing free. "Cheers to that."

CHAPTER THIRTY

LIGHTNING STREAKS ACROSS THE MIDNIGHT SKY IN AN ANGRY bolt. Crisp rain still scents the air. It's a small miracle that the downpour paused, but the reprieve from getting drenched won't last long.

That reminder pushes me to erase the remaining distance. I bound up the three stairs with Rune flanking me. My fist is raised and ready to knock when the door swings open.

Penny props herself against the frame in an elegant diagonal. "Hi, Thorn."

"Hey, Darlin'." I lower my arm and fight the urge to haul her against me.

She kneels to greet her other visitor. "And hello to you, Runey-boy. What brings you by on this dark and dreary evening? It's so late. Shouldn't you be in bed?"

He whips me with his tail while trying to wedge himself onto her lap. Penny flops to the ground with a giggle. They exchange kisses and warmth that sends a pang of longing through my gut. Lucky mutt.

I take the liberty of answering for us. "Did your power go out?"

She nods while climbing to her feet. "About two hours ago."

Her noticeable calm rattles me. This isn't who I was expecting to find. Penny is many things, but being prepared for a storm isn't one of them. That's the presumptuous prick talking, though. Based on her casual attitude, she had every right to accuse me of being such.

"You're okay?" I scrub at the tingles breaking out across my nape.

She gives herself a once-over. "I think so?"

I shove my hands deep into my pockets. "All right, just wanted to check on you."

Her gaze is too keen. "This seems backward."

"To be honest," I drawl, "I figured you'd be unraveling right about now."

She grins, the picture of smug satisfaction. "You know what they say about assuming."

"Yep, I feel like an ass."

"Good," she chirps.

"Where's your friend?" That posh princess should definitely be causing a ruckus.

Penny snorts. "Lou? Oh, she couldn't hack it in Hacken for longer than one night."

"That's a good one," I chuckle. The gruff sound even holds notes of genuine humor. "So, you're alone?"

She nibbles on her bottom lip while fidgeting with the knob. A twist from her wrist and I'd be gone. "Not anymore."

Not ever again, if this goes as planned. "Can I come in?"

"I suppose." She turns to the side and grants me entry with a sweeping arm. "You're the owner."

"But this place is still yours," I remind her.

Rune races inside, leaps on the couch, and curls up before I've taken a single step. My body automatically sways into hers as I pass, combining our heat into one unsettled claim. Penny gasps at the resulting static. The groan I release proves I'm not unaffected.

"Until you kick me out." She shuts the door with a smack from her hip.

That's when I notice the interior condition of her home. Dozens of candles litter every available surface. There's an electric lantern on the dining table. Music croons from what

I imagine is a battery-operated speaker. She's transformed the small space into a blackout survivor's paradise. It resembles mine, only better.

"What is all this?" I spin in a slow circle for a second sweep.

"You sound surprised," she deadpans.

"Compared to a few short weeks ago," I mumble in flimsy explanation.

"I adapted to my environment. Fool me once." She shakes a fist at the blackened abyss beyond the window.

"Damn, Darlin'." I let a low whistle loose. "I'm impressed."

Penny takes a lavish bow. "Thank you."

"There's one major element missing, though."

"Really? The scene looks pretty complete to me." She averts her stare, most likely predicting what snagged my attention.

My gaze lands on the expertly stacked wood still in perfect formation from when she arrived. I shift my focus to the stone hearth that's bare of flames. "Have you ever lit a fire?"

"Nope."

"Don't you get cold overnight?"

"I packed several space heaters, and one is solar-powered." Her shrug is noncommittal at best. "As a Florida native, I expected to freeze my ass off up here. Even in the summer."

"That's all the more reason to get a fire roaring. I provided the essentials. There's a lighter, matches, newspaper, kindling, and plenty of wood." I wag my brows at the last component.

Penny absently chews on her thumbnail. "I do love your wood. It's very… firm."

"Then what's the problem?"

"It's embarrassing," she mutters.

"After everything we've shared, you're still afraid to be honest?"

"Low blow, Thorn." She huffs and rolls her eyes, but

there's amusement in her expression. "I have an unrealistic fear that it's going to eat me."

Humor explodes outward in a sharp bark. "What?"

"Yeah, yeah." Her laugh blends into harmony with mine. "Told you it was unrealistic."

"You should learn to build a fire. What if your space heaters failed?"

"I'd huddle under the blankets."

"Not gonna cut it in the winter when the windchill is fifty below."

A shudder rolls through her. "That's what I have you for."

Primal satisfaction flares in my veins. Not that she needs me. She doesn't, not truly. But an adventure is more fulfilling when it's shared.

"C'mere, Darlin'. I'll show you there's nothing to worry about." My sure stride echoes across the room as I provide us with a momentary distraction to the brewing storm.

"Are you sure? I can just turn on the space heater." She shuffles to where I'm crouched on the floor.

"It won't take long. Can you pass me two logs?"

"That's all you need?" She hands over a pair from the top.

"Just to get things going." I dump them in the box, tucking some newspaper underneath. "This wood is really dry. It catches much faster that way."

"That looks too easy." Penny studies my practiced movements with interest.

"It is that easy," I confirm. Then I gesture to the matches. "Strike one and toss it on the paper."

She gasps when the flames instantly ignite. "My hero. I might need another tutorial tomorrow."

Smoke and ash fill the air, but her floral scent overpowers it all. I drag a deep inhale into my lungs. "Or you could just move into my place."

Her legs fold into a graceful, tucked formation as she sits beside me. "Okay."

I almost startle from how fast she agrees. "Okay? Just like that?"

She must hear the awe in my expression. "What's the big deal? I already mentioned cohabitating with you when we were in the canoe. We just hit a few bumps in the stream since then."

Which serves to remind me why I hauled ass over here to begin with. I couldn't waste another second. Too many have separated us already. My pulse kicks to a marching band tempo.

"I have my own confession to make, Darlin'."

"Just one?" Her teasing tone is warmer than the growing fire.

"At a time," I add.

"Proceed." She encourages me to continue with a raised brow.

"I'm a dick."

Penny gasps, slapping a palm to her chest with a smack. "What? I've never noticed."

My entire upper body shakes with laughter from her dramatic production. "That's a bit over the top."

"Is it, though?" She tilts her head to the side, blonde waves falling in a cascade with the fluid action.

Our knees almost brush, but we're not close enough in this seated position. I slide my palms into hers. Penny scoots forward until her knees overlap mine. A mutual sigh breezes between us.

"I'm also broken," I murmur.

She squeezes our interlocked fingers. "Wait, does that make you a broken dick?"

The pressure at my temples eases. "Are you making a joke?"

Her wince is highlighted by the fire. "Is it inappropriate?"

"Are you insinuating that my dick is broken?"

"No, never." She looks appalled at the thought alone. "Footlong Thorn is man meat perfection."

Fuck, I love this woman. "Then I'll allow the deflection to pass."

She wipes fake sweat from her brow. "Close call."

I clear the diversion from my throat. "What I was trying to say—"

"Before I rudely interrupted." Then she slaps a palm over her mouth. "Gosh, sorry. You bring out the chatterbox in me."

I find that very unlikely. The thought of influencing her behavior—especially in a positive sense—swells my chest with pride. "Don't apologize, Darlin'. Especially about talking to me. I'm a broken man, and you're putting me back together."

"Oh, that's sweet." She blinks in rapid succession. "And I almost ruined it."

"You're capable of no such thing."

She fans her face. "Watch out, Thorn. I might straddle your lap if you keep talking like that."

I drop my free hand on her thigh. "Hold that thought. I have more that needs sayin' first."

"Starting to sound like a southern gentleman." Based on the glowing heat in her eyes, she likes that little slip of the tongue.

I might let the Charleston drawl visit more often. She doesn't know my real identity. It probably wouldn't be hard to find. I didn't bury my tracks. Why bother, when no one cares to look? The change was more for my peace of mind than anything else.

Might as well keep the truth train rolling too. "My birth name is Tristan Hudson Carnash."

Penny takes a moment to mull that over, wheels turning behind her gaze. "That has a sophisticated ring to it."

"Exactly why I dropped it. I can't go back to that world, Penny. Ever."

A frown replaces her soft grin. "No one is asking you to."

"Not yet," I hedge. "But you will."

"Watch it," she warns. "That almost sounds like you jumping to the wrong conclusions again."

"I'm not trying to, but it's hard for me to comprehend how you can willingly choose this place to live. Visit for the summer, sure. But the winters are brutal."

"You're here." She shrugs, as if that's all the explanation I need.

Maybe it is. "But your parents—"

"Can visit, or I'll go down there. You don't have to join me. I'll leave the choice up to you, if it ever comes to that."

"How long will it last?"

Penny scrubs over her forehead. "Let me tell you a not-so-big secret. My parents don't really care where I am. They're happy to have me gone. My mother told me as much."

If I ever meet them, it will be too soon. "Their loss and stupidity are my gain."

"I couldn't agree more." Joy radiates from her expression. "Nash Hudson is better, by the way. Not that it matters. You'll always be Thorn to me."

"Am I still?" I don't bother to hide the vulnerable edge in my tone.

"Thorn?"

"In your side?"

"More than ever," she vows with conviction.

The tension slowly seeps from my rigid posture. "I thought if I pushed hard enough, you'd finally see reason and leave."

"How'd that turn out for you?"

"Not well," I admit. "You provide the comfort I need to forgive myself. I've been isolated and drifting in the shadows of my grief. There hasn't been a reason to stop. Until you showed up."

"Don't give me too much credit. That's something you did on your own."

"Nah, Darlin'. The last seven years proved otherwise."

"I was just a missing piece," she murmurs.

"The only one that matters." I rub my thumb along her knuckles. "You love me?"

"I do," she states.

My nod is slow, but visible. "I'm coming to terms with that."

"You make it sound like a punishment."

For her, yes. That's the divot I kept tripping on. But when the ground leveled out, I could see the truth waiting right in front of me with open arms.

Penelope Winchester is the past. Her voice was silenced, but those days of acting as a muted presence no longer exist. She broke free, and it's about time I do the same. I'm ashamed it took me this long to acknowledge what she's been saying.

Penny Blaire wouldn't stay if she didn't want to. Her whisper might as well be a shout. This is her choice—me and this patch of wooded land. We'll hike and swim. Grow roots to build memories on. Fall deeper in love while living happily. Together. Fucking hell, that's a future I can't wait for. And it's ours.

"It won't be easy, Darlin'. I've already proven to be difficult."

She scoffs, but a wide smile cracks the surface. "You're my eternal challenge."

"How do you do it, huh? You manage to give everything a rosy hue."

"It's a gift."

"One I won't take for granted." The vision she graces me

with steals all the air from my lungs. "All the copper in the world can't outshine you, Penny."

She dips her chin, peeking at me from under lowered lashes. "What a line."

"Is it working?"

"I don't think so." But her eyes shimmer with amusement. "Try another to be sure."

Without releasing her hand, I get to my feet. I use our linked grip to haul her flush against me. "Truth or dare, Darlin'?"

Penny is a bit breathless from the fast motion. "Dare."

"I dare you to stay." I bend until my forehead kisses hers. "Stay with me."

Rather than answer, she pivots the game. "Truth or dare, Thorn?"

"Dare."

Her gaze lasers into mine until she's all I see. "I dare you to try and stop me."

I tower over her, close enough that I can feel her exhales puff against my cheeks. "You drive me wild."

"Ditto," she says on a sigh. Then her throat bobs with a thick gulp. "Is this when the extra freaky apology sex happens?"

There's a pause where we don't move. Hell, I don't think we even breathe. The tension becomes thick like a blanket wrapped too tight. I almost struggle against the constrictive confines.

But it's not discomfort.

No, this is a surrender. A new beginning. Our fresh start.

From this moment forward, it's us against everyone else.

I slide my palms down her sides, along the generous curve at her ass, to the back of her thighs. "You might wanna hold on."

CHAPTER THIRTY-ONE

"**N**O MORE," PENNY WHEEZES. SHE WRENCHES ON MY hair in an attempt to dislodge me.

"One more," I demand into her slick center.

Her hips squirm. "Only if your dick is involved."

My lips barely brush her heat, but she jolts. "That can be the grand finale."

"Take pity on my clit. She's tired." Her husky sigh reveals as much. But she's only been moaning my name for an hour.

I could eat her for at least two more. Her sweet nectar already stains my tongue, but the insatiable beast demands more. "Then let me lull you to sleep."

She thrashes her head, golden waves fanning out on the wood surface beneath her. "No, I want you to feed me."

Desire of a different sort strokes my pride. I'll provide her with everything she needs. "Is my girl hungry?"

She rocks her pelvis, taking care to avoid my roaming mouth. "Ravenous."

"What would you like me to put in your stomach, Darlin'?"

"A baby," she breathes while stretching her arms to the ceiling.

I almost fall on my ass. "What?"

"Just you," she corrects. "And you've made your point."

It takes me a moment to gather my bearings. My mind is suddenly filled with images of Penny round with my child. *Fucking hell.* We'll definitely be circling back to this topic.

I manage to unspool my tongue to ask, "What point is that?"

"Too many orgasms lower my inhibitions. It's almost like I'm drunk," she mumbles. "So, quit with the teasing and get inside me."

"I dunno," I reply. My next exhale whispers across her folds. "I'm thoroughly enjoying you from this angle."

"Please," she whimpers. "No more feasting."

That makes me pause. "You're asking so nicely."

"Don't deny me, Thorn."

My mouth waters for more, but the lady gets what she wants. "Never."

I rise from my crouched position between her legs. The wanton display Penny creates for me sends blood roaring to my cock. I nearly stumble from the unbalanced distribution. My gaze latches onto her as an anchor in the chaos.

Her chest is flush and heaving with labored breaths. A clammy sheen makes her face glow under the dim candlelight. Bleary eyes with hooded lids fight to focus on mine. Penny looks well-loved, sprawled naked on the table.

I yank her to the edge until her ass is hanging in midair. "You need this?"

She's nodding while I grind us together. "Yes, but without the denim in between. Ditch the threads."

My chuckle is as coarse as the fabric pressing against her softness. "My girl is demanding."

"Can you blame me?" Penny struggles to prop herself upright. She manages to rise on a trembling arm. "Why are you still fully dressed?"

"Don't need to be naked to take care of you." I reach back and tug the shirt over my head.

"But then I don't get to whet my appetite with your chiseled frame."

Honed muscles flex on instinct. I almost rip the zipper

from my jeans in the haste to satisfy her. With the elastic band stretched under my thumbs, I shuck both garments with one downward swoop. My dick throbs once freed from the confining material. I give a few trials tugs, hissing at the instant rush to my balls. That'll do.

Lust unfurls in a furious tumble as I straighten to my full height. Wood creaks as Penny shifts to inspect what I've exposed. She's quick to walk her toes along my torso. The warmth in her stare could illuminate this entire cabin.

I snag her ankle, peppering kisses on the jutting bone. "Is this mine?"

She giggles while trying to pry herself free. "Tickles, but yes. You can have that part."

I drag my lips to her calf. "How about here?"

"Uh-huh," she moans.

My mouth moves in an upward trail to stake my claim on every piece of her. I reach the dip in her belly, spending a brief moment there. "Mine?"

Penny's fingers reclaim a harsh grip on my hair. "Of course."

I lick the grooves of her ribs. "These?"

Her nod bumps against the table. "Yes."

She arches her spine, effectively serving her tits in the air on a platinum platter. My touch wanders to the generous expanse and valley between. Her chest thrusts upward into my explorations. I latch onto a peaked nipple, suckling the peak between my teeth.

"These breasts," I murmur into her flesh.

"Are yours," she confirms.

I smile into my next assault on her nipple. "And these?"

She mewls as I flick the sensitive tip with my tongue. "Yours."

Then I'm drifting again. Her collarbone and throat are easily conquered. I nibble a soft path along her tilted jaw. Our mouths collide in the next breath. Tongues sweep to join in the claim.

"Mine," we breathe into the space between our parted lips.

I don't need words to express how much this woman means to me. Each kiss I press into her skin is unconditional devotion from me. She's my heart. The very essence of my soul.

My undoing.

My resolution.

My *everything*.

When I'm thoroughly satisfied with Penny's surrender, I lift to loom over her splayed form again. A crooked smirk signals my approval. "You look like my next meal."

Penny traces my dimple with her nail. "You already ate."

"But I forgot to mark my territory while I was down there," I reason.

She narrows her eyes. "Feed me that footlong, Thorn. Don't make me wait."

Urgency rushes into my veins. Not sure I could hold off another second if I tried. "As you wish, Darlin'."

I drape her leg over my bent elbow. She's pliant and slack, allowing me to manipulate our position however I see fit. That outward abundance of trust spreads pleasure from my groin to my chest. I repeat the process with her other thigh until she's secure in my grip. With a slow stretch, I have her spread wide for me.

"I feel very exposed." Yet she makes no move to cover herself.

"You're mine for the taking."

"What're you waiting for?"

My sole focus is trained on her emptiness that only I can fill. "Can't I enjoy the view?"

"You're staring," she rasps.

"I thought you liked when I watch." I recall very specifically that she didn't want me to look away.

"That was eye contact. Right now, you're concentrating lower on the polite pole. My intimate bits are about to win a gold medal on presentation alone."

"You get participation points too." I nudge my tip into her slippery entrance.

"Finally," she cries.

Just an inch disappears inside her, but it feels like my entire length. Flames are lying in wait to fondle me. I stoke the heat with another shallow thrust. My cock slips to the halfway point before I'm withdrawing again. It takes great effort to rip my focus from her core. Our eyes clash with the next stroke. The smolder brewing between us makes me sweat.

The shock that sparks whenever our bodies join will never fade. But we're not connected enough. She's too far away in this sprawled position. I wrap her legs around my waist before threading an arm around her shoulders, and with a gentle tug, she's plastered flush against me. I bury my face in her neck with a groan. Vanilla, lavender, and the unmistakable scent of paradise fill my lungs.

"More," Penny begs.

"Shhh," I murmur into her throat. "Let me savor you."

She claws at my scalp. "But I ache, Thorn. I need you."

"Thought you were tired." I feed her another inch.

"That was my clit. This is different." She tilts her hips, trying to force my entry. "Very different. You get all of me, and I want all of you."

"Everything is yours," I vow. To prove my worth, I slide in until we're fully cemented.

Penny's moan mirrors mine. "Isn't it sweet?"

"Fucking divine."

I rest a palm flat on the top of her ass to guide her

movements. She's loving me while I dote on her. We rock in tandem to chase what's just beyond reach.

My dick slams forward with a punishing thrust. "Do you feel that?"

"Forever," she sighs out.

Even that doesn't seem long enough. My actions become crazed as the promise of release looms. Our hips smack with the furious pace we set. I'm not the only one chasing those blistering heights. Pleasure seeps from my pores as Penny seats herself tighter against me.

The unspoken demand taunts me. With an arm banded around her back, I scoop her off the table and stride to the nearest wall. She clings to me with fierce intensity to find relief. Our sweaty skin slides together, ensuring we don't separate. The friction is electric, shooting fire directly into my veins. That sizzle escapes me with a grunt when she clenches around me.

Once Penny is secure, I resume my frantic tempo. She moans at the change in angle. I slam to the hilt as tingles spear down my legs. Anticipation soon follows in a fiery streak.

"Are you gonna be a good girl and send us over the cliff?"

"Always," she exhales.

Then the telltale spasms cinch my cock. Blood pounds in my ears as we fling into oblivion, where nothing exists except our mutual relief. I feel complete, fulfilled in the most basic sense. My woman is sated with aftershocks twitching her muscles. The definition of utter bliss, and mine to hold. For eternity.

Penny tucks her face into the crook of my neck. "I love you."

"And I love you." I blindly search for her hand and lace our fingers together. "I knew you were inevitable to me, but I messed up the specifics."

"Fate and destiny."

"You're my unknown that I didn't dare to believe in," I murmur against her lips.

She claims my mouth with hers. "Does that make you mine?"

"Darlin'," I drawl. "I've been yours since you caused a noise complaint."

Her laugh puffs against my feverish skin. "That was your doing."

"Brought us together, right?"

"Just like the rain," she murmurs. "I'm the havoc to your storm."

I brush our noses together with my refusal. "Nah, you're the glue that mends me."

Pure adoration swims in her hazel depths. "Are you calling me sticky?"

Only this woman would make a joke while I'm still buried deep. Just one more reason I'm crazy about her.

"Penny Blaire," I whisper across her forehead. My lips press a soft kiss in the center. "I'm calling you mine, and that's final."

CHAPTER THIRTY-TWO

Penny

"I T'S OFFICIAL," I MOAN TO THE CLOUDLESS SKY. THE inflatable raft crinkles under my shifting weight. "I could get used to floating on our lake all hours of the day."

Nash traces a wet path across my bare chest. "You make skinny dipping sound like a punishment."

I swat at his equally nude form lounging beside me. "Always stealing my lines."

"You're more creative than me. Take it as a compliment."

"Okay, Mr. Beloved Carpenter. Now you're just petting my she-go."

He snorts while turning his head to face me. "She-go?"

"I'll stroke yours if you pet mine."

"Now we're speaking my language, Darlin'." His fist is quick to wrap around his dick. The man is always hard.

I glance at our surroundings with a thoroughly satisfied sigh. The distant splashes from Rune's joyful doggy-paddling provide a soothing tune. A breeze sends a ripple across the water, rocking our shared floatation device ever so slightly. "Does this make me a kept woman?"

With careful movements, Nash turns to his side. His fingers draw circles around my pebbled nipples as a rumble rises from the back of his throat. "I plan to keep you in this exact spot for as long as you let me."

"Very funny." I squirm away from his provocative touch. The last thing I need to do is hop on top and send us flying into the lake.

Nash peppers the arm I slung over myself with kisses. "Is keeping you pampered and happy a problem?"

"No, but I don't want to be a mooch on society." Although, that's precisely what role I'd hold if my parents had any say in the matter. "I'm also getting lazy."

"You run three miles every morning."

"Oh, gosh," I fake sob. "I'm predictable? That's even worse."

"Not to me. I love you just the way you are, Darlin'."

"You're too good to me. We have a great system going, but I need something for myself. I should get a job," I sigh. "Or at least a hobby that doesn't involve your penis. I barely have to lift a finger otherwise."

"If that's what you want." His palm makes a downward swoop to settle on my hip. "Where at?"

I appreciate how he doesn't attempt to dissuade me. "Timbered Tavern?"

His frown betrays the full support he displayed seconds ago. "What about something with your sexy books?"

"Like an erotic read-aloud?" I laugh. Then I notice the genuine gleam in his eyes. "I'm not hosting a steamy romance night in downtown Hacken."

"How about a bookstore? You told me about that one in Tampa. It sounded like something you enjoyed."

I nibble on my lip. Those are few and far between even in big cities. "Are there any nearby?"

"We could build one." His nonchalant tone flies right over my head.

I wait for the punchline, but he remains stoic. "Care to repeat that?"

Nash shrugs. "Labor and supplies aren't an issue. It won't take me long to erect a little shop for you. I could even put it on the north end so you're close to the road."

It takes great effort to sidestep the erect comment. The giddy flutters in my stomach certainly help. "You're serious?"

"Yeah. Why not?"

"I just never would've considered opening a bookstore."

"I bet you also didn't consider permanently moving to Minnesota."

"This is true." I give him an affectionate boop on the nose. "You're blowing my mind wide open with brand-new possibilities."

"It's the least I can do."

I scoff. "Modest man. You're making hopes and dreams come true, Thorn."

"And you're giving me too much credit."

"Only because you don't give yourself enough. We create balance, babe." I slide my eyes shut to absorb the warm rays blasting me from above. "It doesn't get much better than this."

"Sure about that?" He seems to be picking at something, the flicking sound tickling my ears.

"Well," I pause to consider. "There are a few more milestones I'm sure we'll aspire to reach."

"I'm thinking we should make this truly official." His serious tone makes me sneak a peek over at him.

"Wait a hot second." I launch upright, and my hasty movements tip the raft sideways. In what feels like slow motion, we slide downward toward the glassy surface. There's no chance of righting this snafu. The crash is inevitable, much like us. But the lake welcomes us with a chilly embrace and all the irony washes away.

It's more about trying to splash gracefully. As if that's a thing. My body smacks against the water like a bag of bricks. Shock renders me immobile. Nash's botched speech combined with this sloppy mishap sink me straight to the bottom. The sensation of drowning lasts less than a second. Instinct slaps me straight, and I kick toward the light.

I sputter while trying to get my legs steady underneath me. Strong hands grip my shoulders to offer much-needed support and pull me back on board. Rune begins barking, most likely concerned for my safety. These two will have me padded in bubble wrap if I'm not careful.

I swipe at the hair glued to my face. When I finally situate myself back on the raft, I square my shoulders with a rejuvenating shiver. "Wow, that was… strange."

Concern furrows Nash's brow. "Are you okay?"

I clap a palm to my forehead. "Yeah? I think I'm seeing things, or maybe just one specific thing. Super weird."

"Always figured you'd be my downfall, Darlin'." He chuckles while lifting his closed palm. His fingers open to reveal a wooden ring in the middle. "Look familiar?"

I stare at the very distinct—and meaningful—object. High-pitched static erupts in my ears. His lips are moving, but whatever he's saying is a jumble.

"Penny?"

Silence floods in to replace the deafening crackles. "Huh?"

"Are you listening?"

"Trying to," I mumble. "It's a little fuzzy. Maybe I got too much sun."

"If I had known this is how you'd react to my proposal, I would've asked you on dry land." His smile is wide and devastating.

The one I give him in return is most likely dopey and ridiculous. "You're proposing?"

"Trying to," he teases.

"And I'm ruining it?"

"Nah, Darlin'. You're making it ours. I wouldn't have it any other way."

I rub my palms together before shaking out my fingers. "Okay, lay it on me. I won't dump us in the lake this time."

"I'll get you a real ring. This is just a placeholder." Nash holds the priceless piece in a pinched grip.

"What? No. This is a real ring." I almost snatch it from him prematurely.

"There aren't any diamonds." He sounds far too disappointed about that.

"The intricate details are way better than diamonds." I squint at the symbols. "Are these clouds?"

"And lightning. It's meant to be a storm scene." He spins the ring in a slow twirl. "Here's the rainbow and sunshine at the end."

"It's just like us," I breathe. "You made this, didn't you?"

"Of course I did." Nash leans in to bump our foreheads together. "Will you marry me, Penny Blaire?"

"Yes, Nash Hudson. I believe I will." When I offer him my hand, he slides the glossy wood over my knuckle.

"Perfect fit," he exhales with what sounds like relief.

Our bodies naturally meld together in a hug. The shock from his proposal ebbs and flows, much like the calm waves lapping the shore.

"I have a very important question of my own."

"Ask away."

"Will it really be fifty below in the winter?"

A grunt of amusement escapes him. "Maybe even sixty, if you're lucky."

My jaw drops slack. "If I'm lucky?"

His arms tighten around me. "Don't even think about leaving, Darlin'. You already agreed to be mine."

"I wouldn't dare, Thorn. Besides, I have you to keep me warm."

"Thank fate for that," he chuckles.

"And destiny."

Nash's exhale is a breeze of relief coasting across my lips. "Damn, Darlin'. What'd I do to deserve you?"

I stare at this man who's become the unexpected hero. "Built a cabin or four. Invited me to stay. Now you're the only future I see."

"And you're the only one who makes me believe it."

What's half is whole, within each other's arms. I signed up for an adventure. The soul searching has been quite a thrill. And that was just the beginning.

Hacken was meant as a first stop. As it turns out, I didn't need to look further than this tiny cabin on the lake. I came to these woods to find myself, and I did. It just so happens that a secret bonus got tossed in.

Nash was waiting for me while I searched for him. I got lost in him along the way, so we could find each other.

And here we are, living our happily ever after.

EPILOGUE

Nash

A FEW SUMMERS LATER

THE STEERING WHEEL SLIDES IN MY GRIP AS I SWERVE TO AVOID a puddle from yesterday's rain. Most all-terrain vehicles are meant for dirt and mud, but the main purpose of this one is to reliably taxi a certain blonde bombshell. Penny calls the makeshift cab her rugged wilderness chariot for that very reason. Chivalry aside, pulling up to Chase Your Storm covered in muck probably won't be appreciated.

The grin I'm sporting broadens to comical levels just picturing the vision waiting for me. That seductive promise has me searching for a faster gear to throttle. Bumps in the road lift my ass straight off the seat. Rune snorts from his secure spot on the passenger side. I can only imagine the canine curses he's flinging at me.

"Come on, boy. Don't be salty. This is our moment to run wild." I lean over to ruffle his fur.

His mismatched eyes narrow at me before he curls up for the duration of our ride.

"You're no fun," I mutter. "But that leaves more for me."

The wheels skid across rocks in an attempt to gain a grip and correct my reckless driving. Wind whips at my face, but the sting barely registers. I press harder on the accelerator after clearing the final curve. There's only the hill left to crest.

Gravel spits from under the tires as I give the ATV more gas. This luxury model has extra bells, whistles, and padding fit for a queen. Or—more accurately—the woman who chose me above all else. After everything she continues to graciously give me, the least I can do is act as her personal chauffeur.

Rune leaps upright when the building comes into view. Even from his dutiful place right beside me, his gruff bark doesn't carry over the loud engine. But we'll be welcomed soon enough. I crank the wheel, slam on the brakes, and glide into my usual parking spot. My loyal companion lunges from his seat and dashes to the entrance. He paws at the wood, whimpering impatiently to see his favorite lady.

"You and me both, boy."

I feel that same frantic desire surging below the surface. My boots crunch over the ground in an impatient stride. The melodic chime of the bell above the door bounces around the cozy space, announcing my arrival. Penny most likely just flipped the sign to closed, but there aren't any customers lingering inside Chase Your Storm.

The shop feels like an intimate hug after a long day alone. Varnish from the shelves I recently built and delivered packs a pungent punch in the air. I can almost hear the turn from readers flipping through a beloved tale. But my focus doesn't remain on the empty store for long.

Pop music plays from the wireless speakers. The song has a fast beat and seductive rhythm that even encourages me to roll my hips. That's precisely what Penny is doing mere feet in front of me. Her ass sways in an alluring motion that revs my pulse to arousing levels. She stretches her arms overhead while straightening books on a shelf. Rune is already flanking her to offer assistance, just in case she drops a paperback or treat. His efforts prove victorious as she passes him a bone from her pocket.

Then she resumes the hypnotic motions meant to stoke my flames.

Fierce possession rushes under my skin in a fiery burn. If this place wasn't already cleared out, I'd make it so with a savage bellow. That'd earn me a bemused scolding from the shop owner. Penny's territorial streak rivals mine, but she doesn't want her romance enthusiasts to be scared of me.

I prop myself on a nearby table while devouring the view. "Who are you dancing for, Darlin'?"

"You, Thorn. Always you." She doesn't turn, but I can hear the amusement in her voice.

"And how'd you know it was me?"

"Other than Runey-boy rushing in like his tail is on fire?" She spoons extra sugar in her tone just for him.

I roll my eyes to a larger-than-necessary poster showcasing a shirtless male model with too many muscles. "Yeah, he insists on ruining my stealthy approach."

"Puh-lease." Her scoff boomerangs between us. "I could hear you coming from a mile away."

The smile I pin at her back is sheepish. "What can I say? That beast can haul ass."

"Boys and their toys," she coos.

"It's a thrill to drive. You should try it sometime."

"I prefer a more dependable pelvic thruster between my legs. Real girthy." Her tone borders on a lusty purr.

Static buzzes in my ears while I try not to swallow my tongue. The image she serves up so effortlessly makes me break into a sweat. I tug at the collar of my shirt with a groan.

"You don't straddle the seat on this ride," I croak.

"No?" Penny peeks over her shoulder. "Pretty sure that's how I got into this predicament."

Then she swivels on her heel with purpose. From this profile angle, her baby bump is on ripe display. The basketball-shaped bulge protruding from her abdomen is highlighted by the sun streaking through the window. I lose my next inhale from the ethereal glow surrounding her. This breathless sensation only gains intensity with each passing day that she allows me to bathe in her glory. My heart leaps skyward as I fight to remain upright. She blesses me with gifts I couldn't fathom before her.

Most wouldn't dare to assume Penny is pregnant without getting a sideways shot. She hasn't gained much weight after spending most of the first trimester heaving over the toilet. The beauty of creating a life. I held her hair while rubbing her back. Once the sickness passed, I started trying to plump her up. Much to my dismay, she's been fortunate to only add pounds where necessary. Her words, not mine.

Penny spins to face me. The naughty gleam in her gaze reflects the raging hormones she's been complaining about. I have no problem with her increased sexual appetite. That especially rings true when I'm the lucky bastard who reaps all the rewards. She knows the impact on me too.

Penny waddles toward me with an accentuated swing to her stride, and I'm a goner. Only my wife can make a sashay while seven months pregnant look sexy. The sight of her weakens my knees and I collapse into a kneel on the floor. Her chin quivers while she erases the remaining distance separating us. I frame her rounded belly with splayed palms. A strong kick nudges my hand. Two quick jabs follow.

"Hi, sweet baby." I blink at the hot sting blurring my vision.

Penny exhales, the sound so damn pleased. "Our little soccer player has been moving more than usual."

"My girls missed me." I press my lips to her swollen stomach.

"We did, and you missed my mother's call."

The mention of Cordelia Winchester makes me queasy. I don't bother hiding my wince. "How was that?"

"Better than expected." Penny shrugs. "She seems genuinely ambivalent about becoming a grandma."

"Shocking," I mutter.

"Eh, whatever. Her tone wasn't arctic, so I'm calling it a win."

"You're too gracious." A trait that often comes in handy with me.

"I choose to focus on the positive. We have that in bundles." She combs through my disheveled hair. "Speaking of, I can't believe you've been gone for two hours."

Humor tickles my chest. "Are you being sarcastic?"

"Me? Never." But the twinkle in her eyes speaks the truth.

"Don't be coy, wife." I nip at her wandering fingers. "It's a struggle to leave you alone for that long. If you're not careful, I'll stick to your side closer than Rune."

"Like glue?"

"Worse," I vow against her middle. "I won't wash off, no matter how hard you rub."

"Ooooh," she hums. "Is that a promise?"

"Or a dare," I murmur.

Penny taps her lips. "This is sounding very familiar. Are we going to play?"

"Is clothing optional?"

A giggle shakes her belly. "Don't tempt me with a good time."

"That's what we are. Together." I loop an arm around her expanding waist. "Can you blame me for being more protective?"

"No, it's incredibly endearing." She cradles my cheek. "You're great for business. The ladies swoon over you."

I puff out my chest. "Maybe I should become a more permanent presence. Can you get me an interview with the manager?"

"What about your orders, huh?"

The revolving list might as well be scratch paper. "I can quit and be your cashier instead."

"More like security guard." She wiggles her brows.

"Would that be so bad?"

"No, except women go bananas over a man in uniform." The petulance in her voice rouses my laughter.

I flash her a smirk, making sure my dimple pops out. "It's adorable when you get jealous for no reason."

"Uh-huh." Penny sags into me with a sigh. Her slack features are focused on me, but I have a hunch she's lost in the clouds.

"Did you hear what I said?"

"Something about you being super sexy."

I chuckle. "Sure, that's close enough."

"Damn hormones." She shakes off the daze.

My fingers dig into her hips. "Granting me extra sexual favors."

"At this rate, I'll be knocked up two weeks after delivering this one." Her palm rests on the top of her bump.

"Is that a promise?"

Penny studies me for an extended beat. "You want more babies?"

"Yes." Zero hesitation. "I want to build a big family with you."

"And a bigger house," she laughs.

"No problem. I have connections with the carpenter."

Another satisfied sigh escapes her. "You're going to be such a wonderful daddy."

Heat blurs my vision again. The sting makes it easier to ignore the pressure in my gut. "Yeah?"

She's already nodding. "Of course. You already are. Our little girl is going to be loved something fierce. Have mercy on any boys who try to mess with her."

I scowl at the potential threat. "They better not."

"It's bound to happen, husband. Prepare yourself."

My frown deepens. "Have we discussed home school?"

Penny just smiles, as if I'm being unreasonable. "She's going to be just fine. Strong and brave, thanks to you."

"That credit is yours, Darlin'."

"Ours," she corrects me.

"Ours," I echo. "But I'll be having a word with those pee-wee punks."

"She's not even born yet."

"That gives me five or six years to practice."

The hungry sparkle returns to her gaze. "I do love when we practice."

"And I love you, Darlin'."

Penny sways left to right. Her belly swipes my face and reminds me that I'm still kneeling. "With extra sweet every-things sprinkled on top?"

I rise to my feet and wrap her in a hug. "And then some."

That's the end… kinda. I have two bonus scenes for Penny and Nash that you can read for free. Grab them here!

WHAT TO READ NEXT?

If you're in the mood for another small town romance,
I have several for you. ***Doing It Right*** is a second
chance, single mom romance with big rom com feels.
Enjoy this excerpt!

Another swollen beat passes, the internal countdown slowly nearing zero. A raw ache threatens to steal my breath. These last moments are the most painful. It's been easy to deny the upcoming separation—this detrimental force that will irrevocably split us into two separate pieces.

I sniff at the burn in my nose. "Why is this so hard?"

Mason's lopsided grin wobbles ever so slightly. "Because we love each other."

My grip on his shirt tightens, a throb pulsing through my fingers from the effort. "I don't want to let go."

"Me either, Pep." His lips dust my forehead with the words.

"But it's for the best." I'm not sure who I'm trying to convince with that statement.

He hugs me impossibly closer until I can hear the thundering riot in his chest. "You could come with me."

Across the country. Away from my family and the town we grew up in. Ditching the plans I've made for myself.

The offer still tempts me, even after I've already decided against it on countless occasions. I can't leave everything behind to follow Mason's dreams while discarding my own. We've discussed the possibilities for months, ever since he accepted the full-ride scholarship in California. It's the best deal, offering a solid shot for him to play professionally after graduation. That's his ultimate dream—I'd never hold him back. But I also won't blindly follow him.

I recently acknowledged that there has always been an expiration date on our relationship. He's destined to find legendary glory under the stadium lights. There's no guarantee I'll find a permanent place for myself in his next chapter. A visual of me fumbling in unfamiliar territory assaults my mind and I shudder. Mason hasn't vowed to remain with me always, not that I want him to.

We're too young.

Too different.

Too stubborn with our own goals.

That selfish drive is what makes us who we are, and I refuse to let either one of us surrender. I don't want there to be a reason we eventually resent each other.

We could try long-distance, but he doesn't need the tether of a girlfriend rooted halfway across the country. I'd hate to question his fidelity for even a second. It's better this way, even if we're suffering right now. The pain will fade, though. I love him enough to put an end to us.

"A life without you is going to suck, but I can't leave." My tears stain his shirt with agony as I refuse him.

"I know," Mason murmurs against my temple. "You're meant to stay here."

Determined resolve pumps into my slumped form as I push away from his embrace. "And you're meant to be a star."

He tucks some loose hair behind my ear. "Will you still watch my games?"

The idea of that sends a stabbing pang into my stomach. But there's only so much I can deny him. "Of course."

"Then you'll catch my signal." He curves his hands into a makeshift heart, then flares the symbol outward in an arch. It's meant to represent an explosion, as if his chest can't contain his love for me. That's been our shared celebration since middle school.

Another slice cuts me deep. "You don't need to do that anymore."

Mason scoffs. "It's tradition after a completed pass."

I roll my puffy eyes. "From high school. I won't be cheering with my squad on the sidelines anymore."

Hell, I won't even be in the stands.

He adjusts the hat that's seated backward on his head. "That doesn't matter. You'll always be my good luck charm."

A knot squeezes my throat and I wheeze. "No, Mason. That's too—"

"Yes," he insists. In a practiced move, he dips down for a chaste kiss. His lips are salty and wet and mine for only a bit longer. "It's important to me."

I find myself nodding, our noses bumping with the jerky motion. "Okay."

"I'll miss you, Peppy Girl. You'll always be my first love." His voice hitches with the admission.

Fiery moisture pools in my vision. "Ditto, Ten. I'll never forget you."

He swipes at a stray droplet trickling down my cheek. "Too bad things couldn't be different for us."

"I wouldn't change anything."

"Me either, besides this part." Mason threads our fingers together. The soothing gesture is already losing its effectiveness. "I'll try to visit whenever I can."

But he won't. That's just an empty promise to soften the blow of him leaving. He doesn't have a reason to make the trip, since his parents moved to the west coast earlier this summer.

"I won't hold you to it," I murmur.

His chuckle is brittle. "You wouldn't."

With defeat pressing on my sternum, I reach to cup his scruffy cheek. "I'm glad you were mine, Mason Braxter. Even just temporarily."

Continue reading **Doing It Right** with Kindle
Unlimited here!
harloe-rae.blog/2022/04/12/new-release-doing-it-right

Take a peek at *Screwed Up*—a Bayside Heroes standalone.
Penelope Winchester makes an appearance too.

A knot lodges in my gut and I stretch to ease the strain. "Are my eyes deceiving me, or is the busy Doc Belle dropping in for a visit?"

Larsen's posture is stiff. Strictly business. "That depends on what you're seeing, Beast. Reality and fantasy are vastly different."

I paste on a crooked smirk. "Ah, there's the snark I was anticipating. Just as I pictured."

She quirks a brow. "You've been thinking about me?"

A grunt for confirmation. "Hard not to. We seem to cross paths rather frequently."

"Whose fault is that?" The unflinching stare she pins on me is telling.

"It's very tight quarters," I murmur.

Her features pinch into a disbelieving frown. "We have an entire floor."

"Doesn't seem that way to me." Even now, in the open foyer, the air feels stifling. That has everything to do with my present company within reach.

Larsen gives me a lazy once-over. "I can see why."

"Was that a compliment?" I shift my stance, rocking forward with the adjustment.

Her gulp is audible. "You fill the space with your big… shoulders."

"The better to protect you with." My voice drops several octaves for maximum impact.

It could be my imagination, but I swear a slight tremble ripples down her form. "You're confusing the fairytales."

"Nah. I'm interchangeable, babe. You get all the heroes wrapped in one package with me." Minus the romance and relationship. I'll provide the carnal pleasure and let those willing to commit take my scraps.

Larsen snorts. "Ah, I was wondering when your arrogance would make an appearance."

"I didn't want to scare you off with my cock... iness too soon." This one definitely spooks easy.

As if to prove my point, her startled gaze leaps below my belt. She regains her composure with a cough, smoothing a steady palm over her hair. "It's funny you should mention that."

Hushed murmurs from our right steal my attention. A nurse trio zips by, huddled in a tight formation. Their gazes narrow on us before they disappear around the corner. That unfortunate interruption reminds me of where we are. I'm still in the probation phase. Screwing off on the clock won't grant me any favors. Although to be fair, my shift ended five minutes ago.

"Is there something I can do for you?" *Or to you*, I add mentally. Preferably far from prying gossip hounds. Public displays have their purpose, but the things I'm envisioning are most satisfying in private. I manage to stifle that desire behind pressed lips.

She draws in a long breath. "So, I'm done for the day."

"Bragging at this hour, Belle? That's unseemly." I have no intention of making this easy on her. Ruffling her prim and proper feathers is purely for my benefit.

Her huff in response makes me laugh. "I was hoping we'd get another chance to talk."

I cross my arms, a spark zapping through me at her annoyance. "Aren't we already?"

She mutters something under her breath about taking the hint. "I had a specific topic in mind."

"Which is?" I drag the words out, adding a spit-it-out motion with my rotating wrist.

"Do you have a girlfriend?" A ruddy hue stains her cheeks as she blurts the question.

The insinuation of that being possible is comical enough to rip a laugh from me. "No, Belle. I'm blessedly unattached."

"Okay," she whispers. "That's good. Really… good."

Secondhand discomfort smacks me and I get the urge to squirm. "And why might that be?"

Larsen ducks her chin for a moment then returns her gaze to mine. Steely determination straightens her pose. "I'm hoping we can reach an understanding that will be… mutually satisfying."

Wow, she's fucking clinical. Lucky for her, I'm very capable of reading between the lines. "Are you propositioning me?"

"No," she blurts. Then a harsh swallow bobs her throat. "Maybe."

I release a low whistle. "Damn, Doc. Never would've pegged you as the type."

Awkward vibes waft from her in tense waves. Larsen fidgets with the hem of her lab coat. Her fingers drum against the white fabric. I can practically see the rapid flutter in her pulse from where I'm standing. I nearly choke on the stagnant pause.

After several beats, she finds her voice. "What type might that be?"

I study her for a moment, fiery lust licking at my twitching shaft. "A reserved and posh exterior to hide the kink lurking inside. You're looking for some action with no strings attached."

There's no doubting the pleased ripple that courses through her from my crass assumption. Goosebumps pebble her skin, and she shivers despite the October humidity hounding us. She relaxes her expression, a saucy smile replacing the stern lines. "I guess you have me all figured out."

Keep reading **Screwed Up** with Kindle Unlimited here!
harloe-rae.blog/2021/12/17/new-release-screwed-up

NOVELS BY HARLOE RAE

Reclusive Standalones

Redefining Us

Forget You Not

#BitterSweetHeat Standalones

Gent

Miss

Lass

Silo Springs Standalones

Breaker

Keeper

Loner

Quad Pod Babe Squad Standalones

Leave Him Loved

Something Like Hate

There's Always Someday

Doing It Right

Complete Standalones

Watch Me Follow

Ask Me Why

Left for WildLost in Him

Screwed Up (part of the Bayside Heroes standalones)

ACKNOWLEDGEMENTS

Ah, here we are again. I'm always a bit (more like a lot) emotional when I reach this portion of the writing process. It's very overwhelming for me—in the best possible way—to think about the people who choose to read my books. So, I'm going to start this off by thanking you. I appreciate you picking my romance to get lost in for a while. Here's to hoping you enjoyed Penny and Nash as much as I enjoyed writing them.

Speaking of these two, they gave me quite a ride. Lost in Him is my Everest. I wrote this book very quickly, and it wasn't easy. But my love for this story gave me the strength to push through the tough deadline. These characters are very special to me. They spoke to me in a way I haven't felt in years. Cheers to conquering our goals!

In May of this year, I celebrated my five-year publishing anniversary. I need to take a moment and thank the readers who have been with me from the start. You know who you are and I'm eternally grateful for your continuous encouragement. The unconditional support you give me is what keeps me going during the hard times. I owe you lots. For now, please accept this virtual hug.

Huge thanks to my family. I have the greatest husband—my own fairytale hero—who gives me encouragement each day. This crazy magical author life wouldn't be possible without him. We have two beautiful children who light up our life and provide daily doses of happiness. I'm beyond words thankful for their patience and support so I can continue following my dreams. You're my favorites. I love you to a galaxy far, far away.

My little boy deserves his own shoutout for sharing some romantic wisdom. He told me there was a fire between him and his girlfriend. The kid is only six.

My brother-in-law proved that a man can build a cabin by himself, mostly. Thanks for inspiring Nash's craftsmanship.

I probably wouldn't get my books done on time—or at all—without Renee. She's always there for whatever, whenever. Thanks for being the greatest support system and bestest friend. I'm so lucky to call you mine.

Talia and Book Cover Kingdom gets all the praise for this stunning cover design. We've worked together for five years, and I hope for many more. It's always an adventure to discover what we'll create next. I can't wait!

Thanks to Heather and K.k. for being true friends, my bestest beeches. No matter the problem, I can turn to them for unconditional—and very honest—encouragement. I can't properly describe the bond we've formed, but it's simply fantastic. Day after day, you're there for me. I'd be lost without you two, so you're stuck with me forever.

Shain and Kelsey were in the trenches with me while my fingers were flying over the keys. Thanks for the nonstop pushes and shoves. You're incredible.

Extra squishy hugs to Kate. You're such an inspiration and I'm grateful for your friendship.

It can be difficult to find genuine friendships in a cyber world, especially when we're all stuck working at home without much personal interaction. I feel extremely fortunate and blessed to have so many awesome ladies in my corner that I can lean on, and vice versa. I know I can turn to you, no matter what, and that kind of supportive comfort is priceless. Thank you to Tia, Annie, Leigh, Amy, Michelle, TJ, Suzie, Kandi, and many more. Your friendship is irreplaceable. Thank you, thank you.

Harloe's Hotties need an extra loud shoutout. My reader group is the best. Call me biased and I'll admit it. But these ladies keep my author cup overflowing with joy. Harloe's Review

Crew gets warm snuggles too. I'm so thankful you're my people. Thanks for all you do for me. That support is priceless. I love you all!

Thank you to Candi Kane and her team at Candi Kane PR. She's such an unstoppable force and works tirelessly to ensure each release goes off without a hitch. I'm forever grateful. Also, a big thanks to the wonderful ladies at Give Me Books. Once again, your help for this release is invaluable and very much appreciated.

Thanks to Rafa, the very talented photographer who shot the stunning image of Alvaro to become the muse for Nash. Doesn't he make you want to get lost in the woods? Yeah, Darlin'.

There are so many vital individuals who assist in the writing and publishing process. Renee reads as I write and keeps me on track. Thanks to Patricia, Kayla, and Keri for beta reading. Sending a huge thanks to Alex with Infinite Well for editing and polishing Lost in Him until the story sparkled. To Shauna with Ink Machine for proofing. A massive thanks to Stacey from Champagne Book Designs. As always, she once again created the most stunning interior for my book baby. I cannot recommend her formatting services enough!

I need to send out another huge round of thanks to all the readers, reviewers, bloggers, bookstagrammers, BookTokers, and romance lovers out there. Because of you, authors like me get to continue writing and doing what we love. You're who we strive to reach and aim to be better for. Thank you to infinity for continuing to be there for all of us!

And last but definitely not least, if you enjoyed Lost in Him and want to do me a huge favor, please consider leaving a review. It really helps others find my books. Thank you for reading!

ABOUT THE AUTHOR

Harloe Rae is a *USA Today* & Amazon Top 5 best-selling author. Her passion for writing and reading has taken on a whole new meaning. Each day is an unforgettable adventure.

She's a Minnesota gal with a serious addiction to romance. There's nothing quite like an epic happily ever after. When she's not buried in the writing cave, Harloe can be found hanging with her hubby and kiddos. If the weather permits, she loves being lakeside or out in the country with her horses.

Broody heroes are Harloe's favorite to write. Her romances are swoony and emotional with plenty of heat. All of her books are available on Amazon and Kindle Unlimited.

Stay in the know by subscribing to her newsletter at
http://bit.ly/HarloesList
Join her reader group, Harloe's Hotties, at
www.facebook.com/groups/harloehotties/
Check out her site at www.harloe-rae.blog

Follow her on:
BookBub: bit.ly/HarloeBB
Amazon: bit.ly/HarloeOnAmazon
Goodreads: bit.ly/HarloeOnGR
Facebook Page:Facebook.com/authorharloerae
Instagram: www.instagram.com/harloerae
TikTok: www.tiktok.com/@harloerae